Sometimes the unexpected transforms your life. I am one of those people. One Thursday afternoon I was killing time waiting for an interview for the post of Community Facilitator for the Enhancement of Developmental Proactive Non Profit Community Enterprise Units. Somewhere behind the barbed wire where the unemployed live my future lay waiting.

I was sitting by the Liffey reading the Programme for Renewal Government XVIII. It explained how the government planned to reach the EU limit of 85% employment on S.E.S. schemes by 2055 and appeared far more important than the manuscript floating past in the 7Up bottle.

It was the sun which caused all that follows. It shone at a peculiar angle and suddenly I saw with horror the word dole.[1] Immediately I realised the contents were subversive and probably libellous.[2]

What to do? If I ripped it up I would be in breach of EU directive number 3,796,401 B paragraph 2. Only governments and multi-national corporations could damage the environment. I could be blacklisted forever from a job as a government bureaucrat. There was only one solution. I would have to return the subversive material to its own time using my virtual reality cyberspace time traveller D2054. Unfortunately this landed on one of the primary roads in Cavan.

Needing money to repair the machine I sold the manuscript to a publisher. The burst tyre on my machine is being mended by a government task force and they expect to have the job completed by 1997. Meanwhile I am working on a government review compiling a preliminary report on Graveyards, The Economic Potential.

I met Seán Armstrong recently at an EU conference on Government and Enterprise: The need for Review Bodies and Task Forces. Honesty impelled me to ask did he want his name on the book as author.

"Jesus! No! No!" he squawked.

He murmured with some pride,

"I have a good job. I'm useful now. I'm the heritage co-ordinator/academic foreman of a C.E.D.P. scheme. It's called Arts-Shock. The irrelevance of creativity for good literature. Government funded. Please! Pull the book! At least wait until the EU money runs out."

But it was too late. The presses were running and I had to travel back to 2044. 1994 is so different. I think.

---

[1] The word dole had been banned by the Minister Person for Ethics and new un-understandable words in the 14th government for renewal in 2037. The correct term is Employment non-facilitated.

[2] Truth had been banned by the Minister for a free, unbiased and non judgemental press 10th Goverment for renewal, partnership, hope, full employment etc.

INTRODUCTION

This is a book about a year on the dole. It is not solely about unemployment for, as the reader will find, being on the dole impacts on every aspect of your existence.

Although some advice is offered on how to apply for unemployment assistance, the pitfalls to avoid, some tricks of the welfare state etc., this book does not pretend to offer a full guide to the nature of unemployment. It is one person's account of what it is like to be thrown on the scrap-heap of the dole at the age of twenty-four.

Some reasons are offered for the prevalence of unemployment in our society and the possible consequences. These, however, should not be taken as gospel for I am no economist and anyone can be a sociologist.

Parts of this book will shock and reveal. They have certainly shocked me and I can only hope that I am not really as horrible a person as I appear here.

To the sadist who believes life on the dole should be an abject tableau of horror, vice and misery – a warning: it isn't. Much of this text is written in a humorous vein. The reason for this is simple. Humour is the best survival mechanism known to man and the only one outside of anger available to the disempowered. Humour is a necessary crutch to survive the madness and hypocrisy of our society and the emptiness of a life on the dole. The other alternatives are too dangerous and too self-destructive.

Despite this, parts of the text are very bitter. I have tried to avoid that narrowing of the soul. There is, however, much to be bitter about in this country. Some of the text is full of self-pity. I will leave it to the reader to judge whether it is justified or do I really need a good kick up the arse. Much of the text is self-obsessed. That is the nature of unemployment. It turns you inward, often morbidly so.

Finally I hope that, as in all traditional novels, the book both instructs and entertains.

REMINISCENCES

Looking back on it all I was very innocent. I realise now that what I needed was a dole-seeker's guide to survival. Something short and snappy, say nine points, definitely not published by the government. So, financially, how do you survive on the dole. Here are the recommendations of the Armstrong Commission.

1. Don't tell the truth, whatever the temptation, it'll only get you into trouble. Bring your story and stick to it.
2. Act stupid and avoid co-operating. They don't like clever people whilst a willingness to co-operate makes them suspicious. If you can, get them to look down on you, then you have a better chance of getting what you want.
3. Have a good sob story prepared. This is linked to 1 and 2 above. Make sure you appear utterly incapable of running your own life.
4. Bring a few letters of rejection. No problem there. It doesn't matter if they're for the director-generalship of R.T.E. or the I.D.A. or even the I.R.A. so long as you show you're trying.
5. Bring along a bank statement saying you've no money. This will cost you a fiver which is a bit contradictory but then so is life.
6. Dress appropriately. Do not on any account shave or wash and do try to cultivate some bloodstains and Guinness smudges on your clothing. This will re-inforce impressions cultivated in 1 - 4.
7. Assorted children, preferably covered in snot and crying, are an essential feature of a quick and successful interview.
8. Threats of eviction from landlords or Final Demands from the E.S.B. or H.P. companies are other useful props. You can borrow these from neighbours or friendly landlords.
9. Finally, always look them in the eye when lying.

AUGUST

BEGINNINGS 9/8/92

Signed on today. Already this place leaves me feeling sick inside. Footsteps shuffle silently across the dull carpet. Strangers not quite catching the other's eye. Only a few old hands meet and chat familiarly. Their jocularity seems out of place here.

The faces of the welfare officers are cold and supercilious, though this I suspect, is just fancy. Probably they are just bored at the poverty, the desperation, the lies. The dingy paint and shabby furniture merely replicates every other aspect of their existence. I don't fancy coming back here too often. He tells me to come back tomorrow with this, that and the other. I smile and leave. He looks shocked as though I had made a pass at him. I walk away with a sudden haste, glad to be free of the place.

THE RETURN 11/8/92

Go into dole office carrying all the tools of the trade, P45s etc. I am more apprehensive today. My unemployment expert/policy officer has laughed at me for my decision to sign on in my home town. "Not there", he says, with the disgust one normally associates with primary school teachers talking to children with mucky fingers. "I live here", I protest and he laughs again. Apparently there is a hierarchy in dole offices, a hierarchy of dole officers and I am at the bottom with both. Good start, Seán. See one magpie when going down this morning. Oh, we are most definitely doomed.

Inside, I ask how long it will take to sort everything out. He smiles like a reassuring barracuda.

"Three weeks but we will give you an interim payment based on your previous claim".

Great, that was three years ago when I was living at home. Nothing like modern technology for keeping you up to date. I'll probably end up with twenty-five quid a week and then, as your super–soar–away *Sun* would have you believe, begin a life of vice, orgies, and luxury on the Costa del Dole. Ah, the joys of it all, me 'n' Oliver Reid comparing penises in a drunken stupor. I wait anxiously for the plane tickets. More realistically things are going to be tight for the next few weeks but I can always borrow a few quid from friends.

6

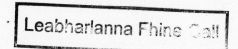

SECOND P.F.O.* LETTER   12/8/92

I received a second P.F.O. letter today. I think I'll keep them beneath my bed, the tone was so nice. Superb qualifications. Regretfully, present economic climate; unprecedented calibre of applicants; will keep your C.V. on file. I feel a surge of pride in my obvious abilities and return to my applications with a will. This unemployment thing should not represent much of a problem despite what the experts say.

NEW LANDLADY   13/8/92

Met new landlady today. Do not trust her. She is one of the others. A user. You can see it in her acquisitive little eyes. Darting, seeking the quick buck, the false effusiveness of her personality. But we smile and grin, pretend cordiality, and you can move in early. Oh, how lovely, and her eyes glint. But how quickly her friendliness goes when the faults in the house are pointed out. Then we are friends no more and it's all business. Only when it comes to payment are we all brothers in this together.

BUS EIREANN MUSIC   14/8/92

Music can indeed calm the savage spirit but this stuff does nothing for the tranquillity of my soul or stomach. Only an hour to go of this. Daniel O'Donnell is singing "Whatever happened to old-fashioned love". The smiles and tears, Momma and Poppa. Grandma and Grandpa. What indeed did happen? These are the things you think about when you are watching a five mile tailback six miles outside of Dublin on a wet morning. Death, decay, the transience of all things human, happiness, sin and murder; these are all things wee Daniel always brings to my mind whenever I am trapped.

I suppose as in politics we get the musicians we deserve. But do we really deserve Albert or indeed Daniel O'Donnell? Perhaps we could swop them. It might work. A burst of excitement dazzles my soul. You know, insane, impractical, dangerously unreal as it sounds it might just work. IT MIGHT JUST WORK!

But will people listen to me. I know Albert is keen but O'Donnell, always seeking status, respect, international recognition, he could be a problem.

* - Please Fuck Off

JOB QUALIFICATIONS 15/8/92

Meet a friend of mine tonight. Honours degree in politics and sociology. He's going for a job as a night porter in a hotel in Bundoran. It's a start, he smiles philosophically. I wonder has he too lost his sanity. Perhaps not, for he's also going for the job of dental assistant. Better promotional prospects and a permanent position. God love him, he looks the part with his crew cut hair, his hangdog expression of intense misery, bearing a vague resemblance to Igor. Perfect for a dentist's office or a funeral parlour, I announce with the pleasure of a personal valet.

WORRIED ABOUT SHORT-TERM PAYMENT 16/8/92

Man behind the counter hands out giro officiously. Feeding time at the Zoo. Fifty-eight quid. I didn't expect this much. With commendable honesty I query the amount.

"It's for two weeks". He adds hastily with experience of long practice, "It's just an interim payment until we get you sorted out".

"It had better be," I mutter. This place really brings out the worst in me. Self-defence is my only plea.

I am a bit worried about this payment of £29. It is suspiciously similar to what I got the last time when living at home. They do realise that I am claiming for benefit, that I am no longer living at home? And if they don't, or if there is a problem, which of course they haven't told me about, what's going to happen then? I don't like this dependency, this lack of independence.

They're hardly going to assess me on what I would need if I was living at home. They're not that stupid, are they? Or perhaps I'm the stupid one and they're playing a little fiddle on me, trying to get out of paying me what I am entitled to in the hope that I won't kick up. They're not that deceitful . . .are they? Are the stories I hear true and not just exaggerations? This paranoia is foolish. Drop it.

WORRIED ABOUT DOLE APPLICATION 17/8/92

Am strangely nervous about my application for benefit. This is not grounded in logic. Perhaps the newness of it all or the reputation of the place is getting to me. Last summer I know of someone who was admitted to hospital suffering from malnutrition before they did anything. They said he was an exceptional case. Consoling.

Whatever about the others they can't do me like they did last summer. I was unemployed six weeks and they paid me nothing because I was a student. That was it. No explanation or justification. They can't do me on that one because I'm no longer a student. Furthermore, the fact that I have been working solidly for three years means they have to pay me benefit rather than the lottery of assistance where they could do anything and hope to get away with it.

But then, when did right ever play any major role in the welfare state, or in our social welfare office. From the stories I have heard perhaps I should have taken that first day's advice and signed elsewhere.

GONE FISHIN'   18/8/92

Decide to go fishing today. Catch the last weeks of freedom. Bring the girl-friend along because I love her and she has a car. This used to be the central freedom of my life, the air, the fields, the soft incurious water. I have lost that freedom over the last couple of years, as much out of carelessness as anything else. It is to be regretted.

The day is a soft rainy one and beautiful for it. I catch a fish, lose it a foot from the bank. A red mist appears in front of my face and I relive my past experience as a Gurkha psychopath. The peaceful tranquillity is broken by a volley of curses and the forbidden word is uttered. Girlfriend tut tuts. "Fuck off", I mutter.

"What?" Mutter mumble, then synchronised sulking. The spell, the peace has been broken. But it is too strong.

The beauty of the day grafts itself upon us, healing and tranquillising our earlier querulous anger, pulling both of us away from pettiness. The grandeur of that scene allows us, in a way that Dublin cannot, to realise the emptiness of our quarrels.

This is so different from the city. There, money, ugly folding paper is the currency of life. Without it you are imprisoned in the grotty bedsit. Here there is so much more to do which is real, is close to the business, the truth of life, fishing, hunting, even a garden. Here, even unemployed, you can be partially independent, not a total parasite.

We return to the claustrophobic city more at peace than for a long time, regretful of our departure from those high mountains, that clear blue sky, the lapping waves of the fertile lake.

PROOF THAT I AM LOOKING FOR WORK   20/8/92

Official looking letter arrives from Head Office seeking confirmation that I am looking for work. Puts the heart across me until I realise what they want. I thought for a moment they were looking for a signed confession or something.

This is the genius of the Irish Social Welfare system, to make you feel guilty even if you are innocent. Luckily I have kept some proof, a couple of letters of application, a few refusals from the last months, otherwise I would have been roasted. But why wasn't I told these would be needed. Normally I would have thrown these out. But, of course, this is always the first rule of the department, to keep claimants in the dark as long as possible and as often as possible. And why do they need these from me when I am applying for benefit?

INITIAL RESPONSE TO THE DOLE   21/8/92

It is a strange uncomfortable feeling being on the dole. You don't know how to react. Hope that it will soon be over is the dominant emotion, mingled with a strange irrational guilt. You say "I'm on the dole" out of the corner of your mouth. Like "I'm in detox," or, "They gave me the Probation Act". You feel in some way cheap. Above all, you hope that this is only a transient phase and that soon things will go back to normal and you will inherit the earth as promised.

The scattered nature of the above indicates that I am not quite sure how I am supposed to feel. It's all a bit too early, though if I am on it for any considerable time all the well-worn phrases will begin to form. "Betrayal of a generation". "We are the disinherited." Etc., etc., etc. Then it will be time to start off the old internal rant of my college days, the sweet tune of self-pity – it's okay for you with your Daddy and your connections, your easy paid-for education. Easy for you to get a job. No wonder there's none left for the likes of me. Take it out on my girlfriend. That's not fair, but neither is life.

It's too early to be anticipating such disasters, to wonder will I end up like those grey beaten failures associated with unemployment in the public imagination. I don't feel anger, disillusion, bitterness – not after three weeks! What I do feel is a dislocation, and with it a hidden uneasiness. What if, what if?

MORE LETTERS FROM HEAD OFFICE   24/8/92
Another letter from Head Office this morning. Don't know whether to be amused or annoyed at the nature of these people. Still on this crap of £29 a week. This should be sorted out by now. If I was as inefficient as these people I would have the head eaten off me in public. They want to know am I on a higher education grant and if so, why haven't I reported it. Well, the answer to the second is easy. As I don't have one there is nothing to report.

I ring them up but, of course that isn't enough. They could phone the local authority but that, of course, would be logical. I take two buses into my old college and my friends in the Registrar's building. They laugh, I laugh at the absurdity. What else is there to do? But slowly, insidiously as I return, the feeling grows in me that something is wrong and that I am not being told about it.

SIGNING ON   25/8/92
Again Dole morning, the same heavy, leaden feeling. There is no joy in this free charity. I get up, body heavy and smelly from a fretful sleep. My head and shoulders are tight and tense and I can feel that familiar bastard of a headache, lurking, sniggering in the background. Usual Eastern Bloc crew, interminable, moving in a sullen grey pastel. God – we spend our lives in queues waiting for money, for buses, waiting, always waiting.

I light a cigarette. It tastes sour in my unwashed mouth. Why are there always queues? Why are they always grey? Why is it always raining in this country? Inside a woman is shouting.

Missus, for God's sake don't hold the queue up. Let family, home, sons, life collapse but don't ever break the etiquette of queues. Don't make me be here a moment longer than is necessary.

The man behind the counter is unrelenting and inevitably the storm peters out. The woman disappears in a series of mumbled after-shocks, carrying her troubles with her.

Thank God the queue has started to move again. I take the form from the woman. Twenty-nine quid . . . again. I feel very cold, like hurting someone unfairly. I throw form and pen back at the woman, snap the money from her hands and stalk out. Petty really, but that's the way I feel. It's going to be a bad day.

THE IMPORTANCE OF PLACES   26/8/92

Everyone needs places, somewhere transcendental, different, somewhere in your heart, your mind, that is a little slice of heaven. It does not matter that to outsiders these things are normal or mundane. I am fortunate in this dour country, this awful winter, to possess two.

So despite all the confusion, the uncertainty, the anger, I am happy. That I have a degree, future, etc. is important but the other things are so much more valuable. There are so many dead people in Ireland 1992. You see them every day in the bubble commuter world of train, bus, car, their eyes hollow and dead within the made-up faces, the suits of the hard sell world.

They, God love them, have no escape, no freedom. I am fortunate, so so fortunate to have these, to have been given the gift of seeing God in the greenery of those quiet fields, Catherine's eyes, to possess connection with both. Sometimes the visions seem to mingle; the quiet beauty of these small wintry fields with their poignant evening-song, mirroring my lover's eyes. Connection and freedom that is what we seek.

"Where are these places?" I hear you, half cynical, half hopeful onlooker ask. Curious, distant, cold, are you not? These places are in fact choices. A field, hedgerow, a kiss, the scent of a lover's back, the comforting of a whisper at night, places, worlds forgotten by the marketing men in their campaigns.

DOGS   27/8/92

Of all animals dogs are my favourite. They are the most human of the four-legged species and the ones I want to see going to heaven. All my pets waiting for me as I go down the long tunnel with the light beckoning. Lassie, Toby, Timmie, all waiting for me with their tails wagging. Awww! Phone Little House on the Prairie quick!

Cats on the other hand are both narky and boring. They are the chartered accountants of the animal world, nervy, claws out, always waiting to strike, and always justifying themselves afterwards.

These deep thoughts are inspired by the fact that there is a bitch in heat in the estate and we are surrounded by incipient lovers, all with the same happy happy calypso type expression that only dogs possess when life is good.

One lover has brought a present. Deferentially and with a wagging tail of love he lays last week's ribs, coated with a delicate breadcrumb of maggots, at her feet.

Their frolics bring great entertainment. There is nothing closer to the delicate movement of a ballerina than the capers of dogs around a bitch in heat. All of human life is played out on the green in front of us. Love, sex, greed, jealously, hurt, hate. Even dogs are capitalists, the bigger ones warning poodles and terriers of their status in the pecking tree of life with menacing growls.

And then, of course, there is that inevitable unfortunate curious child. "Mammy, what is our Rufus doing with that dog?" Smack; and a chorus of inevitable bawls mingles decorously with yaps, whimpers and pants. Most tragic of all, however, is the arrival of the inevitable spoil-sports as yet another chaperon hauls away a reluctant courtier leaving paw-marks in the turf. Aw, go on, let 'im stay. Booo.

BOXES   28/8/92

Am getting fed up of the waiting already. I feel imprisoned in the house, waiting for the letter that says yes. Impatient to get out there, doing things. Impatient also with the waiting for the dole office. I am very frustrated by the lack of communication, as though I, specifically, of the three hundred thousand am an irritation. I am beginning to sense a trap here as though they are waiting for me to get fed up and leave.

My mood has not been improved by the new house. Buy cheap, get cheap. Everything in it is second-hand or decaying, its narrow damp rooms imprisoning like a servants' quarters. Cannot feel comfortable in a world where there is nothing for me to do. Only the aristocracy are educated to enjoy a life of liberty.

The sense of imprisonment is enhanced by the fact that every other house around me is the same. All of us safe in our little boxes. Standardised homes, standardised lives. People spend, waste their entire lives to possess these little boxes. Do they not feel betrayed? There is no difference, no independence or beauty here. Is this it? Is this everything? Do they not want more? I could never dedicate my life to this. The sameness bears in, depressing imprisoning, frightening. I want out of here.

MADWOMAN IN DUBLIN   29/8/92

Go to a film in Dublin. Leaving, we see an old woman waltzing beside the statue of William Smith O'Brien. They make a curious contrast. He, like all the statues of our dead patriots, looks grey and sombre, lifeless in bronze. Her hair flows loosely in the wind, her face smiling beatifically at the gathering of corner boys, gurriers, and curious onlookers. It is a moment, both farcical and beautiful, like something out of Hill Street Blues.

She has no partner, no music except that singing in her mind, peaceful and complete in her totality. I envy her, but not covetously. She has no doubt, no conscience, she is free of all these fretful things. Later the evening sun will calm her. Stretching in it, enjoying, like a cat or bored queen, the elements, rain, wind and sun are her gods. Funny really, ours are more capricious.

CRICKET   30/8/92

I wonder is there that much distance between me and the woman in Dublin. End up playing cricket with myself in the living room today. Everything is set up perfectly. The table acts as the pitch, a wine-glass indicates a wicket, the wall indicates a boundary and a match-stick acts as a cricket ball. Am I writing this down? The pitch/table is seaming wildly. I know my stuff! Decimate the Australian innings thus becoming a national hero. My figures are wildly impressive and I write them down for the record.

First Innings

O	M	R	W	Ex
30	12	78	7	4

Second Innings

O	M	R	W	Ex
19	7	30	5	7

A ten wicket match. Every cricketer's dream.

Only one thing spoils the victory. The Australians are on the point of collapse in the second innings, needing forty runs to avoid the follow on. I am concentrating intensely and bowling like a demon. Suddenly I am disturbed by a low snicker. My girlfriend has been watching me for fifteen minutes. Has she nothing better to do with her time?

"Golf?" she asks archly. I resist the temptation to be rude.

"Cricket", I respond.

"Are you winning?" she asks.

"We're winning", I respond emphasising the "we". Cricket is after all a team game and I depend on my team mates to hold their catches.

"I'd better not disturb you". Silence, heavy with irony, then with a final chirrup, "Well, good luck". Another snigger as she leaves the room indicates that she still has not understood the seriousness of the occasion. My pride falls a thousand times. I return to the match but the spell is broken.

TEACHING INTERVIEW   31/8/92

Attend teaching interview today. Don't particularly want the job. Teaching in modern Ireland is a short-cut to either insanity, or inanity? Heart sinks when I see the interview board. Plonked right in the middle, smiling, is the Fianna Fail Councillor. Job done, job gone. But at least something has been learned from the day. His election photographs are not unflattering. A right little slieveen, his moustache is bigger than his face. He sets his face into a severe mask but his eyes sparkle, enjoying his small power, the summit of his aspiration reached: the interview room of the V.E.C.

I watch patiently. A torrent of words issue through the moustache as he pretends a knowledge he doesn't possess. That's two of us. The questions seem to come from another world. I'm not here. This is a farce, a waste. I come out with all the usual rubbish. The tone of my voice varies from stern to concerned. Yes, I believe in discipline.

"Strict discipline?"

"Oooh yes". This is beginning to sound like one of those 0898 numbers and I wonder briefly am I in the right place.

Then it's time to satisfy the Labour member. My voice begins to resemble that of Monica Barnes crossed with Alice Taylor, as the really heavy spoofing begins.

"We must educate our children in such a way as to foster their creativity and self-esteem" etc., etc. Developmental, experiential, fostering, enhancing, education the nursery of the future. You want it, I'll do it . . . and believe it.

I feel superciliously amused through it all. Probably because I know I won't get the job. Probably deservedly, but our hero butts in just to make sure. The power trip over, he moves into anecdotal form.

"When I was in a school," he begins, (I resist the temptation to ask were the hedges cold), "there was an English teacher who used to talk an awful lot of waffle about everything under the sun except his subject. Would you be one of those teachers?"

I resist a second urge to say, "He taught you well". His eyes twinkle as I answer and I smile coldly returning the message.

The interview ends haphazardly and I escape, relieved in the knowledge that I will not be joining the teaching profession in this school anyway. Thank YOU dear friend, gombeen politician, and saviour! But it is tacky to think that these little wankers control my future, everyone's future, the nation's destiny. Gawd help us! And they say education is not political. Canvassing will be forbidden. Joke!

SEPTEMBER

WHY THE MIDDLE-CLASS ARE SO DISEMPOWERED
ON THE DOLE   1/9/92

I feel very imprisoned and disempowered as if these people can do anything to me. It's as if I feel I haven't the right to protest or complain. After all, the dole is unearned money, charity, like the bread the Romans used to give to the mob to stop them sacking whatever was the equivalent of Dunnes Stores at the time. Dole is nothing more than a bribe to the dispossessed to leave the wealthy in tranquil enjoyment of their gains.

The prevalence of this belief among the middle class causes many of them to hit the skids when unemployed. They are too deferential towards the welfare state, too aware of their charitable status to fight their corner. We are always looking towards that life that exists beyond dole, to purge our guilt through paying P.R.S.I. The ones that fail allow themselves to be screwed because this is temporary. Then they find out too late that it is not and then the tragedies begin.

To survive the dole you have to throw aside all conscience and honesty. Social Welfare Officers aren't interested in it. They don't play by all the rules and they don't expect anyone else to do so either. It's a game of poker and your job is to lie and bluff sufficiently well to ensure your survival.

That, of course, is easier said than done. It's difficult for the model conscientious citizen not to feel guilty about free handouts, the insistent voice hissing charity, charity. You can't defeat socialization and upbringing quite that easily; not until you realise that the social welfare state is worse than unrestrained capitalism. Losers do not survive in these cold offices.

MIKE   2/9/92

This town is full of lunatics. There is one less here now. We wondered why the petrol station was open so late. Now we know. One of the lads who was a bit short of cash copied the keys. There he was happily selling away, when the owner drove by. We believe he was somewhat surprised to see a new man at the helm.

Ten minutes later a police car drove in, filled up, first with petrol and then with Mike. Let us hope he gets a District Justice with a sense of humour or admiration for nascent entrepreneurial ability. The destruction of a talent such as Mike's would represent a national tragedy.

CONTINUED STRUGGLE WITH HEAD OFFICE 3/9/92

More letters requested by Head Office. This is the fourth set of letters all utterly pointless which they have demanded. All of these they could do by phone of course, but it is easier and of course cheaper, to send me running around after them. Now they want a letter confirming that I am not re-registering in college. I ask, snappishly of course, (there is no point in being polite to Social Welfare officers – that I know from bitter experience), how is my claim progressing? The response is quick . . . too quick?

Just get this in and we should reach a decision. I put the phone down. Only afterwards do I realise that there should not be a decision to make. Again that stomach-churning suspicion but surely nothing can happen. I have played by the rules. I push doubt and suspicions to the back of my mind. This is not logical. They are not that dishonest. March on down to the bus-stop.

URGENCY OF APPLYING FOR SUPPLEMENTARY WELFARE 4/9/92

This, of course, I have not been told about by my freedom of information-challenged friendly local dole office. I have been wondering how will I survive on £53 a week. Ask someone about this. They laugh. Have you not gone down to the Health Centre? I know it vaguely – a squat ugly building going rapidly to seed like so many others of the type. He tells me I should go urgently. Apparently the first thing I should have done after signing on was to go there and plead abject poverty and demand both a rent allowance and supplementary welfare.

If the enemy see that you have not applied for these then they assume you can survive without welfare and will use every dodge in their manual to avoid paying out. This could explain a lot of things. It is also important as I am rapidly running out of cash. I go down, but even from the outside the place looks so beaten and defeated, sweltering in the harsh sun, that I put it off for another while. I'll be working soon. Today I am not able for them. Work yes, but not that.

HEALTH CENTRE 5/9/92

Still recovering from the first visit to the Health Centre. The heat, the smell, the intolerable oppressive boredom, this enormous sense of wasted time, all combine to profoundly depress me. The whole place is dominated by a group of gurriers and we are left in no doubt that this is their territory. They can have it with my compliments.

I recognise some of them from school. They were the bullies, the ones who made you feel that terror and fear and pain were natural things. Of course they weren't; but you only learnt that later on. They're still at it here, only so much more pathetic. Now their wives and girlfriends get the worst of it.

Victories are small now. They jostle for the front seats of the queue, jumping it with cynical smirks, knowing we won't complain. One of them recognises me. I sigh inwardly, waiting for the smirks and giggles. They have never liked me. I was the bastard who made it, got out of the estate. In Ireland that's unforgivable.

Fortunately their attention is diverted when a woman walks in. She is immediately privileged with the stare. One of the "lads" feels a sudden urgent necessity to tell his mates in graphic detail about what he did to his girlfriend last night. The boys listen in silent awe. Even I'm impressed. Finally one of them murmurs appreciatively, "Fuckin' slut".

The girl looks away. Obviously she is used to this place. Christ, how have I ended up here? They go into the office smiling. They know they'll get their money; no hassle. The Social Welfare Officer knows she's going to be dealing with them for the rest of her career. She prefers to hassle the softer targets, newcomers and transients like me.

When eventually I go in she is actually quite pleasant. Social Welfare Officers are like cops. They operate in pairs, one good Social Welfare Officer, one bad. I must have got the good one.

Or perhaps her pleasantness was influenced by the fact that I had waited four hours to discover that I would not qualify for a rent allowance until my benefit comes through. Then I will be paid in full, back-dated of course. No such word as front-dated in the English language or the Social Welfare handbook. I leave with the glazed smile of someone who has just left an insurance agent's office. The boys are just going past the office carrying their flagons of cider. Tonight they'll kick somebody's head in.

MATURE RECOLLECTION   6/9/92

Am getting very fed up with all this delay and obfuscation. This latest information on supplementary welfare has really angered me. It so typifies everything. They tell you absolutely nothing in that office. Everything has to be dragged out of them.

They neglect to inform you that whilst you are waiting for benefit to come through that you can get emergency supplementary welfare from the Health

Board. They tell you nothing about rent allowances, about the qualifications for benefit or assistance, about when the Social Welfare Officer will call, one week, three weeks, nine weeks, when she is in a good humour.

These people seem to possess the attitude of mind that we are all born knowing the intricacies of the Social Welfare system. Credits, stamps, queuing – that all you have been aiming for since birth is to rip off the Welfare Department for as much as is humanly possible, for as long as possible. It's a bit like the state's attitude to sex education. Tell them nothing and they won't ask awkward questions. Is this the Minister's policy? If so, it is rather at odds with his regularly stated desire to create a user-friendly service. That indeed would be a revolutionary step.

PARANOIA 7/9/92

Ring up Head Office today to ask when is my claim coming through. I feel like a beggar or as though I am being unnecessarily difficult but things are very tight financially and there is little sign of progress. Am switched from department to department for 15 minutes. After about ten minutes of this I begin to feel I am being laughed at, that there is a group of them all huddled together over the phone chuckling at my growing frustration. Where will we send him next, lads.

I know this is illogical but I am starting to feel very tense about this refusal to give out information or commitments. Eventually I am fudged off again. Next week.

"Is there a problem?", I ask.

"No, no, we just want to clarify some things".

There is a problem. I know it, no, not know, sense, and that is worse than knowing. I can sense it, hear the deceit in the voices. Why can't they be honest with me? It wouldn't take this long if there wasn't a problem. They wouldn't be this secretive. But I can do nothing and the tension and the powerlessness scuttling around my mind in fast, spiteful little circles have left me feeling hysterical and weird. Why can't they just tell me?

KISSES 8/9/92

Memories and love are frightening things. They cherish and sustain but they can also haunt. A song, a passing car, a face. . .reminding. But there can be no fear in real love. We are in a field. I kiss her and in that kiss I know I have created an image, a dream I will never escape.

Today all wariness is dead. The brilliant colours, grass and sky, the leaves gold in their death, flowing sunlight, all the more intense for the knowledge that its span is borrowed, enhance the moment. The clear cold air mingles with the heat of our kisses.

I am on fire for the heat of her lips feed me. I feel like a vampire drinking in the beauty, the heat of another life, to fill me, to know again what living is, something forgotten for too long. Always and always when we kiss I think of the giddy spaces of America, those prairies and clear blue skies and then it is all too much and we break . . . dazed.

There is danger here but the beauty calms and dismisses. It is rich to sleep with someone again at night, so different from this sleeping alone. We are too alone in this world. As I sleep in her arms it is as if I have returned home, returned to childhood in that yielding body.

The one exception to all these joys is what Hitler called the question of *lebensraum*/living space. Life in a single bed is exciting/passionate but it is also very very crowded. At least one thing women have not learnt is the male technique of acquiring space in such circumstances. It is a secret move like that of *Karate Kid I, II, III* etc., passed on from grandfather to father to son, just one move and victory, complete total irreversible, is secured. Then the complaints begin.

But by then I am asleep.

EDUCATION   9/9/92

Out on the beer last night. Met the town bore . . . pissed as a newt . . . again. Ranted and raved about how educationally deprived he had been, his struggle, *Mein Kampf*, how the system had failed him. Nothing of his own weaknesses. Those like the fairies, do not exist.

We laughed at him afterwards, not because the system had been unfair to him – perhaps it had – but at the stupid bathos of his self-pity, the expectation that people barely connected with him would take his struggle into their own hearts and fight his own battles for him. It just don't work that way. The system/society doesn't screw you. It's indifferent, neutral. You only screw yourself.

Part of the laughter for me is self-defence. There is so much of me that wants to take the self-destructive route, abnegate all responsibility, cry out, "I was that soldier too". I feel the old self-disgust welling. Am I like him? More terrifying, will I end up like that empty vessel? Joyce's Citizen, all piss and wind. I can sense that . . . lurking inside me . . .waiting . . . for the first sign of failure. Wanting it?

JOE   10/9/92
Sometimes I think *Punch* and the *Daily Express* are right and that the nation as a whole should not become too upset over articles in either depicting the Irish as mad. The thought is inspired by Joe, a name which has always carried for me a certain aura of mystique and authority, signifying an individual who lives beyond the dull constraints of normal living. Perhaps this is a hidden result of having read Flann O'Brien's *The Third Policeman*. Perhaps it is the beginning of a dangerous monomania. I don't know.

This, of course, all has a point. Met someone called Joe today. Joe has three jobs, bricklaying, betting and signing on and does all three well. At this moment in time Joe's banklink/dole office is being rebuilt which means he has to sign on fifteen miles away. An inconvenience. But what is Joe doing the other five days of the week? You've guessed it. He's rebuilding his old dole office. Minister, you are dopey!

DISCOVERIES   11/9/92
It's four weeks now and still I'm in this shit. He hands the giro out dispassionately as if it is natural to live on £29 a week. I snap at him and he recoils disgusted at this show of independence. "Phone Head Office" is his response. Again!?

It is an experience in the surreal. At the start I had forty units on my phone card. By the end I have five and an angry queue. Am obfuscated gloriously, passed from person to person to non person department, to sub-department, like a rugby ball at a match. They're laughing at me. What is this? Some kind of game?

The thoughts race through my head burrowing like trapped rats. Am almost hysterical by now, feeling the first dull thumps of my familiar friend, the pain, oscillating with my pulsing brain. Finally lose it, exploding a volley of curses down the phone. This is not an act, it is the first time ever I have been totally out of control. The bastards have reduced me to this quivering, crying blob. The woman at the other end is genuinely shocked by the ferocity of my attack. She says she too will check it out. Go on love, join the queue.

When she returns I apologise sincerely for the outburst. It's probably not her fault but this is my seventh phone call and still I have received no information. It's probably not her fault that I have already been on the phone for an hour. And she's probably not responsible for the "Please fuck off, we'll get to you, okay, okay" attitude of her colleagues, invariably followed by a weary sigh when I ask for someone else. "What rights does this wanker think he has?"

All this, however, excuses nothing. I can feel only disgust with myself. I have let them win, let myself down as a man and a person . . . . At last success. She has news and as she tells me the decision I feel the wind going out of my lungs, the bottom of my stomach going absent. Of course, I'm not eligible for benefit, never was. They knew that from the second week. Just never bothered telling me. Why bother? He's a student. He's rich. He'll kick up in the office. Maybe he'll go away soon. Aw, don't spoil his morning. Too lazy. Whatever reason they just didn't bother telling me.

The reason? The rule, paragraph 3, sub-section 9.783. Stamps earned whilst being a student do not qualify you for benefit. You have to work a week after leaving college before they count. In other words the state had been defrauding me by deducting P.R.S.I. from my salary whilst I was in college. This is useless to me now. I have paid into the system. Yet despite the fact that I have over two years' stamps, despite the fact that I am now unemployed, penniless and have finished college, I do not qualify for benefit. These are minor things compared to the rule, the god who must be obeyed. I argue these points with her but it is futile and I am too beaten to put up much of a struggle. She advises me to try for assistance. That will be a joke. I leave the 'phone box laughing.

HEALTH CENTRE   12/9/92

So the bastards switched the rules. Like everything and everyone else. Make it as hard for me as is legally possible. These rules seem to have been specially designed and tailored to ensure the system screws me and only me. Of course this is paranoia. Of course it's illogical. But I am too filled with angry self-pity to care. I don't like taking charity. I don't like taking money I haven't earned, but I've no choice and the first time I need the system it fails me . . . totally.

The Health Centre today is another unique experience. There is always a certain surreal horror attached to waiting there. This morning Gerry Ryan rabbits away happily about knickers before the heartless controller of the radio switches us over to something resembling music for hicks and a wave of country 'n' western music attacks the air. The place is as miserable as before, same gurriers squabbling at the front.

It's forty feet to the office and we move at a rate of what seems a foot an hour. The little pink card is the key to liberty. Those who haven't got one watch the others enviously. They will be out by one. You cannot smoke here, an excellent rule, given that most of us smoke. Leaving your seat is a dangerous risk as twenty eyes covet the space. Going outside for a smoke can cost you an hour.

By the time I reach the office I feel I know the place like my own home. It must be so dispiriting to come to this place week after week after week, these dingy off-white walls stained with sweat and unknown substances. A luminous green fungus, or worse, is thriving on the windows. In the middle there is a square surrounded by glass. A few crooked trees wilt in the baleful space. The glass, the trees, serve only to enhance the oppressive heat, and the whole atmosphere of waste and futility. This place will remain imprinted on my brain.

Go into the office ready for war but I am disarmed by the fact that this woman is actually pleasant. This, however, is poor consolation for the good news. I ask her about rent allowance and supplementary welfare until I get assistance. Guess what? The rule. The all-knowing all encompassing fucking rule, that has no wrong and allows no exceptions. They cannot pay me until the Board is satisfied that I am a *bona fide* case. She should know next week.

I am so confused I am incapable of pressing her. Too honest me, although proud would be more accurate. She takes all the details, half embarrassed at the madness of it all. She assures me there should be no problems and ushers me towards the door.

"Do you want any other letters?" She pauses just for a moment, then says "No" and I am out very quickly, too relieved at leaving the place to think about anything else.

Outside I feel the familiar tight ball of hysteria building and building, knotting my stomach, waiting to explode in my head. But I am too weary for that today. I could smash the room, indulge in a little shouting and screaming at the woman to let her know what I feel but what real good would that do? Bastards, my girlfriend says. Yeah, love, and a lot you'd know about it too with your new little car. Daddy's present.

Rules are strange things. They seem so innocent, so fragile, so irrelevant to the business of living when printed on those slips of government paper. In practice though they are like iron. The man admitted to hospital last year suffering from malnutrition, because of the rule. Only then was the iron grip released. In Ireland! In soft twentieth century Ireland, easy Ireland, according to our good friends the P.D.s. This man was not a loafer or a derelict but someone trying to make something of himself. He too had worked his way through college, paid his stamps. These are the ones they go after. Trying to better ourselves. We'll soon smack 'em down. I consider the option of going on hunger strike. The way things are going I may soon have no other option.

ANGER AND DISGUST   13/9/92

It's all very well trying to be mature and philosophical about this but that's no consolation. Neither does it avoid the essential fact that the first time I ask, really need help from my social welfare system it has failed me. All because I don't fit a pattern, a rule, a typical case, the only one bureaucrats can respect. I wouldn't mind if I paid nothing into the system but I have and it's useless to me. There are people who have never paid anything getting dole with a quarter of the hassle I am receiving. Of course my stamps will come into play after I get my first job outside of college. Fat lot of use they are to me then.

But we can't break the rule. Better let people starve rather than, God forbid, the Civil Service be seen to act justly, be seen to actually serve the needs of the people. Why should I be calm? I'm being screwed. I'm entitled to shout and scream a little.

It's no fun trying to chase a job whilst this is going on. All these C.V.s, folders, etc. cost money, money I do not have. That's another little catch 22 situation my friends have created. If they're so anxious to get me off the dole, why don't they pay me the fucking thing so I can get proper C.V.s and, Eureka! a proper job.

MORE TRICKS AND JAPES OF THE WELFARE DEPARTMENT   14/9/92

Learnt another trick of our Welfare Department today. When you're signing on after college what they do is wait six weeks and then ask you to produce a letter saying you've left college. During that time they don't process your claim. This means that they can wait for ten weeks before paying you. The whole process is facilitated if they accidentally forget to remind you about the supplementary benefits you are (theoretically at least) entitled to .

The idea, of course, is to drive you away from the city to your home town so they only have to pay you twenty pounds a week instead of seventy. I wonder what ambitious little civil servant got promotion on the head of that. Bright wee man. We should get him to run the economy. I wonder has my little friend down in the Health Centre cottoned on to it?

SURPRISE!   15/9/92
I call in today. And surprise, surprise, of course she has. Unfortunately my claim cannot be finally processed until I give her a letter specifically stating that I have finished college.

"Is that *all* that you are looking for?", I ask with a touch of cynicism in my voice. She sounds upset, almost disappointed that I actually mightn't believe her. Good actor, darling. One thing I have finally learned is to trust none of these people particularly the friendly sounding ones. At least the bastards possess the virtue of honesty. I think of asking for a commitment in writing but somehow I think that would be refused.

It's some indictment of our welfare system that I am actually thinking this way. I ask her will the letters that I sent into Head Office confirming I am no longer a registered student and have finished my degree suffice, but of course they won't. I flash her the sweetest of smiles as I leave and just when she is at her most defenceless ask very nicely could she not have asked for those yesterday. She is confused for a moment, then replies, "I thought we mightn't need them". I smile knowingly and leave. Hypocritical old bitch.

SEPTEMBER AND MORE DEPRESSION   16/9/92
When you are on the breadline everything combines to depress you. It's enough living on the dole but the actual squalor of the house enhances the sensation. It is one of these places which can never be clean, no matter how often you wash it. Middle-class people have no conception of what this means. They think that working-class estates are dirty because the inhabitants are slovenly. They think our homes are the same as theirs . . . just wash it and it's clean.

That's easily done if the house isn't damp or rotting. That sort of house is never clean no matter what you do. As I write I can see the paint bubbling up from the walls. The carpets below are shoddy and rotten. A hoover would belong to the wrong century in this house, whilst it is hardly comforting to see half the fuse-box swathed in bandages. That looks as it if is going to go up soon. It should solve the problem of the damp nicely.

I feel trapped and enclosed here as if this place is a nightmare or a vision of the future. The whole squalor and damp and rot enhances the claustrophobia of the place, turning us in tightly against ourselves. It is a place that can never be cleaned, that can never be called home.

EXAMPLES . . . 17/9/92

See someone lose their head in the dole office today. A pathetic, flailing, stupid sight. Utterly pointless with the inevitable results. Climbing down faster than a cat meeting a bear in a tree. It really copped me on. There's no point in paranoia or hysteria. You've got to keep your head or the bastards will just laugh at you. There's no point in screaming at these people. They are as bound by rules as you are. Besides, if you antagonise one of the pettier ones nothing more assured but that they will tie your application so tightly in red tape that you will never get even what you are entitled to.

DEFEAT LITHUANIA 18/9/92

Ireland defeat Lithuania or some other Baltic country today. Another great day for the nation, national uplift, fillip for national morale etc. etc. Perhaps we could send Reynolds or Haughey or whoever is our present great national leader over there for the celebrations. Perhaps they might keep them. Now that would do a lot for national morale.

What is that awful squealing tuneless sound I hear in the background? Has somebody been knocked down? Someone quick, call an ambulance and bystanders. Oh Sweet Jesus, it's the first World Cup song.

"The ghost of World Cup Songs of past returneth. Myself and Scrooge bail out."

The only thing that keeps me in the country is the cartoon section of the *Irish Independent.* It's full of excitement these days, what with the Baron going mad in Curly Wee. No, I can't explain. It's too big a story.

27

ANOTHER KICK IN THE TEETH 19/9/92

And, of course, we have more problems. The letter, surprise, surprise, was unsatisfactory . . . They want another one. Until then, unless the S.W.O. gets around to seeing me or I get the result of my degree they are going to categorise me as a student. It is not the nice Social Welfare Officer today. Instead it is the bad cop.

They can't do this. Yes they can. I have three weeks to wait for my results. That's another three weeks of £29, another three weeks of charity. It means eviction. I cannot afford the rent for the house.

I tell her it wasn't like this before. She looks at me coldly. Obviously I am a professional loafer. We've had a lot of fraud by students. We've had to tighten up the rules. Tried, guilty and convicted. It's all legal. There's nothing I can do except feel bitter. Pointless even shouting and screaming. She'd love that. Another victory. I feel for the first time in my life so utterly helpless, apathetic, almost waiting for life to happen to me, waiting to be a victim. I go home to bed and sleep for the day. There really is nothing better to do . . . .

CHARITY 20/9/92

Yes indeed, excellent sentiments those of the 17th but sometimes difficult to maintain. This is particularly the case when one is officially dependent on the charity of friends. Can't pay the rent, can't pay the coal. I've always been proud of my self-reliance, the *soi disant* legend of the man who paid his way through college. That's well and truly dissipated.

Instead I'm just another parasite living off my girlfriend or more accurately her parents, just to plunge the knife in a little further. In circumstances like that it's hard to be calm with these anonymous indifferent people on the phone with their permanent jobs and their dammed inflexible Chinese rules, all seemingly specifically tailored towards someone like me . . . .

HOUSE I 21/9/92

House is turning into a disaster area. Now we know why it was so cheap. This place is claustrophobic, its narrowness choking and repressing. We seem squeezed in around each other, intruding, grasping everyone else's space. The tension is intense, almost visible. Now I can see why so many marriages on the poverty line break up. The constant proximity results in people overpowering each other.

The place itself is falling apart, combining damp with intense cold. Last night the electricity went, joining the cooker and the grill. It's depressing enough being on the dole without having this ramshackle hole collapse all around you.

Interestingly enough the landlady is proving very difficult to contact. This is perhaps not as bad as first appears. Thanks to our great social welfare system about which I learn more and more each week, it doesn't look as if I can pay any rent this month. It's just one more thing. Put it on the rest of the pile. God, this is embarrassing. It's more than embarrassing. It's beginning to become slightly frightening.

GOLF   22/9/92

Sometimes I worry about the fantasies which dominate my interior world. Have been playing golf with myself for the last few weeks to break the boredom. It all ends in agony as I lose the British Open and with it the chance of the Grand Slam by three strokes. First of all, psychiatric problems, then an assertiveness deficit, a crisis of confidence and now juvenile dementia.

Back, however, to the drama. The year starts off well. Win US PGA with a sizzling final round of 62 – this on a course I don't like. The US Open follows and the world watches in silent awe. When I win the Irish Open by a record 28 shots it all looks set for the hat-trick. Burdened by favouritism I open poorly with a 76. Come back strongly with a 64 and a 62, both course records, to become joint leader on the final day. Go out in 31 to lead by three at the ninth.

Golf, however, finds out a man's innermost soul, that and the fates, and it appears that this year I am not destined to win. A few loose shots and a sizzling (is this about golf or sausages) 64 by Greg Norman leaves me needing a birdie on the last hole to tie for a play-off. A poor first shot leaves me gambling all on the second. It nearly comes off but I bogey to finish third. Still, one can't complain about a cheque for £50,000 and anyway it's nice to see Greg winning something. Still haven't told the dole office about my golfing nixer. Am starting to feel guilty about this, given my millionaire status.

This is soon resolved. Return to a government reception. Tell Albert about my dilemma. "Don't listen to the meeja," he really is a lovely chap. He says,
"Listen, you've made Ireland proud, you've made me proud".
The tears are falling down both our cheeks.
"Keep the dole in perpetuity, it's our gift to you".

He leaves, his final words,
    "Just do it for us in the Ryder Cup".
Brian Lenihan asks me about the cricket.
    "Game ball Brian", sez I, "I'll have the Ashes wound up next week".
    "Any chance of you declaring for Ireland?"
    "I will", sez I, "You get me a team and we can enter the world cup".
    "No problem, I'll fix it with Dick".
    Later that night it is announced that in return for Ireland taking over the six counties, the U.K. will allow me to play for Ireland, this despite tearful protests from the Queen and Maggie Thatcher, both of whom are concerned about the decline of the U.K. cricket team. A nation celebrates and on this happy note we end this edition of Ballymagash virtual reality . . . .

WORKING CLASS EDUCATIONAL
DISINCENTIVES . . .WHY? . . .   23/9/92
    It's wonderful the incentives you get to make something of yourself in our charming republic. I have just finished working my way through college for two years. No grant. Not because I am outside the financial limits, nothing as simple or logical as that, but because of *de rule*. Now because of another *de rule* I am going through this.
    I wouldn't mind if I were alone in all this. I could mount a constitutional challenge or appeal to Europe but hundreds, probably thousands, face the same disabilities and society finds this acceptable. We compete against all these nice middle-class boys 'n' girls with their financial security and their pocket money. Heaven help us if we complain. Then we face the unpleasant noise of parents and siblings in their hereditary posts screaming at us to be grateful and not to be such moaning minnies etc. etc.
    So we continue to fight our unequal wars with our attitude problems. Bad news in this nepotists' paradise. I strongly suspect the motivation behind many of these hindrances. Is it all down to bureaucratic stupidity? Or is the big idea behind these restrictions to engage in a little selective pruning to ensure that all their nice sons and daughters do not face too much competition from the un-couth masses competing with their own scions for jobs, honours, places. Truly, like so much else in this awful republic, we have the shadow rather than the substance of equality. Certainly they could not have made it any more difficult for me if they tried.

The Irish state is no longer confessional. Yes. But forget all this guff about the triumph of pluralism. All that has replaced the old oppressors is a middle class oligarchy dressed in the decent drapery of social democracy. The state is their property, education within it free, but not too free. Otherwise everyone would use it.

PASSION   24/9/92

We make love this afternoon. Catching time, holding it, creating memories. That is the essence of love. These days are precious now, more than the others which went before, days full of the sweetness which plays so short a song in our lives before the gods take over, work, responsibility, mortgage, residents' associations. So we indulge in our last sips of the sweetness of freedom, the last of the lightness of being.

The greyness of that week, of that house is lost in a moment. I am drinking tea, she leads me from the kitchen, that strange violent fire lighting her eyes. We undress silently as though conscious of the sacramental nature of this . . . for us. It is as though she can see through me completely, those eyes burning through the evil, guilt, deceit, seeing a truer, purer me. All fears are gone.

I am carried with her, half dazed yet passionate, desiring possession so strongly, so fully. She gasps, her eyes away in that far distant country. Her passion frightens me sometimes, drawing a heat from deep within me. I no longer possess myself. I am soft first then thrust, hard, wanting only to be freed from the intensity of that desire, the gape of wanting.

Gone; swallowed by that intensity. Normality returns slowly. I see the room now. Dark in the afternoon light. Outside a world is surviving. Nothing more. But this room with its heavy scent, its cries of passion is a little bit of heaven hidden within the socks, the shoes and the earplugs. Outside they are waiting for the buses.

Our eyes are calm now with the hidden song of a lark in a childhood summer. It is dusk now. Hours have gone. Unnoticed. The fading light reflects our cooled bodies lying, poised, at ease. We sleep. Connection. What we all seek in the rush and the heat.

HASTEN VISIT OF SOCIAL WELFARE OFFICER   25/9/92

Back to reality. Still waiting for the Social Welfare Officer's visit. I am by now totally fed up with this shit. This is my pride, my life, these dozy wankers are playing with. Nail deference to the wall today and kick up a rumpus for ten minutes in the Welfare Office. Even brave the wrath of the queue. I strike a nerve somewhere between publicity and going to my local T.D., probably the latter, and surprise, surprise, I'm to visit her tomorrow.

That's the problem with most of us here. We'd starve out of politeness. We should be more ruthless in dealing with these people. They take advantage of everything but particularly politeness and ignorance to deny us everything they can. Really they're wasted here. Most of them would make excellent capitalists.

INTERVIEW WITH THE VAMPIRE   26/9/92

Health Centre was too crowded yesterday so I am told to come along today. After all, what else have I to be doing with my time? My interview is an unforgettable experience. What a battle-axe. Yes, I know it's sexist but this woman was a younger version of Norah Batty. I knew she was trouble the moment I walked in. The face was set with the cold determination of someone who just knew I was a chancer. She complimented me with a grunt that I think passed for hello then glared at me with cold self-regarding eyes. Pleasantries over, the interrogation began.

The interview confirmed the accuracy of first impressions. There are two types of Social Welfare Officer. One is unpleasant because of the nature of the job. The other is unpleasant out of choice. This was the latter. The questions were coldly spiteful and at this stage in my life I'm not sensitive. Perhaps on recollection it was the tone which got me.

"Why aren't you working?"

"Why can't you get a job?"

"Are you trying?"

"Why don't you emigrate?" Then finally, the best one of all.

"Why don't you go live somewhere else!" . . . and I thought only Cromwell was into rural resettlement. I mean how do you answer a question like that. I began to explain that as I had lived here for seventeen years it kind of felt like home, that my girlfriend, that all my friends live here, but that all seemed very irrelevant in the teeth of those eyes. Why bother? I am only a thing, a nuisance. That is abundantly clear. So I mutter something about better job opportunities and leave it at that.

I leave feeling like a piece of shit.

"Pretend you're stupid, that you know nothing". That was my amateur solicitor's advice before entering. That wouldn't be too far off the truth. But I, of course, was stupid, too proud to play the thick Paddy in my own country. That's not an acceptable luxury amongst the unemployed today. It wasn't even anything she said. No, she's too cute for that, just the attitude of distaste. Clear as broken glass.

They wonder why people cheat the system. Two reasons, necessity and revenge. Strangely enough the unemployed do not want to spend their lives living like a higher caste of animal. But there is also the element of pleasure in our cheating. Revenge at people like her, revenge at being forced to pretend to be humble, obeisant, stupid, in order to cater to the arrogant superiority of madame la vampire, anger at being judged slaves in their own land, free only to use the methods of slaves as revenge.

C.McCREEVY AND THE RESPONSIBILITY TO CREATE WORK   27/9/92
Charlie McCreevy, part-time conscience of the nation during the Haughey era is on T.V. Lecturing us. Another one? We have to create jobs for ourselves. They, (by this I presume he means the unemployed, for this is the term traditionally used to describe us) cannot just depend on others to do this for them. For a moment I feel guilty. Must invent something dazzling and new next week. Employ a thousand people. Save the country.

There's just one problem, Charlie, we're not trained to do that. Too much of the emphasis within the academic system is geared towards providing us with solicitors, civil servants, teachers, even accountants, a professional post, the sole aims of the Irish bourgeois. Actually, Charlie, you're one of those, aren't you. How many jobs have you created?

Anyway, Charlie, tell me how do you start a business on the dole? Where do you raise the capital? I mean it's hardly a great advertisement for the budding entrepreneur.

"And what do you do young man?"

"Um, I'm on the scratcher".

Even all these government schemes you're inventing to massage the unemployment figures don't train people to set up their own business. All in all it appears very easy for the likes of Mr. McCreevy to draft a sexy press release, shout about the need for self-reliance but beyond that he appears as toothless as the rest of us. What about red tape, taxation, all these things, government inspired, which make self-employment the last refuge of the deluded or the masochistic?

CHICKEN THIEF   28/9/92

After discussing the problems of the nation, today it's back to the normal business of living. Deterioration of my character continues apace. Buy six quarters of chicken. Price £5 – not thrilled. Bring them to the counter. No-one there. Walk out casually. Five pounds saved. And I will meet the shop owner tomorrow and smile at him as though I have not robbed him yesterday and never would.

That was really stupid of me. Don't tell my girlfriend. She would have me shot. Why did I do it? Fuck the morality of it. I could quite easily have been caught. What would I have said? I forgot? Yeah! My character in the town would have been destroyed. Not that I seem to care much about these things. The anthem of "Don't give a fuck" has entered my soul. After all, I am only on the dole. Who cares or expects anything better? Not me evidently.

GIRLFRIEND STARTS COURSE   29/9/92

Girlfriend starts pre-work course today. Am acting the good boyfriend – cooking, cleaning, etc. Actually enjoying it particularly as I am a better cook. It's nice for her to come home and have nothing to do, although my domestic education seems to have suffered a bit of a lacuna when it comes to washing and ironing clothes. She's actually quite uncomfortable about the whole thing. We're both very conventional when it comes to sex roles. I could see myself becoming uncomfortable also – the whole thing too close to being that embarrassment – a house husband – for comfort. Still it won't be for long . . . hopefully. Meanwhile, better put the spuds back on, Andre.

No, let's cut this crap, these socially acceptable sentiments. The house has become imprisoning. I feel trapped in here. Nowhere to go. Nothing to do except clean and cook, clean and cook. Have no money to go anywhere, wouldn't know what to do anyway. We are not educated to enjoy liberty. We prefer enslavement, the chains that bind. The mortgage, family, commuter route provide us with roots that secure . . . and imprison. I despise them yet want them also, the security, status, thoughtlessness.

That sort of imprisonment is different to the one that I feel. Theirs is a chosen one, like a vocation, obediently following the dictates of socialization – what the T.V., press, education tells us we must do. Mine is not chosen. I don't want that other imprisonment but I would prefer it to what I am experiencing now.

The house itself feels like a prison, shabby and decayed. It's like a Fine Gael manifesto, all doom and decay. I fucking hate these walls and frayed carpet. I feel edgy and trapped the whole time now, the house is like a Pharaoh's tomb with me fossilizing inside. I feel instinctively this will be a cold, grey winter.

I remember once seeing a middle-aged woman drying dishes by a window. She had the patient, happy-stupid look of one who had been defeated early in life and had really expected nothing else. She had spent her whole life behind that window, those walls, cooking and cleaning, cleaning and cooking. That is not my future . . . But it is my present? Or will I learn to like it?

AT THE BRINK OF EVICTION   30/9/92

Being in this rotten house has depressed us beyond belief. Your home defines the quality of your life. We have none. Now another disaster as two tenants have just done a runner. This will be fun.

The landlady is a hard bitch, typical of the type. Safe job in the bank, forty hour week and of course still the world is against her. It's a tough world trying to run two jobs, a '93 registered car and build a little nest-egg. I would say she will be fairly frosty when she hears our news. Is it not amazing that these are the people our society and the P.D.s tell us we should respect. And then we wonder why there is no social cohesion, no sense of community in Ireland.

OCTOBER

TRIALS AND TRIBULATIONS

1/10/92

She is not impressed. The news that I do not have any money causes the situation to deteriorate further. She leaves and returns with busily sobbing mother for further reinforcements. She informs me that I am evicted and my deposit confiscated. Great. From the others she demands the full whack, five people's rent to be paid by two. The deposits of the escapees and mine will be confiscated but will not go towards the rent. Mother cries enthusiastically during all of this. Lacks sincerity though. Both leave in a flurry of threat, tears and ultimatums. Landlady warns she will be back tomorrow and if there is no money then it's eviction for us.

She's well out of order. But I am silenced by my shame. I have no rights here, no better than the runners the others are criticising so bitterly. If it wasn't for my girlfriend I would be out too . . . and with nowhere to go. I feel ashamed of my powerlessness.

We could remain in the house for the rest of the month as of right. She, however, has chosen well, knows her victims will not fight. Too soft, too middle-class. Not used to the language of desperation, of conflict, of eviction.

It is an unconditional surrender. We sit around for two hours then scarper in the face of the descent. Fortunately we have somewhere to go. The next day is spent skulking around No. 11 grabbing our stuff surreptitiously. We are moved by the evening time, my good self also, even though I won't be paying any rent there either. They say nothing . . . thank God. I would not like to ask for charity, to admit verbally that I am practically destitute.

I feel useless, a total parasite. This is the lowest ever. The others have been evicted, lost their deposits because of my uselessness. I can offer nothing. Ah well, another slice off my pride and self-respect. Some boyfriend I am, good only for sex; a prostitute living off my girlfriend.

EVICTION

2/10/92

Eviction is a loss of pride. Life on the dole is that, a cumulative series of little losses every week. The signing on, the shabbiness, cheap houses, cheap clothes, cheap food. Everything on the dole becomes cheap, including yourself. At first it's just the little things. You hardly notice most of the time. You begin to dress sloppily, change your clothes less regularly, don't shave or wash. Why should you? There's nothing to do it for. You start to sleep and gradually before you even know it you have become a nightmare. The malaise has gripped and the anthem of your life has become "fuck it". Jokes become coarser, your voice louder and inside every day you carry a small secret pain, a small seed of self-disgust gnawing and biting. But the anthem eases the pain.

If you don't care, eviction is just another joke, robbing a shop, sponging off your friends, a sign of intelligence. And the beginning is so imperceptible. That's why it's important to dress well, why it's important to keep doing the shitty small unimportant things like shaving, getting up early, washing, for these impose order and discipline, keep things under some semblance of control. Lose these and you start to slide irrevocably.

The eviction has left me feeling so low. Landlady continues to promise fire and brimstone. We'll all meet again in the High Court. Fuck it. Everyone should get evicted once at least. For the experience. Staying in a new house now. Again on sufferance. If I had any decency I'd go to O'Connell St. and beg the rent. When, when will this nightmare end? Everyone looks at me imagining the happy pillar of society, the boy who done good. Joke! Now I'm just a loser who can't pay his way.

HEALTH & EFFICIENCY   3/10/92

Great to see so many people in Ireland concerned about Health & Efficiency. The country needs more of this. Become like Germany. It is particularly good to see men so concerned about these issues and reading the magazine so diligently. Does this indicate a renaissance of the tidy towns ideal? I note that another magazine on Outlaw Biker Woman, obviously a feminist analysis on the status of women in the motor-cycle industry, is also popular.

The man reading these at the moment looks like my bank manager, faceless man made flesh and dwelt amongst us in a heavy serge suit. It contrasts strongly with the oceans of black leather and white flesh he is engrossed in. I move closer and he shifts slightly. I decide to be cruel and snigger surreptitiously. ZOOM . . .

Am off cigarettes too and my bout of moral superiority is thriving. Only sex left now. Of course, the cost of cigarettes is influential in this new chastity of outlook. Tobacco is a constant drip on your finances – £3 here, £1.50 there and for what, a puff of smoke, a flicker of ash. I blanch realizing that I sound like the converted, then continue my research into nicotine poisoning, fingers, arms and legs being amputated, gangrene, heart disease.

A slow delirious smile spreads across my face. Selfish? Yes, and I love it. For once I am amongst the chosen few. I. . . I have been spared this drastic fate life had marked out for me. I must lecture my girlfriend on these evils so she also can be spared.

SHORTER QUEUES   5/10/92

At least the queues for signing on are not as long as they used to be. I suppose with the bigger numbers they've got more expertise in crowd control over the years. I am old enough to remember the misery of queueing in the rain for over an hour. That appears to remain one of the eternal features of life on the dole. Waiting to sign, waiting for Tuesday, waiting for the welfare officer, waiting for rent allowance, for a job, for life to come back and grab you by the throat.

Recently everything appears like a drugged dream, life suspended, hanging unfinished in air. At least the old embarrassment of wondering will the neighbours see is ended. They're in the same queue.

STEPHEN'S GREEN   6/10/92

The city sickens today. The sun glares as though angered by the indifference of these magpie crowds, the heated rays reflecting off the arrogant tower blocks, striking the dull crowds below. This is unnatural, wrong, this crowding and hemming, seeking the swallows' hour of freedom in these crowded cafes at lunch. We duck into St. Stephen's Green exchanging concrete for grass, dancing amongst the trees protecting us from the oppressive sun.

We stand by the pond. A child and its mother, most beautiful and enduring image of all, are together laughing, the child throws bread into the water, trying to attract that imperious swan swimming by, oblivious to the squabbling ducks.

These provide the real entertainment. There is neither pride or unity amongst the duck population. It's every drake for himself. The ridiculous nature of their skirmishes is enhanced by the harmless nature of the protagonists. Show me the duck who can send an opponent into oblivion with a right hook. A drake swipes viciously but pointlessly at the tail of a retreating foe then flaps vigorously, quacking the triumphant song of victory. There is no chivalry here either.

A jerky waterhen skirts nervously around the periphery, circling until trust is established with the golden-haired child. It feeds gently . . . grateful, unlike the brattish ducks.

We watch, the downy touch of her hands warming. The sun is softer here, refracted by the greeny leaves throwing them into a fantastic light. The querulous rush of the traffic is drowned by bird-song. It is outside, a million miles away, but still present. It is darker now. We check and realise with some shock that an hour has passed in the reedy calm of that pond.

FIRST INTERVIEW   9/10/92

At last! Escape! Now I can begin to move to make something good, something positive of myself. An ironic job given the little nightmare lying at the bottom of my soul.

Interview next week. A.I.D.S. co-ordinator. Ah, the glamour – an A.I.D.S. co-ordinator in the inner city. I actually do want this job but I will not give the diary a resumé of my C.V. At least this is the break at last from this tedium of wasting away, the beginning of this new world.

This has all come just in time. After forty rejections, confidence was really beginning to suffer. All I want is one chance and I know I will succeed. Just one. Does that sound a little desperate?

DIANETICS   11/10/92

Life moves from the mad to the ridiculous. In Dublin today I decide to try a new way of worship, the Church of Godknowswhat. They appear to be nice people, promising to cure all my problems and revitalize my life.

Unfortunately, as I begin the test to determine my leadership qualities etc. etc. I am possessed by the spirit of Homer Simpson and fail miserably. The leader, who looks like Gonzo the Great on speed, looks at me coldly. Drat! I haven't made the elect . . . again.

I smile and leave, amazed that these people are allowed operate . . . openly. Why not ban them instead of cannabis. Why are these people allowed destroy minds and lives? But then to ban them would be logical. . . and we are never that far away from Swift.

HONESTY IN MY DOLE ASSESSMENT   13/10/92

Ten weeks and still on £29 a week. This shit is no longer a joke. I snap at the counter attendant. When is my claim coming through? He looks at the file surprised.

"It has come through".

"What!" I snap, feeling the first tuggings of that hysterical confused insanity that only the Department of Social Welfare can inspire. He looks at me coldly as though to ask am I retarded, then thinks better and reads the file in a flat monotone.

"It came through this week. You're living at home and you've had means of forty pounds a week assessed against you."

I can only gawp, too shocked even for abuse. I haven't lived at home since my parents moved away four years ago. The other statement is a plain lie. I haven't means of forty pounds a week. Simple as that. Fact.

Realisation quickly comes. I smile because if I don't I'll either cry or scream and they'd love that. Now I see what's happening. Now I see the rationale, should have understood why the Social Welfare officer asked, "Why don't you go home?" Of course.

If they lie about my means, grant me a totally inadequate dole payment and then just sit tight, I will have to move home, and it's all legitimate. The equation is simple. One lie equals a saving of one thousand pounds a year. One thousand pounds! Yippee! Promotion will soon be on its merry way. I can do nothing except ask quietly for an appeals form. I am too angry and upset to do anything else. He gives it to me, a sardonic half smile flirting with his lips.

APPEAL   14/10/92

Ring my T.D. about the appeal today. I know I am a big boy now and should be able to do things on my own, but I'm taking no chances with these people. This is serious trouble. My savings are well vanished. All I have to live on now is the £29 a week and the charity of people I know. Where am I going to get next month's rent? I cannot continue like this. Am getting headaches every day from the tension and snapping constantly at my girlfriend. She is being remarkably tolerant for someone who knows absolutely nothing about living life at the edge. It's a real learning experience for her. That's not an edge of cynicism in my voice, is it?

Am all piss and wind and self-righteousness when I get through. His response disconcerts me. I had not expected laughter. This is not a joke, but then he explains to me just how it is. The whole thing is in fact a jape, a stunt, hence the smirk on my friend's face yesterday. First of all, it will take thirteen weeks to come to a decision. Secondly they won't change their decision because they are responsible to no-one. It will be one of them, possibly even the same person who made the decision, who will be reviewing it. No wonder the bastard handing out the form was smirking.

He explains it's all to do with reducing the numbers. It doesn't matter if the people go elsewhere so long as the numbers are reduced in my area. A bit like the E.C. quota in reverse. I'm not alone. Hurrah! He tells me of one case where a man was driven berserk in a health centre because of their refusal to grant him a rent allowance. This was because he already possessed a home. What they neglected to add was that this was a deserted cottage possessing no roofs, windows, doors or running water. Luxuries.

Needless to say he was imprisoned and fined by a sanctimonious judge. That sort of story is hardly comforting news for me. The T.D. says to leave it with him. I am glad to do so. These are people beyond my comprehension. They have me well tamed by now. I no longer have any confidence in myself. I need others to do things I would normally be capable of.

Later on that afternoon I tell the Social Welfare officer I am appealing the decision through my T.D. She winces. Good, he must be effective if they can't stand the sound of his name. It is the first sign of humanity apart from a dour misery I have seen in her. A breakthrough for civilization! Time to ring the scientific journals and become famous . . .

ANGER   15/10/92
Still ferociously angry at this bastard's system. I cannot believe that these people, with the connivance of the government, can treat you like this, make up lies and leave you with no come-back. That meeting with the vampire was a joke, a formality. She had decided how much she was going to give me before I even entered the room. These are the people who whine in the pub that the unemployed are screwing the system. The fraudulent liars should know. Give me the opportunity in the future and I'll screw them too. Bitch. . .

SULKING   19/10/92

Throw the docket down in front of the woman at the cashier's desk. No smile or hello or thank you. Good man. Revolution! That will really shake 'em up. Impoliteness at the dole office. Unprecedented! It's all so petty of me really but I don't care. I'm not in the humour for the social niceties, and this pleasant and inoffensive, if rather stupid woman will do for a start. Recently everything in my life is petty, so why not this?

I envy her, covet her stupid, mindless, petty little monotonous job, a job which I, with all my qualifications (joke!), cannot aspire towards. I snatch the cash away brusquely. She looks at me with brown bovine eyes, not even noticing the grandiose gesture. I walk out head held erect.

Satisfied with yourself?

STILL DOING THE DISHES AND THE HOUSEWORK   20/10/92

I have resigned myself to becoming a new age man and all the angst that this involves. Will have to take hormones to make my breasts bigger for suckling the baby. Perhaps I should get one of those rucksacky things for carrying it around so it can hear my heartbeat. Maybe that's where I went wrong, maybe it's not an Oedipus complex after all.

It's strange. I've always seen myself as being progressive yet the thought of being a house-husband makes me quiver. I feel a real threat towards my virility/ masculinity in such a concept. Housework signifies failure for my sex. It is that rather than the work itself that makes it so depressing. Those of us who cannot cut it in Ireland c.1992 are branded by the mark of the iron and the hoover.

Fortunately my girlfriend is not politically correct either. Both of us are equally uneasy with the present situation. She realises I'd never be happy as a house-husband unless this was voluntary which the present situation manifestly is not. Is this attitude of mine wrong? I don't think so and neither does the girlfriend and she's no doormat. That is the release of an unspoken tension. I thought she was happy with a situation that is slowly killing me.

I don't know what will happen. Perhaps I'll end up forming one of those New Age Male movements like in America. Imagine it: taking the lads out of the local down into the woods to rediscover their masculinity. You know, male bonding, howling at the moon, camp-fires, pissing on trees, that sort of thing. If that's the alternative I think I'll stay a house-husband.

ADVICE   21/10/92

We are treated to the views of another expert on unemployment tonight on T.V. The usual cheap self-help philosophy. Victorian drivel married to Thatcherism. You can climb Mount Everest if you want to, become a millionaire, a best-selling author! Easy.

I sit and watch as the pointless flow of garbage continues, the pointless tips all repeating the old middle class deities. If you work hard you'll get your reward, promotion, acquisition, leadership qualities, communication. If the unemployed really put their minds to it they could get a job tomorra, dole's too soft for 'em. All busted dreams twisted and scattered by today's world.

As the woman rabbits on I feel a growing awe as though I am in the presence of some form of divinity. During the uncritical interview she emerges as an expert on everything outside of the story of Adam and Eve and the creation of the world, etc. etc. Pity really for these are things I am curious about.

None of these highly successful people actually have a clue about the reality of unemployment, of a world where you scrimp and save just to be able to send off C.V.s as distinct from faxing off applications from the pleasant comfort of your parent's residence. The poor dear with the manky hairstyle and the incredulous dress sense doesn't understand what's going on today. She belongs to a different generation.

I think of writing a letter of protest into Arthur Murphy but decide this is one blow my reputation cannot take. Instead, sickened by the pontificating, I switch over to the old black and white movie on RTE 2. It's more relevant.

FOOD FOR THOUGHT   22/10/92

Feel so much better after that little outburst of bile. Amazing how a little dart of hatred can re-invigorate one so. Yet it's funny. Most of what the woman said is true. I'm just scape-goating. Looking for someone to take out all my bile on. Looking for someone to blame for not rescuing my world. Still she does have a manky hairstyle.

Today I am reading a Sunday newspaper food column. The woman who writes this is slightly deranged. It must be all that food. She's probably a walking tube of cholesterol, walking around the place puffing and snorting like one of those over-fed Pekinese, that always seem to belong to old women. She certainly possesses a similar personality.

My eyes dilate as she describes first, second, third, fourth courses and naturally the sweet. The meal is disappointing and inwardly I offer my condolences. It all seems a bit rough given that she forked out a hundred sovs. for it. Still, life is tough and we cannot just throw our pity away at everyone. Anyway, inspired by this encyclopedia of gastronomic knowledge, I tear into my plate of sausages and grilled ovenpack chips with a will, part of my mind wondering would I get a good review from the cuisine expert.

WORRY ABOUT JOB   23/10/92

No word about the job yet. This is not looking good, in fact it's looking all too familiar. Please don't tell me this is all going to go down the tubes just like everything else. What is wrong with me? If I don't get this there goes my self-confidence. Fuck the wankers anyway. It's not as if what they're offering is so brilliant that they can afford to be choosy.

Am fed up of living on my nerves. Even more fed up of having to beg for what is mine and feeling pathetically grateful for the opportunity to beg. It's a bit sad when you have to use a T.D. to get the dole, let alone a job. Getting nervous again today so I ring him up. This is so self-abnegating.

Please Mr. Grown-up Man, help me to survive in the real world. He must be sick of the likes of me. Failures asking him to rescue our lives. He tells me it should all be sorted in a week. They are simply delaying things to pretend they had a realistic argument for refusing my assistance. They are also apparently fed up with the sound of his voice. He has thirty cases going at present most of which will be settled in favour of the claimants. But, of course, we don't need an independent social welfare appeals tribunal.

The Minister is correct. The present system works perfectly in his eyes. The Minister is not concerned until the media become concerned and there are far sexier stories than the plight of a few thousand social outcasts being shafted by the state. It's bad enough to have a parliament of whores without that parliament having a fellow traveller as its conscience. Meanwhile I settle down to wait until the Department of Social Welfare decides if its pride will survive giving me my dole. There is nothing else I can do. . . .

PATRICIA REDLICH AND "CROSS-DRESSING" 24/10/92

Jesus . . . my sanity . . . Please! There is a plot out to get me. Please, please, not cross-dressing again. But of course it is. Apparently half the men of Ireland at it. I worry lately about how many of my friends I can continue to look in the eye.

Seeing as everyone else is doing it I decide to try on my girlfriend's knickers in my continuing search for secret sexual perversions. They are a bit on the small side. After a struggle I decide this is doing nothing for me. This is apparently a fetish best suited for small men with large girlfriends. That narrows the field down a bit.

Girlfriend comes in the middle of the struggle. She is neither aroused nor horrified. Just laughs. I decide this is a perversion I can live without and that we should just continue to survive with bondage, whips, leather, mirrors, videos, wife swapping, Nazi regalia etc. etc., the main features of sexual activity in the normal Irish family.

REJECTION 25/10/92

Often it's hard to retain a dispassionate mask when writing about unemployment. No matter what you do the silly, stupid, emotive language of betrayal, hurt, anger, keeps on creeping in. Employers, the employed, everyone successful, becomes the enemy because they have what you haven't got. It's never your fault, it's society's, or employers using you, tantalising you with promises of jobs, then spitting you out. Poor me. It's an easy comforting line.

One of the things unique to being on the dole is how easily and how quickly you lose perspective. After a while you become desperate, placing greater emphasis on certain jobs, believing that if you don't get them you're doomed. Every near success is a failure magnified a thousand times by your previous failures. When you are close to a job you place all your faith in it. You magnify its importance in your life beyond logic and with that your suitability for it. How can they pick anybody else but you?

And when you fail it's because of a thousand things completely unconnected to you. It was because of pull, you didn't have the right politics, go to Mass often enough, they were biased or you were too independent for them. Before you know it, you've become a social psychopath. Often the simple basic fact that there were 200 others going for the same job or really you weren't good enough is forgotten. Odds of 200/1. No sane gambler takes those. We have to.

HATRED   26/10/92

This considered response to rejection is all very well but not when the real things strikes. Fucking wankers . . . Fucking tosspots . . . There, that's made you feel better now, hasn't it. That's really cured everything. Got the letter today right on cue. Sorry, good, but not good enough. Surprise! I don't know what I can do anymore. Is this going to go on for ever? Am I going to evolve into one of the miserable crooked little people I see flooding the town every day. Society's cast offs wearing the clothes nobody else wants. Same lives.

Sometimes it's just nice to let loose the older primal emotions, hatred, envy, greed, jealousy. Why didn't I get the job? I was well qualified for it. I did well at the interview, I know I did. The reason?

The reasons are dangerously complex. In the old days if you were up for Dev and you voted F.F. you got the job. Now, however, your enemies are more subtle, the language of acquisition more coded. Now, to belong you must speak the vernacular of social democracy. What these interviewers want is miniature versions of themselves. They're not interested in originality, in fact they dislike it, see it as a threat. They're not interested in ability. The problem with the liberal conscience, particularly in areas bordering on social work, is that they cannot accept difference. Anyone who disagrees with them is an enemy. So they build their little empires.

The perfect example of this is teacher training. That is now dominated by the ideology of the 1960s. Progressive education and all that stuff. The fact that this is useless in the classroom is not recognised. The fact that the trainees who agree with them in the lecture hall act in a completely different way in the classroom, out of necessity rather than perversity, is ignored. That is okay. But anyone who publicly disagrees with them is out, or no honours. It is the liberal way.

The same in that interview. Agree to use the clichés of social democracy, social empowerment or you're out. And what is most frightening is that these people do not realise that they are imposing an intellectual dictatorship. At least F.F. were honest about their corruption. These people believe they are acting in a scientific manner, that people are rejected because they are just not suitable, rather than out of any attempt to impose an ideology, a way of looking at society that allows no dissent.

BORES   27/10/92

There is something evil in me, always lurking below the surface, waiting for the bore to arrive. Once that occurs goodbye self-control and politeness. Today I am domineered for an hour by a bore on the crisis in eastern Europe. It is very nice of him to perceive my total ignorance about the Eastern European situation and my genuine anxiety to learn everything I can about it. I sit quietly in the position he has manoeuvred me into as the complexities of the whole situation unfolds and I am educated into the names of the German, Bosnian, Serb and Croatian foreign ministers and their views on it all.

He's a very lovely, earnest, uptight individual, the sort that goes to Nicaragua today, joined the American Peace Corps in the 1960s. Eventually he asks my opinion on it all. I look at him and smile. What can I be but honest. After all, is this not what the good book tells us.

"Well Martin, to be honest I don't give much of a fuck". Disappearance of bore. Job done.

Unfortunately, bores like deaths tend to come in threes. What next, I quail, some drip telling me.

"Ah shure, life on the dole's not all bad". I take no chances and return home to bed. It's safe there.

MULLAGHMORE   28/10/92

"A victory for the community," intones one of the leaders, placid in his triumph. That this view is not shared by the community is unimportant. They want the centre more for what it symbolises, jobs revitalization, hope, an end to emigration than the economic reality. They want to keep their village as a living entity not a place possessing old men's memories, having to amalgamate with other parishes to even create a junior football team. They have been denied even that small dream.

But, of course, these small people do not matter in the eyes of our leaders. Like all true Liberals these despise the people they profess to lead. The majority are after all stupid, dull, benighted, lacking in culture, unable to appreciate the unspoilt natural landscape which they grew up in. They listen to country and western for Christssake. We can't leave this in their hands. And so, with a heavy sigh, our heroes ride into the West to save it from Interpretative centres.

Unfortunately, they have come too late for the bungalows, peasants living in the countryside, blighting it with their tasteless dwellings. Underground bunkers, that's what we need. Then we can drive around a countryside unspoilt by people living there. The West, Ireland's own Indian reservation.

These people are in every town. In my own they managed to successfully ruin a development which would have created 200 jobs. And for that they expect the thanks of a grateful people. Twenty of them against the will of the whole community. What a spineless people we are. Complaining, always whingeing, allowing others always to control the levers of power, the local press, county council, and then we wonder how they grab and shape everything to their own will. That's how they work, our new colonists.

Who are these people? What the fuck motivates them in their small victories, their desire to domineer and control even in their spare time. They decide who are to be our Arts Officers, our A.I.D.S. co-ordinators, our new gentry. What convinces them, what tablet or truth drug have they taken which convinces them they are always right . . .

Celebrate your small victories.

DOLE SORTED   29/10/92

My dole has finally been sorted. Olé, Olé, Olé etc. I am thrilled. Full dole. There is, however, one catch. I will not be getting any rebate for technical reasons, something to do with the college year. I should query it but I am not capable of another battle with these narrow little people. And now I am even entitled to full rent allowance. Honestly this is the best new year's present ever! I will settle with these bastards yet.

Girlfriend and family congratulate me. I feel like I've just received a first at Oxford though Oxfam would be more accurate. This is all a bit insane. I never expected to see the day when I would be celebrating getting the dole. Things surely can't get any lower than this thanks to my friends in their dingy little office.

ACCEPTANCE BY THE HEALTH CENTRE   30/10/92

Trailing clouds of glory and not a little spite I go proudly down to the Health Centre today. My hearts beats a triumphant song. I fit in at last, at last I fit in. I am more thrilled about this than when I got my degree. I beam at the assorted gurriers and inert forms as I enter. No longer can I be tainted with the slur of non-conformity.

I go in to meet the Social Welfare officer. It is the bad one. Her eyes glitter with a strange greedy lustre when she sees who it is. She is soon crest-fallen, realising there is nothing left that she can do. She does possess a final ace up her sleeve, sending me back to the college for a letter, but it is a Pyrrhic victory. I cannot resist a final shot. I name the T.D. noting that he sorted it out, smile then leave. She looks nauseated. The staff at the Registrar's office burst into spontaneous applause when I tell them this is the final visit. A tear glistened in every eye.

THE BLACK ECONOMY   31/10/92

Poor Brendan McGahon. The "Just William" of Irish politics. Always in trouble with his nice parents the social democrats. Today he is in the dog house . . . again . . . stating that he couldn't blame anyone on the dole doing a nixer and not reporting it to the relevant authorities, consisting of six government departments and forty civil servants. This, of course, is a threat to both the economy and the security of the state and must be countered. As a result those unfortunate listeners to daytime radio are treated to a long sonorous debate about the evils of the black economy.

All opinions possess a suspicious uniformity. Indeed, after five minutes the level of their expertise about life on the dole, and the economy of the working class family is abundantly clear. So also is their attitude. These people are the experts, the ones who will save us from the error of our ways and ensure the continued growth of our economy. It's not an easy job but they must know their stuff. They've been at it for decades.

Anyway according to these people it is of critical importance to the future of the national economy that an unemployed painter with five kids declares a nixer of £100 to the dole office. He is acting immorally if he fails to do so. So all of us doing nixers on the dole to avoid living just above the level of animals are like humanity after the fall, living in a state of sin. Our actions are, of course, much more immoral than the actions of a tax consultant earning sixty grand a year to help those unfortunates earning two hundred grand a year avoid paying tax. But this, of course, is legal and the law is made by the social companions of these people.

McGahon is brought in to be sneered at by the Minister's friends in R.T.E. This is the man who's supposed to be a lunatic. His view is simple and humane. Why should a fellow be persecuted for doing a few days work to get his wife and family something for Christmas. This argument, however, is simplistic. No exceptions can be made in the law. The man defrauding the state for a £100 must be treated in the same way as someone defrauding it of a £100,000. Otherwise you'll reduce respect for the law and the state. Actually lads, don't worry on that score.

NOVEMBER

CHEAP TOBACCO   1/11/92

They're selling cheap tobacco in Dublin today. Lung bursting stuff, the packets glued together by the tar oozing from them. Purchasing it adds a bit of excitement to life. The stuff is illegal so there is a slightly bigger thrill in buying it than going to the local tobacconist. I approach the woman conspiratorially, imagining myself in a heroin deal.

"How much?", I whisper out of the corner of my mouth.

"Three for a tenner", she bawls, shattering my eardrums. I grab the goods and make my escape.

NEW HOME   2/11/92

A man's house is his castle even if he is only renting it courtesy of the Health Board. Am finally fixed up with a roof over my head. That is a release. This staying with people and not paying rent is destructive on the spirit. Self-respect doesn't last long in those circumstances.

The sneaking around is the worst part, sneaking away from landlords and house-mates. Even home becomes a prison, every morning wakening with the same sensation of failure/entrapment, the same suppressed panic. Is today the day they tell me "Sorry mate". And the same pathetic gratitude, "Thanks lads, it won't be for much longer, I hope".

That helplessness is now gone but the memory lingers like a smell. My bitterness with our brilliant Social Welfare system will not depart easily. I'd like to get them all. It doesn't matter. I'll get a job soon. I've never been out of work for long before.

CHANGED ATTITUDE ONCE DOLE SORTED OUT   3/11/92

Now that my social welfare has been sorted out I have decided to become a new man; refreshed, reborn. My attitude towards these good Social Welfare Officers has been changed, changed utterly. No longer are they bloodsucking vultures. Instead they are decent people trying, and with little gratitude may I add, to do an almost impossible job. How could I have been so wrong!

Actually most Social Welfare Officers probably are fundamentally decent. If they are ignorant it is because they are beaten down by the dismal nature of their job, ten thousand days spent studying the same dismal office, the same dismal people. They are incapable of coping with the numbers of this new human tide. Then there are always the gurriers, the liars, the bullies, dragging down a whole class. It's no wonder their view of human nature coarsens and weakens, tainted as much by the system as we are, until they become replicas of who they deal with. It was probably a bit hypersensitive of me to expect to be treated like a real human being amongst the other three thousand. Now I've said it. Can I go kick old ladies for the rest of the week after that bout of sensitivity?

THE P.F.O. LETTER   4/11/92
This literary form is now rapidly reaching cult status in informed circles and is probably due a summer school next year at the latest. Contrary to public belief and previous statements of my own, this literary style is not uniform but possesses a whole range of sub-genres. The most popular one is the middle-of-the-road genre. This is used for those jobs where you were not considered totally useless for the post, nor particularly close, but surprise, surprise, somewhere in between. It congratulates you for the host of qualifications you have, wishes you well in your future career (what!) but many of the others, generally two thousand, that applied, were better suited. It is a letter which inspires neither hope, ecstasy nor fear.

Then there is the letter which asks "How dare a chancer like you even ask for a job as important and valuable as this!" Brief and generally signed by the tea-boy it usually goes as follows:

"Your application has not been considered".

That's it, no thanks, regrets, compliments on your achievements to date, nothing, nada, rien. That sort of letter either merits an effusively apologetic response for having bothered anybody, or the finger.

Then there is the hard luck, "You nearly made it to the first of our six interviews" letter. This praises your abilities and qualifications so enthusiastically that you feel like going in yourself and telling the manager to fuck off, you're taking over; personally. At the end of this litany of praise it is, however, announced in funeral tones that you just failed to make it. However, as a special favour they will keep your C.V. on file for six weeks before throwing it into the bin with the rest. The latter is my little addition in the interests of honesty. They do urge you not to call them, they will call you. As a special sign of favour this missive is signed by the owner.

We read this letter with a mixture of cynicism and pleasure. Although it is as useful as a forged cheque it is nice to have your true worth recognised and some day you may get that job as an assistant manger at McDonalds.

Finally, there is the fourth and most effective type of P.F.O. letter. The non-existent one. Why do employers not bother acknowledging applications for work? It's quite simply a matter of economics. It costs a lot of money to type and send two thousand refusals.

These are the white telegrams of the 90s, each the death of another little dream. You feel a small sorrow and then the merry desperate circle continues, another dozen arrows awaiting another dozen little telegrams each singing the same tuneless song, just different chords . . .

FREEDOM   5/11/92
Arriving at the house she is just up. Her eyes are heavy with sleep and sensuousness but bright also with the fresh unspoilt enthusiasm of morning. I can scent her, the smell of the bed, and I kiss her first tenderly then violently, turned on by the sensuous promising form.

Her body tenses, lips open, possessing, surrounding, greedy. Her power shocks me and I become recipient rather than aggressor, defenceless, wanting and loving this. She strips me quickly, efficiently, then leads me into the room. The coldness makes me flinch, then I am oblivious and it is replaced by a fantastic heat. A movement, rustle of belts, stockings, she is on me, taking. She gasps, then smiles, her eyes glittering, hard with lust but not cold, too warm for that.

I cry, "Jesus"! as she caresses me with that soft warmth pulling the heat from deep inside me, rising so fast. We move faster now, rocking, her breathing short. I am frightened by her passion, not in control here. Lost and caught in the maelstrom, turbulence then reaching for the calm, a squeal, then the landing, spent, the storm ceased, ending as I spiral into the warm darkness.

Peace. Outside the cold rain tap-dances on the roof. A bird sings in the quiet housing estate, its song only interrupted by the cries of distant children. We are at one with their laughter. Fulfilled we sleep, hiding from the cold grey rain in the heat of our stilled bodies.

It is both terrifying and exhilarating to love without caution, bargains, rules. Yet in some ways it is the most secure, the most full of all. My life has always seen such strong contrasts and never have I needed such contrasts more than now. To return from a wintry Dublin morning to this. There are indeed the years worth living.

MORE DYNAMIC GROWTH   6/11/92

Read today of dynamic growth in the aero-space industry. That is indeed good news, though fuck all use to me. It would be nice if for once I could read about dramatic new growth in my own areas of work, but always there is something else growing, expanding. Twenty-three and obsolete already. Fit only for the knackers' yard or the civil service.

Employers don't want people who are sophisticated or imaginative. They want nice little young people with narrow little qualifications in marketing or computers who will obey the corporate law without question. I would be an employer's liability in today's risk free world. Mindless little robots carrying out the task allocated to them, incapable of anything more. It is my own fault for thinking otherwise. I wish I had never caught the bug of ambition trapping me between two worlds. I would have been happier if I had stayed in my own social class and taken a trade or something.

DUNBOYNE – LAND OF THE GURRIER   7/11/92

Visit Dunboyne this evening, the land of the gurrier by all appearances. They slouch around menacingly, eyes blank and cold like some poor pastiche of a vampire movie. The uniform is uniquely unlovely, *de rigueur* pump trainers, tracksuits, staring eyes, and of course the crew-cut hair. They are more and more prevalent these days in our towns and villages, particularly obvious on Dole Tuesday, all knocking back the flagons of cider and waiting for someone, generally themselves, to kick around.

Their rise is linked inexorably to the rise in unemployment. Before these people had jobs, generally stupid jobs for stupid people, but at least they had worth, some sense of use, of value, in their lives. Now they have nothing. That is why their eyes are empty.

They're beginning to hate now, hating the successful ones, the snappy dressers who own the cars, pull the birds. They want to be noticed, want the successful ones to recognise that they are here also, want the birds and the cars. They want to grab their attention with fear.

Life is becoming more dangerous recently, mindless violence, theft, rape, their only attention grabbers. We are lucky in one sense. They are too stupid to ever organise. For that reason the violence will remain sporadic, illogical rather than organised, but growing; all the time growing. Still, however, as the English say of the North – at acceptable levels.

CHOICES   8/11/92

When you are on the dole you have two choices; eat poorly and have an okay social life or vice-versa with very little vice. This week I choose the former with the consequence that I have a sore head mingled with an empty stomach. At least each distracts from the other, a condition the poet Keats called stasis . . .

Boredom is the most dangerous aspect of life on the dole. It is the absence of anything to do which leads to crime, to drugs, the kick of hash, sex, violence, breaking the interminable lethargy. There are so many people coiled around this town simply waiting to unleash their desperation and their hatred. Can we really do no better than create a society which offers nothing other than survival/subsistence for one quarter of its people?

It is this absence of focus which leads to so many welfare pregnancies. These are not happening because of the money . . . let me assure disgusted tax-payer of Foxrock of that. Neither are they caused by any breakdown of morality or ignorance of sex. This is for the benefit of those disgusted mothers of 28. It is because having a child brings focus and worth to a person's life. It is the only opportunity for that, available for so many in our society.

Albert, is this right? Could you write to me and give me your opinions. I'd really value that. Frame the letter on the wall, beside John XXIII. Albert, I'm waiting.

CRAP . . .   10/11/92

AAAAAAAARRGGHHH!!! I mean isn't it absolutely awwwwwfullll. The nation is shattered, black flags everywhere, syntax and grammar in my writing style totally shattered, this from an already low base. Yeats rises from the grave to point sternly and Europe, worse still the Brits, are laughing. Yes Albert has said "crap". Horror and disgust is the only appropriate national response. Is this really happening? Let's just put a banana on the national flag and have done. This is just too surreal.

You can run an economy into the ground, do nothing whilst slaughter goes on in the North but say "crap" in a land where even nuns curse and you're a pariah, the Noriega of Europe. In England, poor debauched lost Engerland (sic), a good sex scandal preferably incorporating whores, homosexuality and three in a bed is necessary for such a furore. Here just one "crap" and the fabric of society is ripped asunder, Shakespearian quotes from Lear and Richard III in *Irish Times* editorials, the Curia of the Irish press. Don't worry Al, I agree with you, it's all crap, all of it, crap, crap, crap.

PROSPEROUS   11/11/92

Am shocked this afternoon. We enter a church. The presence, the heat shocks, disconcerts. The church is so like Yeats' poem, cold, yet I sense passion also. I seek refuge in logic. This is all the result of a change in temperature, in light. This is physiological, too many sausages this morning. Then accept, for if you have faith then a divine presence is not illogical. I do not stay long. Scared by the connection with something outside of me, bigger than me, knowing it offers fulfilment/warmth, but scared because I am used to my small world, not the grandeur of this.

We leave, smiling with a warmth rare in this grown-up world. I know something now of those people smiling at Mass. We remain separate from them, bored and annoyed by their participation in something we are kept out of; keep ourselves out of. I want that, want the greediness of their tongues flickering at the Eucharist.

Outside the burnished autumn landscape is transformed. Rich. Now I know the truth of the richness of harvest, the fullness of those dying fields. Soon they will be bare, leaving only stubble but even in winter there is a promise contained in those fields of the certainty of growth, renewal, spring.

I feel only peace. The horrors of that week are past, gone. I smile at a grandmother and child, finger-locked in the dying sun, seeking the shadow of the sensuous grey wall. They too are the same as those rich fields, growth and harvest, spring and autumn, poised together. It is good to see happiness, beauty in the ordinary. Peace be with you too on this autumn's eve.

PROMISES, PROMISES, PROMISES 14/11/92

More promises from that nice Mr. McCreevy. Forget the dirty dozen. Forget retrenchment. It's election . . . oops sorry Christmas time and, like Scrooge, our man has obviously been visited by the ghosts of elections pasts. The after-shock of this is so serious that he has even been promising humanity in the Social Welfare system. What, I wonder, could be the cause of this admirable but sudden urge? And does this imply that there was no humanity in the system prior to this? Ooops! Anyway, we are all to get one stop shopping and sophisticated electronic fund transfers. Joy! Of course all these new gleaming dole offices. . . sorry, employment centres, will boost the tourist industry. Come to Ireland. A friendly place. Fairies, leprechauns, the most visually attractive dole offices in Europe.

Even better still, guess what Santa Charles has promised? Yes! We are all to get our Christmas bonuses early. Yippee! The economically challenged of the nation swoon gently into his strong gentle arms. When did he make that decision? In a fit of remorse after watching a Christmas Carol and his little son lisping into his ear, "Daddy, does there have to be poor people?". Awww!

The decision on the Christmas bonus is the most nauseating of the lot. I personally do not mind being conned by unimaginative politicians. What I do sincerely resent is being told I'm easy, the implicit belief that the unemployed can be purchased as cheaply as this. Is that all we're really worth, the early payment of a Christmas bonus? More bread and circuses and the party strategists up in Mount Street snickering.

And what of this stuff of more modern facilities. What of it? Let's be blunt, these are not being offered because the Minister is concerned for our health. It is because these drab grey queues embarrass ministers. They remind them of their collective failure. These drained men and the ramshackle buildings they go into are frighteningly similar to Eastern Europe. Build them new employment offices, pretend to be doing something. Above all hide them away. Bad for national morale and the tourist industry. Much better to get them in and out nice and quick. Discreet like a brothel.

That final image brings Fleet Street to mind. I wonder should I attempt to sell my story to *The News of the World*. Give Max Clifford a ring or something. I can just see myself starring in the centre pages with the sad-eyed whores, a tasteful photograph of my good self draped over a bed in a see-through dressing-gown. The headline: "Kathleen Ní Houlihán took me and used me".

Then the sub-headings: "The lies she told me". "She was insatiable – I asked her for work seven times a day". Possibly centre pages of the *News of the World* is a bit optimistic, but page twelve of *The Meath and District Chronicle* is an option.

OVER THE MOON   15/11/92

I see we are to be the grateful recipients of a rainbow coalition at the end of this election . . . whether we want it or not. This is all too reminiscent of the Wizard of Oz. I amuse myself with a bit of amateur casting, John Bruton as Mr. Cowardly Lion and who better than Mr. Dick Spring as the Wizard himself, a small man masquerading as a giant.

Barry Desmond will do as Dorothy for, as it is a sequel, Dorothy is now an old woman, just like Barry himself. Alan Dukes possessing all the charisma of Mr. Tin Man also gets a part. The Wicked Witch of the midlands – who other than Albert. Tut, tut, such irreverence. Looking at it all, its' not so much a case of over the rainbow/moon as sick as a parrot, Brian.

THE WASP   16/11/92

Wake up this morning after a massive bender. Jesus, I sound like a country 'n' western singer. After five years of college has it come to this? No food for the rest of the week. What do I care? Christ, I'd love a pint! Is there anyone I can scrounge money from?

I hear a faint buzzing. What's that?! I am immediately alert and fearful. The sound is horribly familiar.

Logic is not strong after two bottles of sherry, and phobias are definitely heightened with a hangover. The harsh droning sound continues to send slivers of cold glass running through me. I have a phobia about wasps, those hard little glittering balls of malice, waiting to sting, to hurt. I dive under the bedclothes to consider my position, then re-emerge. I would be best advised to keep my eye on it lest, unbeknownst to me, it flies under the bedclothes to launch its attack at my weakest points.

It is resting now, watching me with cold unerring eyes, waiting the moment of weakness. It is a massive thing, a queen wasp. Dopey in the glittering autumn sun. I peep out warily. This is embarrassing.

It is seeking a place to hide and hibernate from the winter. The mind races. Next spring a nest of wasps in my room. With that thought my stomach does a delicate somersault sending its contents perilously close to the roof of my mouth. Courage, no, necessity demands that the thing be despatched. But how, without causing danger to the indigenous population.

I consider calling in the fire-brigade. As though sensing my treacherous thoughts it buzzes, again sending me under the bedclothes. I feel the beginnings of a seedy headache. The noise ceases and I re-emerge timorously from the bunker. There is no sign of it. This, however, unnerves me further - for now it could be anywhere, skulking, breeding, gestating, waiting to pounce. The wasp must DIE.!. . .

I grin crookedly, a fanatic light in my eye. I can see it now, discern its shadow behind the curtain and the fiendish method of its death. The utmost caution and delicacy is required. One mistake will be fatal. The curtain is pressed tight against the outline of the window. No muck-savagery here, no uncouth swipes with a newspaper. This is to be a precision job.

I press the book hard again the window pane. A faint buzz. Then a satisfying scrunch. I keep it held against the pane for ten minutes. Arrogance has proved fatal before. Finally remove it, wiping the sweat from my brow. The task is done. I lie back exhausted. There will be no more work done today.

NO DOLE BONUS   17/11/92
Received dole payment today. This should put me in good form. Christmas bonus. Debauchery and drunken revelry here I come. But of course I am disappointed. Another joke, this myth of Christmas bonus for everyone. It is in fact like everything else, only applicable to certain categories, those who fulfil the criteria of *de rule*.

So *de rule*, master of the universe, has struck again. Petty really. But then, Christmas, like respect, is now for other people. I think I should hire Charles Dickens as my P.R. consultant on this issue. It comes as a terrible shock, when I find out that he is dead.

HOUSE 2, THE SEQUEL   18/11/92
New house is grand. No central heating so the place is bitterly cold. This is dangerous for it creates an incentive to lie in bed all day long. There is after all really nothing else to do. Some unimaginative people, the type who write into Arthur Murphy to tell him how good R.T.E. is, wonder why people on the dole stay in bed. Well, for you fine people, there are five easy answers:

1. Some are dispirited, particularly when they see the sort of people who are employed and who waste their valuable time writing in about the unemployed.
2. Some are bone idle, Ooops!, better not let the Irish National Organisation of the Unemployed see that. The I.N.O.U. are the unemployed people's version of 1.
3. It kills a lot of the day.
4. If you get up late you eat less food, smoke fewer cigarettes and spend less money.
5. If it is bitterly cold, staying in bed is a lot cheaper than fuel.

But I digress.

It is great to have your own home again, a luxury almost. It has all the necessities, cooker, fire, bed, roof. Yet apart from the aforementioned central heating it also has deficiencies. This realisation is informed by the views of my girlfriend, my first middle-class girlfriend. I have learned from her the utter contrast between what the working and middle-classes take for granted in the areas of living standards, comfort, expectations, be it cars, holidays, videos, central heating, careers. The gap is very great for our classless society, often as much an attitude of mind as physical living standards.

On that level there is a real clash of cultures between us. She, for example, has learnt to drive. We have never owned a car. This thing replicates itself in every area, computers, confidence, presentation skills, adaptability to new technology, networking. The old boys' network is as influential in the Republic as in Britain. I am fortunate in having made half the leap: or is that unfortunate? Am I not in fact a bastard in both worlds now. But this is a long way from Mick's central heating.

THE P.D.s AND ELECTION '92   19/11/92

P.D.s are promising us a National Community Employment Scheme. Is this election time or what? The aims are lofty and inspirational as is typical of those documents which are to be dropped quietly, once the party joins Dorothy and the others in government. The primary objective is to increase the participants' skill base. This is to be achieved through cutting nettles, weeding cemeteries and hanging flower pots.

I can just see the I.D.A. brochures now. Ireland at the heart of nettle containment technology. Of course, you don't get paid anything extra for joining these schemes. These aren't real jobs, after all. Uniquely Irish, isn't it? A political party's job creation strategy centred around the creation of imaginary jobs. Alice in Wonderland politics, more expert wall-papering. And, of course, such a scheme will never become compulsory. Oh Noooo!

ELECTION '92   20/11/92

Election continues and still I feel very separate from all the process and hullabaloo. Really, only good tax-payers and wealth generators should possess the right to decide. I feel like a cuckoo in the electoral nest.

I have no stake in this. No party is relevant to me, not even Democratic Left whose concern appears disingenuous. Fine Gael is trying to make unemployment the issue but somehow I feel their concern is centred around the cost of this to good tax-payers rather than the unemployed themselves.

All the others are offering plausible solutions which I might believe if I knew less. Perhaps if I didn't know so much I might participate, get enthusiastic about the goddamned thing, at least be grateful for having a democracy and the right to vote for politicians whose words I don't believe. Still it's good to know so many people are concerned about me. It's only at a time like this that you realise it.

BRUISES   21/11/92

Wake up more suddenly than expected this morning. Looking and stretching I see my reflection. What is that? I look. She stirs. "What's wrong baby?". My eyes, voice betray. No. No. No. It's a bruise, only a bruise, nothing else. Please. Why will this cough not go away? I am full of fear now, the shadow growing. I leave to sit and think. What do I do, where will I go next. Surely I am not going to get this thing. Yes, it's a bruise. Ten to one my odds. My luck?

SOCIAL EMBARRASSMENT AND THE DOLE   22/11/92

This unemployment bit is getting embarrassing. All my friends are teachers, lawyers, computer salesmen, even accountants, all getting on in life. I sit envying wistfully as they go on about cars, mortgages, share options, all foreign deities to me. I feel reluctant to talk around them. What worth is my opinion? How can I talk confidently about politics or society or literature, me who has failed miserably in the matter of my own upkeep. A dependant, a well-groomed beggar, living on the taxes out of their wages. What civic rights do I deserve in a society where I take everything and give nothing.

I would not have survived in Victorian times. Weakling, the runt of the litter, my father's disrespect palpable. He's good at that, a star in making me feel small and useless.

My mother's concern suffocates. God love her, she means well but I freeze like a trapped rabbit at her concerned pity. Yes, I'm all right. No, I won't starve. How can I tell her to Fuck off without cutting the head off her. I can't, so we achieve the classical Irish family solution, puzzlement and a voiceless confrontation. As voiceless and as felt as the disapproval of my girlfriend's parents. The evidence for the prosecution mounts M'lud.

As for my friends, I continue to worry. When will I finally lose their respect? When will they start talking about me in corners, when will I become "poor Seán". Will I deserve all that?

WORMS . . .   23/11/92

Yes, indeed, dear diary, I tell the whole story warts 'n' all. No favourable editing here. Announce triumphantly to all my friends today that I have worms. They blanch. What? Yes indeed. I confirm. Little round fellows breeding in the nether world. "How do you know?", they chorus. Fools. By the time I finish recounting the evidence there is not a dry eye in the house. God I love to shock. Sometimes I think I may have been Gerry Ryan in a past experience.

THANKS FOR THE EIGHT BILLION ALBERT;
NOW PLEASE F***K OFF   24/11/92

The nation is to get EIGHT BILLION POUNDS. I repeat EIGHT BILLION SQUIDS from our good friends in the European Community . . .WAAHAAY YIP! YIP! YIP! You must be joking.

I hear the muttered epithets already. Miserable Git. Why can't he join in the mood of national celebration? Another fuckin' begrudger. Why have I not joined a grateful nation in its homage?

Well, dear reader, the answer is simple. This eight billion is a fraud, a myth. Nothing will change as a consequence of this money. One reason for this is that the eight billion is quite simply a bribe. Open competition suits the large E.C. states and perpetuates the poverty of smaller peripheral nationals such as

Portugal, Greece, Ireland, etc. The eight billion is like a trinket being offered to a savage to sign away his kingdom, or in our case, to allow every other European state access to our economy. As a result of this free competition our economy is drowning. The E.U. money acts as a buoy, kindly allowing us to tread water instead.

Worse still, the present government, like the last one and the next one, will simply waste the money. This they have already made clear, with some pride. More money for FAS, more money on roads and infrastructure . . . Again . . . Infrastructure appears to have replaced the language renewal movement and draining the Shannon as the White Elephant of the party manifesto. Now we are draining Europe instead.

Now lads, let's get a couple of things clear. All that guff about the value of training is drivel. We don't need to train employees in this country. We need to create employers to hire the tens of thousands who are already trained and are still jobless. Then, boys, we can go and train more. Yes, we can. Promise.

And if the government are incapable of creating real jobs why don't they show us the respect of admitting it instead of playing games with us and pretending training is the key. So also for infrastructure. Again a grandiose word is used to mystify, to pretend something is . . . can be done. Sometimes it appears we are following the path of the communist states and that in twenty years we too will have nothing but great highways, deserted factories, an empty country whose youth have left its deserted towns, testimony to the folly of those who are its leaders.

STILL DISINTERESTED   25/11/92

Election continues and as it reaches a climax just like all the best novels so does my disinterest, and we both come together. I am too bored and depressed to care about such a sad shower of wankers. A career of housework does not promote interest in the political process. Is this what has happened women through the years, the constant diet of drudgery, trivia and Gay Byrne destroying interest in anything outside these imprisoning walls.

All my political interests are centred on the forthcoming elections in Fur and Featherland. Will Curly Wee defeat the evil machinations of the fox? (cf cartoons section *Irish Independent*). It's a frightening parallel. Are there any differences between the two? If not, should this not tell us something? Will Fintan O'Toole please save us by writing an article about this.

SOCIAL ETIQUETTE AND ROUNDS IN THE PUB   26/11/92

It's difficult being in pubs when you're on the dole particularly when there's a group of you. I am, of course, talking about the social importance of the round. Even if you attempt to buy your own, there is no escape. Stupid bovine questions from civil servants and national school teachers: "Are you not joining us? What are you having?" If you buy into that one you're down twenty quid. I hate the hassle of pleading with twenty drunks to be allowed the privilege of buying my own beer. For some people it's a dereliction of etiquette not to be able to buy a round in company, but by this stage I'm pretty thick-skinned about the whole thing. You have to be.

It's a minor thing really but life on the dole is so full of these minor things that eventually they seem more important than they really are. Something else that kills me is being paid into discos by my girlfriend. Talk about reversing gender stereotypes. It's a real diminution of masculinity. You feel embarrassed and cheap wondering if all the bouncers are laughing at you. Now I know how women often feel.

Recently I feel as though I am becoming more and more feminine but in a negative way as though I am acquiring the worst traits of the sex. I am economically dependent, possessing neither freedom or virility. Even in bed my girlfriend is dominant. That is all building resentment and quiet self-hate, all unspoken.

CHARLIE McCREEVEY VICTORIOUS   27/1192

The people of Kildare showed their opinion of the unemployed by electing Mr. McCreevy top of the poll. Fair boy you are and all, Charlie. Four more years to bash the lazy and unemployed, to hear your bog accent lecturing us.

A clever man. He gambled on the lowest emotions of the employed, greed, fear, and avarice and it worked. Get those scroungers out. Here is yet another man with two jobs complaining about the unemployed siphoning away the wealth of the state. Yeah, Charlie, I feel your pain. Man of the people himself. Good P.R. job, Charlie, but I don't buy it anymore.

ELECTION RESULT, WHAT CARE I, ME, MOI..   28/11/92

Yes, the people have spoken. God help us all. People and elections are like children and matches. They should be kept apart for their own good. One thing is abundantly clear – F.F. and F.G. have gotten one big smack in the chops. This is nothing more than my old friend Charlie McCreevy deserves and I'm delighted for him.

The collapse of F.G. is more interesting. Poor John Bruton, so separate from society today and boy does it show. He comes from a time when Ireland was more stratified. He has never mixed with people outside his own social circle, U.C.D. in the 60s, the Dail from the 70s. As a result, even though he is a good man who cares deeply about concepts such as injustice, unequal opportunity, social exclusion, he does not know what these mean to people on the ground. He doesn't like and isn't comfortable meeting the people who theoretically he most wants to meet. Out of synch with our time, his tragedy is that he is a Redmond or a Dillon rendered obsolete by the *zeitgeist* of the day.

One man who is in synch with the times is Dick Spring. The cleverest move Dick has made is to get Fergus Finlay to write his speeches for him. Dick is a chancer, a rhetorician using the language of change to keep things the same. Dick, for all his talk of change, will reform nothing. He looks good, sounds good, the politics of marketing. Nothing else. He wants the window box vote, the gobshite/floating vote.

Some socially concerned individuals may ask why F.G. with their emphasis on jobs and unemployment did so badly, given its importance as a national issue. The answer lies not only in the lack of cohesion and solidarity amongst the unemployed, most of whom are too hassled in the search for work to care about their compatriots (the rest are too dispirited to vote), but in another more fundamental belief.

People know unemployment is here to stay. They know that politicians can do nothing about it and if you're one of the 300,000, tough. F.G.'s employment agenda was seen as a gimcrack or at best a bad sign of political naivety. They voted Labour because they wanted divorce, homosexuality, abortion information, etc. They wanted to become respectable in Europe. The belief, that Labour is the party most capable of achieving this agenda, has caused the surge to Labour; not any old drivel about the working man. That belongs to the bad old days under Frank Cluskey.

It's a good result for F.F. The rest will do them good. It's a hard job saving the country the whole time. They will enjoy their holidays, find out what the people want and lead from behind as usual. As for the P.D.s and the Democratic Left, now let me see, which one is the hard left socialist revolutionary party and which one consists of the right wing Thatcherites who have just broken the mould of Irish politics by going into coalition with F.F. Ooh! how radical! So now the P.D.s are going into coalition with their sister Thatcherite party, F.G., or is that the D.L. So it's the D.L. which are the real mould-breakers in Irish politics or is it the P.D.s? Ooh! It's all so confusing. Now once more it's the D.L. which is the mould-breaking hard right Thatcherite party. Isn't it. No. Wait. Let's go through this one more time. I thought . . . never mind.

HOW TO DRINK ON THE DOLE   29/11/92

People, fools, ask how can you drink and draw the dole. You know the sort, the ones who write to Arthur Murphy and appear on Winning Streak . . . without any shame. My response? Conscience-wise no problem. Financially the story is different. Most survive through various scams, nixers, not paying the rent, claiming rent allowance for non-existent addresses. The latter two are a bit like government policy on foreign borrowing. Generate an immediate cash flow but at a long-term cost.

I manage it through a combination of budgeting and nixers. I drink less recently. Don't like what it does to me. Drinking in my case is the child of boredom, self-pity and envy. Every time I succumb I feel it takes from my character. I know the symptoms, I know the consequences. Sometimes however you can't defeat the urge. Well, you can if you want to but you just don't.

Tonight will follow a similar pattern. The plan is a miracle of financial engineering. First, I will buy two bottles of cheap sherry. Despite the fact that old ladies drink it, this stuff is dynamite, much better than cider, the more popular brew. But then I was never a populist.

Knock that back, add five pints and you're pretty close to Nirvana for little more than a tenner. Then you can be the centre of attention, all your insecurities forgotten, your wit and repartee leaving the whole pub in tears . . . genuinely. No need for conscience, no come-backs, "Aw shure, Pat, I was locked". You can tell that prick what you think of him, "Did I meet you last night? Jayz, I can't remember a thing". That simple. But at the end of it all you're still the bollocks because you're so envious and insecure that you feel the need for a cheap victory, an easy laugh in a pub that both you and the loser know is worth nothing.

But sometimes these small victories are so tempting. Finish the first bottle. It sits heavily on the stomach. The second will dissipate that, bringing only that lovely familiar darkness that signifies freedom temporarily purchased. Look out town, respectable wankers, rich snobs. . . Seán is about!

DECEMBER

LOCAL ALCOHOLIC I 3/12/92

"The farmers, do you see?" Silence. The frightened silence of a cornered man. "Well, they won't let you go across their land to get the logs out of the water". "Yep?"

"And they rot in the water."

"The farmers?"

"No, ye eegit, the logs."

"Oh." I respond, chastened. I realise I am sounding like Dustin and make a conscious effort to modulate my tone.

"And that's what turns the water red, what you call the red water . . . Dat's what's causing the hole in the ozone layers".

Ah Science. Queen of the intellectual pursuits. Genius allied to madness, the clearest sign of greatness.

The local alcoholic asks me for my views on this theory. What can I do but temporise. Silence again. Silence of the lambs. I suggest he consult more expert opinion and leave hastily vowing never to enter a pub before twelve noon. Have we really moved far away from the apes?

IRISH EDUCATION AND THE CULTURE OF WORK 5/12/92

I read today that Irish students are not given a work outlook in our educational system. That is one of the rare pieces of truth I have read on the job situation in Ireland. My case is a perfect example. I can complain all I want, boast about my much vaunted abilities but I am irrelevant to the world and needs of employers.

I have not been trained in anything which could be useful to industry. It's a bit late to discover this now. My failure is that I took that choice. I should get on with living, with the consequences. Enough of whining self-pity. That is not healthy. Get on with the business of life.

Really we should close down all the universities. They're a danger to the country, producing only solicitors, lawyers, politically active primary school-teachers, and civil servants. The lecturers? We can employ them cutting grass on the side of the roads. Harmless and progressive work, enhancing the quality of society. Just like an Arts Degree.

SPUDS   7/12/92

Read today of a German organic gardener arrested for growing cannabis. His defence was that as an organic farmer he could not spray his spuds against the blight, but that cannabis acted as a natural deterrent. Well, if it does as much for the spuds as it does for me I'll be first in the queue when they are sold.

One thing I cannot understand is the illegality of cannabis. There again the state always likes to ban that which it cannot control. Alcohol, despite the fact that it has destroyed more lives than hash can ever pretend towards, is okay because it can be taxed. Moreover, if the state legalised hash then it would be admitting its previous position was wrong and Irish governments have never been prepared to do that, no matter what the cost.

Meanwhile, I continue to watch the case with interest. If my German friend is not convicted, in go the spuds.

BEGINNING OF CYNICISM RE. P.F.O.s   8/12/92

Am starting to get cynical about the P.F.O. letters. Great flocks of them pouring in letter boxes all very complimentary and all very negative. At this stage the arrival of the postman no longer brings undiluted excitement. Now it is tempered with a mixture of nervous cynicism. This is dripping away at my confidence; another little sting, every day. It's amazing how similar each letter is. Perhaps there is a standard P.F.O. form. That is not good news.

HEALTH CENTRE   9/12/92

Back in the glass-house today. At least the moss on the windows is thriving which is more than can be said for the rest of us. We are as pale and nondescript as the ugly brickwork outside, reflecting the bureaucrats' vision of what this place and its inhabitants should look like. We swelter in the hallway whilst the bureaucrats' successor sits in an air-conditioned office despising us, particularly those of us who are more intelligent than she is.

The usual variety of people are here, some of the more prosperous looking ones impatient, in a hurry to return to work after collecting the bonus money. Good luck to them. Anyone who can screw this rotten system has my respect and support. A child cries and we all glare. The tired wailing only enhances the dinginess of this forgotten corner of the world's hell, city of the failures. Time does not exist here, the forlorn tick of the clock pointless, for us who have time, a world of it, to spare.

At the front are the usual assortment of gurriers, all harsh vowels and conso-
nants. Empty. Several of the lads have been in prison already and are proud of
it, an introduction into manhood, the gurriers' bar mitzvah. One of the lads is
first in the queue again. It's his sole ambition in life to be first in the queue
every day. He is quarrelling with another shaven-headed companion, more
for excitement and effect than anything else. Then the magic door opens
and everything stops.

Beside the lads are the groupies first serving as girlfriends, then wives. None
of them are attractive, the choice of women for the lowest in society rarely are.
Still, they are convenient for sex, admiration and occasionally to thump, releas-
ing frustration and drink. They all chatter and brag, happy starlings in the reservation society allows them. We are treated to a recital of how much they drank,
what they puked up and when and if they pulled woman. Length, details and
activities indulged in. Ditto for the girls.

Beside these masters of the Health Centre sit the older gurriers. Past their
prime these are incapable of either violence or sex. Now they are just habitual
wasters. They like to sit beside their younger compatriots and reminisce. They
too have no proper names, all being called Harpo, Mickser, Watser, Hego, Lego.
Anything that finishes with an "o" or an "er" is the badge of initiation.

For these the Health Centre is a social occasion like the pub. They have their
own seats, order of precedence, status, a bit like the Dail really. The rest of us
are a rather nondescript bunch of has-beens, will-bes, never have been and
never will bes, an eclectic mix of building workers laid off for the winter (some
voluntarily), salesmen, clerical workers and assholes. Some look bored, others
nervous and uncomfortable, the rest cynical and detached. I, of course, fancy
myself amongst the latter but is that really a compliment?

The queue moves with interminable slowness. These days are etched irretrievably into my brain. Eventually, thank God, liberty. It is my turn. Ten minutes and I'm out with my cheque for £15. Is it worth it? No, the day is ruined
now. That waiting around, that atmosphere of defeat saps and destroys, extract-
ing a heavier price than the few pounds charity. Some people seem to think that
waiting around shouldn't be a problem for the unemployed. After all they have
nothing else to do. Do they want it posted to them whilst they lie in bed eating
chocolates blah, blah, blah.

What people fail to realise is that if you acquire the passivity that they want
then you are certain of remaining on the dole in perpetuity. It's a battle to make

sure every day has a purpose, that it just doesn't die slowly. If you fall into that trap then your enthusiasm just dies. Then you certainly won't get on your bike looking for work, you'll just wait for your charity every week. Those of us still alive really don't need this slow death for £15 every week.

X AND SUICIDE   10/12/92

Friend of girlfriend calls around tonight. Unemployed, depressed, suicidal. Great, this has all the signs of a brilliant night. The sad tale is told. We listen and listen and again listen.

She turns towards me. "Oh. At least Seán understands. He's in the same boat as me". My girlfriend nods her head in enthusiastic agreement. I look shocked at the lazy self-pitying creature that has bored me to tears for the last two hours. Am I fuck! No way! No thanks! If your solidarity with the unemployed means this then you can stick it. I'm not like her, am I? Am I also this boring incessant complainer?

When she leaves I punish my girlfriend for the implication with a cold silence. We Irishmen are great that way.

IRELAND VERSUS LATVIA   11/12/92

What are those lines by the poet Keats?

My hand trembles
And a dull ache hits my brow
As though of Hemlock or of Guinness
I had drunk too much

Don't know and don't care. All I know is that I can't do that sort of thing much more often.

It all started so differently. Went into the pub to watch Ireland v Latvia. The bar is soft and warm in the glow of the dying afternoon. The beer flows and I feel a strange content I haven't known in months. A good session now would be nice, a good proper feed of beer. I love this, the release from normality, convention, depression, the not caring, freedom to do or say whatever you want to whoever you want.

Ireland win. Yahoo, Olé! Olé! Olé! U.S.A. Eu Ess A! Now the real drinking begins. Covetous, selfish drinking. I go to the jacks. Throw up to clear more space. Return. Great rejoicings and laughter. "I can drink any of youse under the table". By this stage the table possesses more intelligence.

At this stage the girlfriend arrives. Oh Fuck, she's wearing her "I love you but you're making a mess of your life look". Defensive. Inevitable row. Leave me alone, you've got drunk often enough. Fuck off, will you. Tears. She slaps me on the face. I slap her back. Impulse. I am drunk enough not to be shocked by what I have done, drunk enough only to want to return to the drink. After all, I am nearly there. Two more and then black out. More tears then disjointed sentences, then she leaves. Thank God. Fuck you.

I wake up next morning in a pool of puke. The whole bed is soggy and covered in it. The closest I have come to a rock star's life-style yet. Death by asphyxia. Not surprisingly the girlfriend is in the next room. I receive a cool reception. Apart from the vomiting I almost killed myself twice last night in falls when I got home, not to mention the incident in the pub. I am sent over to a friend with the decorated duvets. Humiliation combines with hang-over, a heady brew.

I know the cause for this excessive drinking and it is not only unemployment. Every time I make love to my love I betray her most fully and completely. I cannot survive this much longer. It must be told soon and completely or we will both die.

ESCAPE   12/12/92
We are always in our lives searching, cherishing dreams, some of us more than others. Or perhaps it would be more accurate to suggest that those of us who cherish most deeply have the most elusive dreams. The country has always offered me a fragment of that dream, a peace denied by the flux of normality. I have not shot much over the last two years. Too many hassles and encumbrances, relationships, work, even unemployment. Walking these fields now, this small narrow landscape, I remember a time when I felt a unity, a connection that was almost complete. I remember when young, dreaming of leaving it all behind, living in the woods, free and away from it all. The intervening years have severed that dreamy attachment.

The rupture hurts me. I can only hope it can be recaptured. The dole is a strange imprisoning experience. Nature may yet serve as a release. My girlfriend cannot understand, doesn't realise that you can hunt and kill, yet love nature. Killing is what consummates the tie for then you are a participant. You are no longer that bystander watching. Her concept of nature is dominated by that which is scenic, what is pretty. Mine is more visceral, feeling nature as a reality, not a picture. These fields have entered my soul, filled my memories. I know the beauty but also the terror, the squeals of a shot rabbit, the pathetic flutter of the dying pheasant, its power and flight ebbing with the freckled blood. Beauty and pain mingling, each irretrievably entwined.

GIRLFRIEND OVERDUE   13/12/92

Girlfriend is overdue with period and I am rightly terrified. How did I not sense this? Am full of worry and recrimination. Have I the right to have sex with Catherine, risking getting her pregnant, when I am unable to provide for a child, to look after her or it? I run no risk but her career and reputation, even in today's Ireland, are on the line. This will destroy her family. Have I acquired the right to run these risks? I don't think so.

It wouldn't be quite so bad if I was working. On £53 a week what can I promise when I mouth the platitudes, "I'll look after you. We'll be okay." A single mother's allowance, a council estate, that would be a marvellous contribution to a person's life. And the destruction of another family. Sex, the creation of new life is a serious adult business. You need to be prepared. Until then it's just selfish pleasure, two greedy children playing at being adults.

I mutter platitudes, lying to myself and her. It'll be okay. I love you. Fat lot of good that is. We are very separate on this issue. This is very personal to her. I wring my hands suffering the unfelt agonies of the liberal conscience. This is such a fucking mess. We are going to have to seriously consider giving up sex until things are more certain, more settled. Her childhood will be well and truly shattered now. Is that my present, her screaming pain in childbirth. What will I do? And what of the other thing?

That night I dream, all my guilt, my hidden guilt surfacing, bubbling. Childhood dreams possess such innocence. I remember during a particularly severe bout of puppy love I dreamt of saving my Irish teacher from being raped. Rape, I hardly knew what sex was but I knew that after she was rescued by me she would see the real me and we would live together etc., etc. . .only after marriage, of course. I would protect her, keep her safe from that outside world. Well, how things have changed.

The dreams are more frequent now. Yet I know I should not be concerned. The chance is minimal. But it is there and I have said nothing. Afraid to lose what I have. Were I more cynical I would not worry but I am cynical enough to satisfy my conscience by worrying but saying nothing. That is the essence of evil; fear, banality and covetousness.

Dreamed again last night. Am afraid of talking in my sleep. I was in a church at night. It was peaceful. This nun came in. I felt only peace. She moved astride me then quenched the seven candles one after the other and as the soft light died, I felt only terror.

I walked down the river this morning, watching the swans, partners for life. Are they a mirror image of us? Is that us? That rat swimming below. Is that me? This cannot go on.

WEIGHT   14/12/92

Am putting weight on at a frightening speed. Not bad for a man theoretically on the poverty line. Too much sitting around and comfort eating. This is also affecting my confidence. It is bad enough to be unemployed but fat and ugly with middle-aged spread as well, this does not enhance the quality of one's life.

I need to go on a diet but I seem to have such little will these days. What exactly is wrong with me? So much of what is destroying my self-esteem could be rectified quite easily yet I just don't seem to posses the will to do so at the moment. Always tomorrow and tomorrow and tomorrow. At least I am not losing weight. Then I would really be worried.

PREGNANCY   15/12/92

What can I say? This is her problem. Not in the sense of "I want nothing to do with it" but in the sense of how can I help her. I, the hero, the man who will solve all her crises. Not this one, love.

We walk, attempting to "sort it out", attempting to calm, pacify, resolve, face, begin anew. All these things you try. What can I offer but the old cliché "I'm here", "I'll support you". We are both terrified but there is no bitterness, no hate. We love too much for that.

Or do we? Will that too break and decay, and what of my guilt? I stifle fear. This is no time for some narcissistic release through confession. My role is to comfort and strengthen her. But is it not terrible that in Ireland today when we have a woman president etc., etc., that the same terror holds now as for twenty, forty, sixty years ago. This is wrong. I will stay with her. I love her. That is all.

I kiss her as we hug seeking warmth in the frosty air. What if it is true? There will be no kissing then. What is my full gift to her?

POVERTY   16/12/92

I am living in the poverty trap. Tragic, is it not? I know I am not starving, have my luxuries, a home, girlfriend. Yet I still feel poor. This is because poverty is about more than starvation. Poverty means never having enough, the always never feeling safe, the scraping to survive until Tuesday, the ceaseless counting, always having to accept second best in food, clothes, life, grinding away, softening you up, preparing for the second and worst surrender. All very well for Yeats to speak arrogantly of the greasy pence. He didn't live in the slums or fear the fall.

Then there is the second surrender, the fall. Poverty is not solely a matter of physical hunger. It is as much a state of mind, a sense of entrapment, of blocked opportunities everywhere you look. No escape from the trap with the rest of the rats.

Poverty is essentially an absence of choice. It is about the death of aspiration, the absence of hope, love, faith, optimism. This is what Kavanagh brilliantly defined in *The Great Hunger*. The peasant Maguire is a slave because he has nothing to aspire towards. Because of this he could never possess freedom. Like so many in our society today he would not know what to do with it.

We are in the process of creating a nation of Maguires today. Only the locations are different. The sorcerer's apprentice in all of this is the culture of unemployment, corroding the self-respect of all who measure self-esteem in terms of work. Like the North of Ireland we have created acceptable levels. Full employment is no longer an electoral manifesto. It is acceptable that a quarter of our people possess no self-respect so long as enough of the electorate are happy with the new icons of social democracy, lower taxation, growth, divorce.

It is only when the true tragedy of unemployment, the ghettoisation of a quarter of our people becomes apparent in terms of violence and crime that something will be done. But this is not apparent yet. The unemployed do not protest because they are slaves to the welfare culture. They are no longer free but possess the traits of slaves, the apathy and the alienation. That is the lowest form of poverty.

I have not yet reached that stage. If I feel it approaching I will emigrate. I would leave even my lover before I would surrender to that non-life. Of course, by then it may be too late.

BEER 'N' SAUSAGES 17/12/92

Well, I've done it now and with just as much style as usual. On the beer again. Welcome to the world of poverty. The usual drunken blather about the hard time I've always had, how unfair it all is and how the world and society have specially picked on me. Go back to someone's house and drink a bottle of their vodka just to even up the score. Thrown out after decorating their kitchen floor and stumble away laughing. Oh! we have no conscience when drunk. That's the attractive thing about it.

Fall into the local shop at six thirty in the morning. The owner is there, pompous and grandiose as only the emperor of a corner shop can be. I summon the last relics of my pride and sobriety and in my best Eton accent ask my good man for a pound of his best sausages. I decide not to stretch it by asking him to add it to the bill and wander out circuitously clinging to my pride like a surreal Daffy Duck. Home James.

Back at the ranch my mind swims with visions. Lovely pink sausages nestling warmly in the pit of my maternal stomach. Yum Yum! A fitting end to a glorious night. Turn on the cooker and wake up four hours later. Jaysus! Rush outside but no, the kitchen hasn't blown up. There are, however, eight black things strewn around the back garden which I believe to be the remnants of my breakfast. Pathetic little things, a bit like myself. Even the crows won't touch them. I retreat to my room to sit it out and regroup.

Later on in the day the full story emerges. A housemate settled in the sweet dreams of innocence smelt the sausages cooking. Sighing he returned to sleep only to be woken an hour later by a far less lovely smell. He dashed downstairs, saving cooker, house and all of us from immolation whilst gobshite snored on. I smile at the good of it. All of us do. And we all remain the best of friends. But inside I whisper stupid fucking shite, I've done it again.

LOVE 18/12/92

In so many ways I am foolish, for despite everything I possess so much. That is easy to forget. I am so fortunate to have love, despite all the guilt, the pain. That is valuable, yet ironically it is the easiest thing in the world to forget. Sometimes the ordinary, the squalid become so pressing. And there is above all the guilt but how do I tell her. Do I just leave? That will destroy her twice as effectively. And the chance is so small. Still waiting.

How do you find the language to describe love, the delicacy of word, metaphor, simile? It is easy to describe despair, hatred, the darker passions. In writing above love I always feel like Caliban blundering around stupidly, too rough to describe, knowing enough to want to.

All I do know is the importance of kisses, short snatches of heaven where the world is no longer harsh. I gasp for them like a fish in air, seeking return to the soothing water, seeking to be full again. I, thank God, have that repletion.

TURKEY PLUCKING   19/12/92

The Irish welfare state remains as generous as ever. Local headline screams *Swoop on Welfare Cheats.* Apparently some people on the dole had been plucking turkeys to earn extra money for Christmas. Presents for the kids, that sort of stuff. Debauchery.

This, of course, is a serious threat to society and well worth the attention of the state and the Gardai. We can't have the unemployed and their families enjoying themselves to excess over Christmas. Besides, this work is needed by people such as Gardai, National School Teachers and other lowly paid groups in society. Well done lads, you're a credit.

JAYSUS, YOU'RE NOT STILL ON THE DOLE   20/12/92

Another fucking person says it again today: another fucking bright-arse.

"Jaysus, don't tell me you're still on the dole, with all your qualifications. Was it worth it? Well, there you go".

He leaves, smiling mysteriously. I know that smile. It says another victory for the little people, more proof that education is worthless and there's young Seán to prove it.

"Look at him and all his college and his degrees and he no better than the rest of us". Bully for all of you.

Well, it's consoling for me to know that everyone agrees that it's shocking. A young man like that. So well qualified. Someone should write into the *Evening Herald* or Gay Byrne about it. Better still tell the employers. Everyone write into them and tell them what a swell fella I am. Gather signatures outside the G.P.O.

I've become everything I've always been terrified of becoming. You know the joke about the fellow, the M.A. working in McDonalds. The fellow they all point to, see him, see him, the fellow with the M.A. and he's only working at

McDonalds. I could become a tourist attraction. Build a heritage centre. That's me, useless fuck, wanker, failure. I call myself all the correct names.

What's wrong with me that I can't get work? I should have got myself a trade. Stupid this jumping out of your own class. College is too big a leap for the likes of me. Is it because I'm lazy or stupid or gormless or is it the fault of society, this unemployment thing? The latter's an easy option. I won't take that, at least not explicitly. Better to blame yourself. I can hate me better that way.

GUILT   21/12/92

She is safe. Or is she? At least she is not pregnant anyway. I know why I am drinking so much these days. I am drinking to get away. The bruises are gone now, thank God . . . but still this permanent cold fear, and what if they return. What will that mean and what will it mean for Catherine?

She will leave me if she knows. But if I love her I will tell her. But why tell her if I am not H.I.V. Positive. Why, when the chance is so so low. Genuinely. I must think, must decide soon. If the bruises return. Drink is an escape, a revelation of my real self, the ugliness of a person who cannot reveal to someone they love that they are afraid of being H.I.V. Hoping she will see and leave me.

What is that fucking spot! Are my armpits distended? Oh God, this is foolish, stupid. This should not happen! Leave it. It will be okay.

CHOICES AGAIN   23/12/92

Go Christmas shopping. Cheap presents acceptable only. Head straight for the pound shops. This is the reality of Christmas on the dole, the hating of the cost, expense, shredding your budget, breaking the old safe routine. Everything affordable is cheap and garish. I do not want to be mean about things. I hate it, the lying and deceit with the parents but I do not possess a choice. Purchase the least expensive of the stock and leave with the defeated gait of the cheapskate. The day ends fittingly as I am squashed into a train with a thousand drunken civil servants on their merry way home.

Mother, as ever, delighted to see me. Relations with my father do not seem to have changed much from five years ago. He is as unpleasant as ever and we continue to communicate at the level of spasmodic grunting. We're not as yet at the point of breakthrough into complex language systems. He can't understand me, what my ambitions are, what motivates me. And because of this he cannot respect me:

"His age and still in college. Why isn't he working? What bloody good is that old M.A. anyway. Leave your girlfriend alone and don't be mauling her". Our relationship is a series of peremptory silences and dismissive grunts. We do not have what can be termed a normal father/son relationship. Does such a thing exist in Ireland? Not from his generation and we are too separate now to ever meet.

I have schooled myself not to care by now, not to notice the absence of communication or praise or love. It is normal. I have seen too many people fucked up by this. All I can do is laugh. It is the safest route.

Strange – I used to worship him as a child. He did leave one gift, the love of nature. Apart from that nothing. Perhaps that is enough, as much as could be expected, for that was a deep gift. Perhaps when the worship ended and the scales fell from my eyes he couldn't hack that. Don't know. Don't care anymore, thank God.

Today is not without its humour. I make spaghetti bolognese and in an evil moment fill the plates with spaghetti only. The white globules glisten with the evil hue of boiled worms and he murmurs miserably for five minutes before I put him out of his misery.

Miserable bastard.

He comes from the old school. The man is the most important person in the world or at least the house. His word is law, the Bismarck of the living room.

CHRISTMAS EVE   24/12/92
Feel only dread as another disastrous day enjoying a family Christmas looms ahead. Bring on the Joe Locke and the James Bond movie.

CHRISTMAS DAY   25/12/92
And thank Christ it's over. Mystery and mystique pass by again.

RELEASE   26/12/92
St. Stephen's Day. Patron saint of televised football. Joy! Celebration! Go home to Dublin.

JANUARY

HAPPY NEW YEAR! 1/1/93

And a happy new year to all of you from all of us, three hundred thousand of us. Yes, sales in your super-soar-way unemployment office have rocketed to 300,000. That's a new record folks. Now don't forget to say thank you to the politicians and trade unionists. It wouldn't have been possible without them!

PROGRESS 2/1/93

We are supposed to be fortunate. According to some, the end of civilization has been reached; this is the peak, the high, we can't go any further, do any better. That's it. Looking around Dublin all I can do is to question that, to doubt.

Innocently I once thought . . .was taught to think that progress made everything better. But today, and every day the city looks miserable. Everyone I know is under pressure, be it at work or college. People working eighty hour weeks in shops and supermarkets, teachers at the point of breakdown, frightened salesmen and marketing executives all hawking false dreams, the sullen adolescents of the SKY/Nintendo generation, the fear of violence, mortgages, unemployment haunting every face, a society where no one knows certainty or control or security. Where is the progress, the point in that?

Everything is so out of control in this world. A.I.D.S. is the metaphor of a generation, afflicted by viruses they cannot see, wasting their lives away. Everyone is so greedy now trying to claw and scramble over everyone else, everyone the enemy; holding three jobs, trying to reach the magic figure of £40K a year.

There's no solidarity in this periphery of Britain, the U.S.A., Europe, only a rush of greed and whining chorus of discontent. Sometimes I think I'm better off to be outside, to have escaped all of that. Who would want to be successful in this work where the price of success is only yourself, your dignity, your humanity, minor things. All those things which chain stores take as a reward for that permanent job.

Or is this just me engaging in yet another delightfully rhetorical cop-out.

DULL HATRED OF THE UNEMPLOYED 5/1/93

This dull hatred frightens you. The hatred of a generation that has never possessed hope, that has simply never possessed. A society that has lost confidence in everything. You see it in the Health Centre, the Dole office, the pubs of this dead town after closing time on Dole Tuesday, small ferrety eyes, arrogant voices challenging, hating, seeking fights. They always only fight among themselves for only amongst themselves can they win these petty little battles. You call them "they" because you are the narrator, still outside, thank God.

One place, a grey wall on a cold housing estate, symbolises all that narcissistic hatred. A single word printed out in bold perfect strokes, CUNT. You wonder what small hatred warmed the hand smearing the walls. What dark fretful mind conjured up this as a symbol of his hatred and defiance? What dispirited community allowed it to remain there as a testament?

The word on the wall symbolises everything. It is his masterpiece, an epitaph to a mind and life incapable of comprehending progress, love, life, hope. The cold dank wall with its curse is a mirror to a state of mind so constricted as to be capable only of hate. There are too many of these people in Ireland today.

Life is becoming more and more dangerous in this town. Last night someone was raped for three hours. I was out that night. It was a beautiful, tranquil evening, silent with that beautiful calm present only on a winter's evening, everything peaceful – even me. Yet half a mile away someone was being raped repeatedly. That is how close the madness is. And the tragedy of it is, we are shocked but not surprised, indeed our only surprise is that "it" has not happened sooner. Who was it? Perhaps the cold hand that daubed those capitals on the wall has moved on.

UNIVERSITY EDUCATION   9/1/93

Everything in this society is a lie. Meet one of my former University professors today. He plays the benevolent *pater familias*, "And what are you doing now, young man?" I reply bluntly, too fed up to apply the salve of pride, the muttered "This and that," or by way of contrast, "Oh bits and pieces". He put on the mask of shock and concern then walks away dispassionately. I have spoilt his breakfast. Somehow I think he'll survive.

University education is the great lie of my generation. We were promised. Get a degree and you'll have a job . . . a good one. Haw! Even today the promotional literature carries the same old fairy tales. With a degree in Anthropology and classics you will have no difficulty in securing . . . etc., etc. Then when you get your degree they tell you a postgrad. is necessary. It's like a timeshare option, or a bad government monopoly.

The truth is that a B.A. is no longer worth the paper it's written on. It's almost as useless as a certificate from FAS. In terms of numbers, and employability, it is similar to the Leaving Cert twenty years ago. But the concerned university doesn't tell you that. So we continue to churn out graduates in utterly pointless disciplines who after three years and fifteen grand are basically unemployable, because they are qualified to do nothing.

It's all a waste of time and of money unless you are aiming for one of the great karmas of Irish life, the professions, the civil service, teaching. University, the finishing school of the professions. It's time universities ceased being disingenuous about all this and admitted most people would be better off doing their post-graduate diplomas first.

SEX LIFE PRIOR TO A.I.D.S. TEST 10/1/93

Sex life is horrific recently. Cannot maintain an erection. I know the cause of it and it scares me. I do not like making decisions, not these ones, but I cannot continue on like this much longer, that fear every time I get a fever, am I losing weight? What is that swelling, that bruise? I jump when she catches me looking at myself

"What's wrong, baby"?

"Nothing."

Guilty bastard.

Even she is beginning to get suspicious, to probe, ask questions. Why at this first point of happiness does this old terror recur. This will kill us, kill her, but I cannot continue like this much longer. I must discover how to be brave but not now, not yet . . .please. Christ, I am scared.

RELATIVE ISSUES 12/1/93

Public censure, the best way, and most common, to bury private guilt. I decide to do a bit of ancestry tracing in the national library today. Fifth cousin six times removed to a back-bench T.D. should be enough for a job as a Dáil usher . . . strictly without canvassing, of course.

It's good to see the old continuities in Irish society thrive in an uncertain age. The old Labour party always took the high moral ground in opposition, before grabbing every job in sight in government. Sometimes I think they go to such extremes to identify and root out corruption when in opposition so as to be handily placed to know where the real action is when they return to power. It's good to see that Labour and F.F. are united in one issue, something which far over-rides piddling matters like economics, divorce, abortion.

That issue . . . The importance of the FAMILY . . .

NOVEL   13/1/93

Am working hard on a novel. I have invested a lot emotionally into it. It's bloody hard work. The first draft is four hundred and twenty pages long. What will I do if it fails? That will crush me, destroy the rags and tatters of my self-belief. Good but not good enough . . . again. A failure. One of those useless dreamers all good girls are taught to avoid in *Bella* or *Cosmo*. The thoughts crowd around me accusing like pointed fingers. What will I do if it fails? Is this all just a placebo to hide my present state, my inadequacies?

GROWING CYNICISM OF P.F.O.s   14/1/93

During the first couple of months the wait was an anxious one. By now it has become cynical. Yet the worst days are when he doesn't call. It's hard, however, not to be cynical, not to mutter "more rejections" when the little white missives of death float through the letter box. The first ten or fifteen rejections weren't so bad. When it reaches a hundred it becomes harder to stamp down that desolate cynical little voice telling me not to fool myself, that acceptance will never come. Go on the beer. Give up, it's pointless. The other part of me says to keep on going, to plough on through and like everything else the corner will turn. I must listen to that voice or everything I have won so far will be lost; even that little.

TELL GIRLFRIEND THAT I AM GOING TO
HAVE AN A.I.D.S. TEST   16/1/93

Another failure. This cannot continue, fear, guilt, hatred . . . . Conscience can't take it anymore. I hadn't told her before because I only loved her enough not to want to lose her. Now I have to tell her because I love her enough to risk losing her. I can no longer take this guilt, even sex, tainted by my fears. Am I a murderer killing to keep. It is that fear which is leaving me impotent, unable to consummate something which is rapidly becoming a lie.

I break the news as delicately as I can. Breakfast – no better time.

"I'm going to be tested for A.I.D.S."

Silence. Her reply shocks me.

"I know".

Women know so much more than men and so easily. What shocks me most is that despite her knowledge she loves me so much to risk all. This is deeper territory than I have ever known before. I feel a vivid guilt at my lack of faith, at my irresponsibility. This is a life I am playing with. She asks me gravely:

"Do you think you're positive?"

I answer as truthfully as I can – "I don't know . . ."

It's over now. That guilt, my weasel's knowledge. It's safe. We're using condoms. Playing ducks and drakes with a partner's life. And, of course, the other line, I'll destroy her if I break from her now. Clever worm. You'd hurt her more if you give her A.I.D.S. as your love's present. And all the time the wondering and the watching. Why that cough, what's that sore, that mark, is it a bruise or Karpsis Sarcoma. I tell her all this, tell her because she should hate me. But she does not buy it, leaving, yes, but only to go to work. I am glad for . . . I . . . need the space. I think she does too.

I would almost prefer it if she fucked me out of it. That would be easier to deal with than this outlandish love.

We go our separate ways. In truth what is there to talk about in something like this? I feel guilty as though I have brainwashed her into a position that logic denies. That day I walk. There is nothing else left to do. When I return she still has not left, is there, waiting.

The evening is a blur. The shock of this morning has left me dislocated from time and space. I cannot articulate the chaos inside of me. Part of my mind is in shock switched off from the implications of what I have said, what I may become. I am running from myself and my future.

The night is over before we know. She wants to make love. I resist but am caught up by those eyes, her need, scent, everything we have been and are, connections in a dead world. We discuss what to do, where to go. She wants to go with me. I don't resist. How can I? There are some things you cannot do alone. She has earned the right.

We hug and cuddle for the whole night.

My test is scheduled for five days' time. Five more days of normal life. Then what? How will I tell my parents, some mysterious disease, then trust to their innocence. Christ, this fucked up country even has hierarchies of death.

SOMEONE GOES BERSERK IN DOLE OFFICE   19/1/93

After tragedy or at least high drama . . . farce, as ever in this world. The event is so poignantly farcical it is almost tragic. It is never fully funny to see a person stripped of all human dignity. Someone goes berserk in the office today and starts singing the Ave Maria. The sonorous notes of the old hymn bounce against the suspended ceiling. Half amused, half pissed at the show off, the self-pity, we wait for the performance to cease so we can get our money and go.

He continues on. Not embarrassed. Why should he? What does he care about dignity or worth? He has none to lose. A number has no pride and there's no harm in a little madness. We laugh at his madness but edgily. Too many people here are not a million miles removed.

It turns nasty. It always does. He starts hurling abuse at a stony-faced welfare officer. I feel sorry for both. The language indicates his degradation, his lack of self-respect. It also lays bare the hidden tensions, the unspoken hatreds at this clearest of meeting places, possessor behind the steel grill, the dispossessed outside. The man sits, implacable behind the grille, as he is called a "whore's cunt". It's not his fault the man is unemployed, defeated, it's just that he's available. No wonder they don't smile anymore.

Public opinion has turned against the man at this stage. No-one likes to see someone making a bollocks of themselves and by implication us. This wanker thinks he's doing what a lot of us would love to do. Instead he's what we all dread becoming. Poor deluded bastard, holding up the queue. Someone mutters "Shut up, you prick". He deflates like a soufflé. His eyes widen in childish shock, his face wrinkles like an old man's and then he is gone in a volley of defeated murmurs.

The new silence is oppressive. And amongst the sordid ordinariness of it all, tomorrow waits like a coiled snake. And then I am out of that dead place and if this were a novel I would be running, but this is not a novel and there is nowhere to escape. The theme from the 60s cult film dins through my head, " I am not a number, I am a human being." Yeah!

A.I.D.S. TEST EVE   20/1/93

It is the night before. We hug and cuddle, kiss a lot. Our eyes shine with a strange hard fire.

"I love you" she whispers. "I love you too," but still the cold voice questions

"Do you or is it that you just didn't want to go through this alone. Why didn't you tell her earlier? Why are you putting her through this?" I have very few answers.

This is so difficult to write about. Hatred, envy, the break-up of relationships, these are easy subjects, but need, vulnerability, that is different. Even kissing in public is an embarrassment for poor little fucked up me. Perhaps living in a family where love was never shown, where we never even knew of its existence, explains much of this. That is sometimes the worst form of abuse, the withdrawal, or even worse, never-existence of love and affection.

I know why I didn't leave my girlfriend. How could I, just walk out, no explanation, just leaving her, a quick flit, as though the last nine months had mattered for nothing. That would have devastated her just as effectively.

But still the cold little voice persists. Fancy yourself, dontcha. She can't live without you. Maybe she won't live because of you, lady-killer and still the Grecian chorus of this little tragedy. Why not earlier? Why not earlier? But then earlier would have given her a choice, wouldn't it, and Irishmen are not good at that, are they?

At least this way she has me to hate if things go wrong. This is insanity. Lovers like us should not have our bed a battlefield, each wondering if the other is or will become a casualty of war. I am too tired to think or write anymore. I will seek sanctuary in sleep, that is the only escape left open to me.

A.I.D.S. TEST   21/1/93
The condemned man eats a hearty breakfast then off into Dublin we go on the bouncy bus. A beautiful clear blue morning, the laughing sky inspiring the first lustre in the earth after this grey winter. It is a strange setting for a journey into death. I would have liked something more dramatic than a cheerfully bored selection of bus passengers to witness my final hours.

Girlfriend sleeps. A deep exhausted slumber. Her unlined features indicate she is too young to be put through this trauma. Am very calm rather than nervous. It is the calm, however, felt only by those who have burnt all bridges, who have nowhere left to retreat. The only escape for me is that finally I will know. I am truly glad for the telling. No longer the guilt, the furtivity, doubt, fear. This more than anything proves my love exists beyond the easy realm of words.

We go for a walk prior to the test. The canal is beautiful, reminding me of autumn, gushing with life, yet death also, barely hidden beneath that deceiving growth. Autumn, most poignant season. Harvest. The fields heavy and ripe waiting to be stripped, becoming barren and dead before the cold winter.

I light three candles in a grassy verge. For me they are both symbol and prayer, an affirmation of faith in the real beauty of life, something I have not always known. I feel very light-headed. Whatever way it will go I will not give up. If life is short I will live these years more fully than what has gone before. I kiss my girlfriend softly once, twice on either cheek, then a soft kiss on the lips and I go in.

The place is fine if containing a slightly used air. I ask the attendant to look after her. Part of me wishes vaguely that we looked especially tragic but we don't. Inside there is an element of farce when I fill out the questionnaire. You are always supposed to give a wrong name in these places. This is to protect your identity. Typically I begin with a false name then lapse into the real one confusing all of us. The woman knows what I am at but says nothing and eventually we arrive at a suitable compromise, first name right second one false.

Then the needles. I watch avidly as the blood swells up. I had never known blood was so purple. It looks so vital, so alive. I wonder will it betray me; will that filling syringe sentence me to death. The woman smiles dispassionately, swabs and then it is over. I realise with some irony that I have been more nervous of the jab from the needle than its consequences.

Leaving, I feel a great sense of freedom but also separation. I smile wanly at my girlfriend. Now I know the distance women feel when pregnant. I am so grateful for her support but how I feel now is something she cannot experience, or enter into, no matter how much she desires. Outside the cold air is fresh and beautiful on my cheeks. Even the surly city is calm, seeming almost shocked by the quiet beauty of that afternoon. Refreshed. We stand in rapt attention of its peace, the streets cleansed by the rain which has fallen. We go home . . . quietly . . . Home where it is safe. She sleeps exhausted by it all. I remain numb.

THE MORNING AFTER   22/1/93

Over now. I push it resolutely from my mind. No point in wondering and worrying. I have sickened myself on that for months. The time to start that again will be in a week. No point in clouding and destroying the freedom left to us.

We have become so much closer these last days, making love as if every night was the first; the hugging, touching, kissing; sacred and revered. This may be an interlude, a memory to be cherished in times of pain and isolation. Strange how times have changed. Twenty years ago couples used a child to bring them together. Now in these modern times it is the fear of A.I.D.S. rather than the parish priest that is keeping them together. I wouldn't mind but I probably am not H.I.V. Positive. I was always a careful boy even at school. Safe cross code crossing the road and safe cross code having sex, a model citizen. But I'm not taking any chances with this woman . . . or no more anyway.

I'm also bracing myself for the worst should I be disappointed. Such a nice moderate word. I think I'll be more than disappointed if the result goes the wrong way.

Will we survive? I am more dubious than her on that one. I won't take the responsibility of giving someone a death sentence. She protests but I temporise.

"We'll wait and see". Greatest weapon for delay in Irish society. I wonder how she would live with the reality if I am positive, every kiss poisonous, every caress carrying the stench of death.

Part of me knows that if she were H.I.V. Positive I would stay with her. I am sincere in that one, though I have not told her. That would be putting too much pressure on us, too close to being disingenuous. But it is true. Things are too serious for lies or flattery.

The dole is very irrelevant now. Life is far more important than jobs or social status. That's only something we realise when life itself is threatened. I used to think life was cheap. Now I know that it is just short.

NO ESCAPE IN EMIGRATION   23/1/93
Emigration used to represent a potential escape for me. Not after this week. You can escape geographically. You cannot escape your mind, your past, your fear, your guilt.

Even geographically there's no escape anymore. U.K. Germany, U.S.A. all escape routes for the rats are blocked off. No alternative now except the same grey stodge of life, the gimmes at the exchange. Enough just to go on like Beckett's tramp. Same faces, weather, news, conflicts, statements, press releases and spins. Emigration was never welcome but it was at least an option, the promise of something new, the promise of promise.

Not that emigration was often brilliant. Irish emigrants seem to always get jobs below the level of their abilities. The brilliant Irish education system is partly to blame for this. We produce too many gentlemen and not enough players. We are not prepared for the speed, the aggressive competitiveness of London or New York. Too often brought up in an unambitious society security is all we settle for. Little enough but we are happy in the deal. In many ways so little has changed. Still the foot soldiers, never the officers. Only the location is different. Today our educated graduates ply their trade in offices, word processors rather than shovels, the tools of our new navvies. Still under-achieving as a people.

CHEATING THE SYSTEM   24/1/93

Am still not being a model citizen, still riding the system and loving it. No horror or guilt about cheating something which treated me the way they did. Even with the nixer I am still only coming out with a disposable income of £90 a week after rent. These people who squeal about a life of luxury on the dole spend twice that, some in a night. They have their luxuries, why begrudge us?

I don't feel guilty. I broke my back working through college whilst these people were being subsidised by Mammy and Daddy with their relatives waiting like vultures to take them into jobs.

I had no advantages. Now after all that struggle I'm unemployed. I'm entitled to feel a bit pissed. I feel cheated by society, the false promises "Anyone can be president", "Work hard, be good and you'll have a job waiting for you when you're finished". All that crap . . .sorry Albert. All the disadvantages I've faced and overcome and still nothing. Well, if society has lied to me like that then I have no problem whatsoever in cheating it blind. The more the merrier.

Alas! I'm not always as courageous as I sound. Recently, as the nixer draws to a close I have become increasingly nervous about being caught. I have now reached the stage of catching different buses every week to throw them off the scent. Those opening paragraphs, that defiance of Minister Woods was only false bravado.

Last week there was a stranger on the job. She is too good-looking to be a dole officer. According to myth these are all hard-eyed with thin cynical mouths and ash-tray faces. But what if this pleasant affability is a cunning disguise, what if she is Michael's Mata Hari. I consider my alternatives, do a runner, false names, an emotional plea for clemency and a promise never to sin again.

There goes pride. Eventually I settle for an edgy waiting game. Fortunately nothing happens and I do not have to leg it over the outside wall. Just as well for nothing in my experience or fitness has prepared me for such an activity.

This fear is really rather silly. I shouldn't be a social enemy for working one day a week and legally it should be worth my while. Which, of course, it isn't. The attitude in our system is why pare a pound when you can pare a tenner which you can claw back into the hand of the attentive . . . and voting . . .tax payer. And then having worked hard; in fact damn hard to create absolutely no incentive for an unemployed person to declare any income, they wonder . . . sincerely, bless 'em, why people are fiddling the system.

They're fiddling it because it's an unjust system and they're not being caught because people realise it is unjust. They may hate welfare cheats in the abstract but the neighbour trying to earn a few quid for Christmas, or the family, they recognise he has a right to more than just existence. Ironical really, the Irish welfare system is in the process of replacing the British and the R.I.C. as the common enemy. That's some achievement for a welfare system.

A.I.D.S. 26/1/93

I used to think life was cheap. That was easy. Now I know the truth that life is not cheap. It is instead short, transient, rich. Oh God, I would not die yet! So many brilliant things to do, to live, so much loss if I am positive, the child loving her father, the heat of a lover's body at night, laughter, sex, creating, nature, all these things which in our stupid, stubborn blundering worlds we do not notice until it is too late.

The thought chills. Is my body decaying, betraying me and others? Is this what it has all been for? Will I go mad? Is it eating at my mind already? Where are you? Come out you bastard! Leave me alone and let me live. I have so much still left to do!

RESULT 26/1/93

It has been a weird half-life. Everything has been very much on hold, waiting for the test, then the results. I seem to have felt everything so much more intensely this week despite my attempts to place it all elsewhere.

We go in by bus. A hearse passes us out. Well, Dublin Bus is that slow. It's not a comforting sign. We say little. What is there to say? All the pledges, the promises have been said. Both the kissing and the tears have been done, the guilt admitted. There is nothing left, except truth.

We move briskly towards the clinic, the canal as beautiful as before with all the cold fertility of early spring. Enter the hall-way, possessing that weird disconnected sensation you always feel in hospital corridors, as though you are in some place you shouldn't be. I feel empty, hollow, uncaring. I am not afraid. If I am H.I.V. Positive I might as well know and have an end to it. My relationship? That decision is not mine. Now there is just the result, the world, my whole life revolving around that one sentence.

I go into the room. My girlfriend waves bravely, her lying smile of confidence so stabbingly reminiscent of my mother when I left home on my own for the first time. That was so long ago and very different.

There is a trainee nurse in the room. The woman asks if I mind. I laugh. Why should I, but what an introduction for the poor girl. She speaks. Everything is narrowed down to that voice, the brisk professional tone deciding life, career, future, love, hope. She has undoubtedly seen awful things in this small room. The sentence is brief and my mind whirls with the words. Your tests are negative. I try to grasp the exact meaning of the words. Negative. What, where, confusion, translate. I realise I am free.

I feel a dizzy relief but almost immediately a great sadness for the others who hear the opposite who have everything quenched in that small room with the peeling paint.

I walk out unsteadily. For me at least the trap door has not opened. My girlfriend's face is distant, anxious. I smile a little half smile. Obviously it creates the wrong impression. She faints. That's my girl, always wanting to be the centre of attention.

When she recovers she tells me that she thought from my face that I had been diagnosed positive. Can I be right to put her through this much so young. But I feel such a release. I cannot feel guilty for long. That can come later. For now I celebrate the release from a black presence, a fear that has haunted me for years. Free but still guilty. Guilty of deception, of not telling, of fear itself. Is there nothing in this world we can celebrate fully. Not if we have already spoilt it.

I take the free condoms and run, leaving behind, forever I pray, that peeled paint, the nurses who have seen too much torment.

LIBRARIANSHIP . . .   29/1/93
Back to earth again, if this is earth and not some awful aberration as a result of a time warp. Get a response today to my application for the post of Clerical Assistant or Librarian in Leitrim. Permanent job!!! Unfortunately I didn't make the cut for the post of Clerical Assistant but at least I am still in the running for the post of library assistant. I am . . . wait for it . . . 274th on the panel. Yahoo! Well, whaddya expect with only a B.A. and an M.A. Me and my foolish pride.

The solution is clear as a dastardly plan evolves in my mind. I must kill off all 273 rivals and then the job is mine, mine, mine!!! I had better be subtle lest the finger of suspicion fall on me. How to ensure the grisly deaths of 273 library assistants does not become a media event or arouse the curiosity of the police. That is the difficulty. At least I have time to plan.

MISTAKE ON RENT ALLOWANCE FORM   30/1/93
Make a mistake on rent allowance form. Okay, stupid but does this really merit being treated like a total idiot. Get replacement form covered in red slashes like a prison letter being censored. The tone of the advice is arrogant and unpleasant. Sign here. Don't forget to fill this. Fill out this correctly or allowance will be refused. I imagine the chuckles of the arrogant little clerical assistant. We'll make it fool-proof for the idiot, Haw! Haw! I feel like a child getting back an essay and scribbled on it those dread words "repeat". Yep, things are indeed back to normal . . . .

CATS   31/1/93
Break the boredom today by meowing threateningly at the landlord's cats. They scatter and I enjoy for just a moment a sense of what it means to have power. Then I wonder am I beginning the road to madness. The neighbour watching from across the road certainly thinks so. They are getting the shutters in next week.

FEBRUARY

RELIGION AS HOPE/ESCAPE   2/2/93

Religion represents one escape. It is about hope, faith, belief, things alien to being on the dole. I feel a strong fierce joy in belief. Atheism is a dead creed, a cynical *reductio absurdum*. Atheism is easy. Its cousin agnosticism a cop-out, religion's version of the Liberal Democrats.

Faith is difficult. Marx may have been right in defining religion as the opium of the people but we all need our dreams, illusions, escape. That is often the hardest, that leap beyond the safety of pragmatism, of logic, that our society inculcates so intensely these years. It is hard today to say you believe in God to your cynical friends, to believe that some unseen deity possesses in itself all growth, knowledge and perfection in this unimaginative age which knows so much. It is tough on your pride, worship.

I do believe. I have felt a strange warmth in prayer and contemplation. I know His presence and its warmth, feeling both all the more strongly for having known the cold desolation of that previous time. I would not return to that cold ache of the negation of hope, that lifeless logical cynicism.

SOCIAL DIFFICULTIES OF UNEMPLOYMENT   3/2/93

Small talk becomes increasingly difficult after a long time on the dole. I mean, what do you say about your day? What is there to talk about . . . nothing . . . and day after day, year after year of it. Other people get to talk about the job, personality conflicts, pressure, exhaustion, mortgages, cars, holidays. You can talk about none of these things, because you have none of them. Poor Baby!

What do you have to say? Got up. Watched Breakfast T.V. Zig & Zag were funny. Went down to the pub and met the human versions. Applied for ten jobs which you won't get. Went home. That, current affairs and sport, is your lot. Not exactly the genesis of eclectic or sparkling wit. No wonder people on the dole are often characterised as good listeners who care. They've no option.

CLAIMS AND POT-HOLES   4/2/93

Read in the paper today how people are using the claims' system to make vast fortunes out of falling into pot-holes and things. Yeah, right, okay, okay, I'm horrified. Look, I can't even eat my food.

I take these shock horror headlines with the seriousness they deserve. Whose agenda are they pushing this week? It's like those stories about bus drivers or postmen earning fifty grand a year. Some poor bastard working one hundred and twenty hours a week to pay off gambling debts before his knees are rearranged, manages it. The rest are a lot worse off than the horrified columnist. Next week it will be the dole and how we are all ripping off the good tax-payer, the week after drugs, the week after crime. What goes around comes around.

Still there might be a career for me in all this, the pot-holes you fool. Certainly we have the natural resources for it. I start to practice my screams of terror and pain. As the landlords cats flee *en masse* I can see the neighbours looking at me apprehensively from a distance. "I really think it's time we moved, dear".

TO ALL FEMINISTS   5/2/93

Girlfriend is having a period this week. This on top of all my woes. Feminists of the world bristle at this latest manifestation of unsympathetic man. Irrationality, tears, loss of self-esteem "You don't love me anymore". Not when you're having a period love. I blanch, sit back and await it all.

Am I an unsympathetic bastard ...? Probably. I think God created periods to test the institution of marriage ... then there's the menopause. What will that bring ...AAAAArgh.

EASY   6/2/93

Have I not slipped very easily, too easily into this language, this cloak of despair, of failure. Sometimes failure has its own security, the victim complex, poor working class me, a nice little niche. It is often more frightening to succeed for then you must question, must challenge yourself and that is not easy. It is as hard as getting out of bed at eight o'clock on a winter's day to face nothing. Much easier to snuggle within the covers.

Perhaps it is because I have settled into that frame of mind that I will never work. Don't spend my money on C.V.s and layout. It doesn't matter. Don't visit employers personally. They will see you are working class and throw you out. Don't buy the self-help books. It's easier to bitch about how much they cost, how useless they are. How useless are you, Seán?

STILL SCREWING THE SYSTEM 7/2/93

Michael Woods is on the T.V. tonight, assuming his guardianship of the people/I care profile. His nick-name is Dr. Goodnews. Any positive announcement at all and you can't keep him away from a Press Release. His main concern tonight is . . . of course . . . the hard-pressed tax-payer. Even though he is Minister for Social Welfare it rarely seems to occur to him to make public announcements on behalf of the hard-pressed dole sponger. Ooops, I entered the Minister's mind for one second there.

Anyway, Michael appears to have overdosed on the *Daily Sun* editorials again. Managing an approximation towards a tough face he lisps about cutting out fraud. We mustn't let these people screw the system. Of course he's right. After all, with everyone else screwing it, doctors, lawyers, solicitors, auctioneers, planners with their little networks and monopolies; planning deals, a job for the nephew, the friend; we can't afford the unemployed joining in also.

So sorry Doctor but don't bother appealing to my conscience because the system is/has screwed me and I've no problems with a little corrective action. I tell you what, Michael. I'm so nice I'll even do a deal. If you can convince me the system's fair; if you can convince me that equal opportunity exists in this country then I'll re-acquaint myself with my social conscience. I'll accept my failings and play fair. Until then, tough! Meanwhile, excuse me whilst I continue with my frantic efforts to enter that system so that I can join the rest of you pontificating about those who screw the system. I know about my full potential in the areas of bare-faced hypocrisy.

NOVEL . . . SLOW PROGRESS 8/2/93

Novel continues, but slowly. Am treating it like a nine to five job although lately it is more like twelve to eight. Have to force myself to write every day. I would do anything to avoid it . . . even work. Joke! Anyone who says they enjoy writing is in my view a dosser or a chancer. It's the greatest risk of all, worse than betting. If I fail then that's a year's work gone for free. It's an end to all dreams, no escape then from the rat race I hate so much. Yet part of me desires to participate in that race, so intensely. Which part of me is true. Sometimes I empathise so strongly with James Dean. It's okay. Joke!

We are like lemmings, those of us who chase dreams. One of us succeeds but a thousand are destroyed by the effort. But then, are the others in their little tunnels, the office workers and salesmen, the national school teacher, pillar of the community, any better? They also are worn away by the fret, the effort to achieve . . . What? Will one of them say at sixty what they have done, what they have achieved which was of real value.

I will continue to chase the dream, self-important as that sounds, because if I lose that, then I will lose the core of what I have become. I will risk failure because defeat is better than the stigma of surrender, the allowing of the little people to win . . . again. I will not accept that; not just yet.

LOCAL ALCOHOLIC I   9/2/93

Go into the pub this afternoon. The local character is in quite munificent form. We watch in silence, awed by the performance, as he proceeds to eat a whole bag of raw vegetubbles (sic.). The horses duvet (sic.) or should that be (hic) consists of a few leaves of a raw cabbage. An onion goes, unpeeled of course. Real men don't peel their onions. More onions are followed by mushrooms and brussels-sprouts in a Guinness and Whiskey sauce. It is an unnerving sight, particularly as he is wearing sun-glasses and a Russian hat. Gerry Ryan come here quick.

A generous man, he offers some of the vegetubbles around but the offer is politely and unanimously declined. Not good territory for vegetarians this. He unveils a turnip. Obviously the piece de resistance, the main course as it were. Unwashed (the turnip) it glistens in the soft reflected afternoon sun with the pink delicacy of a bride on her wedding night. But now the terrible consummation is nigh. He feasts his eyes on the helpless victim, but only for a moment, then the terrible struggle is on.

We watch avidly wondering who will win. Crunch, Crunch, Crunch, three bites and the war reaches mythical proportions, the sound of battle echoing around the silent room. Will he eat the whole turnip? Will he lose all his teeth?

But he falters and we sigh disappointed. History may not have been made but we leave revitalised by the courage, or is it madness, of the attempt. Self-centred as ever I sigh, for how can one concentrate on the misery of unemployment, one's own petty concerns in the presence of greatness such as that.

MULLAGHMORE . . . AGAIN   10/2/93

The fuss continues. Our liberal élite are incapable of celebrating their triumphs quietly. They have indeed won a notable victory. The countryside can remain clean and pure for them to watch as they drive through it in their '93 registered cars, on the autobahns sanctioned by their relatives in the Dáil.

The views of the "little" people count for nothing in their agenda. What are the losses of the jobs of a few builders labourers, the voice of a small dying village, compared to the march of social democracy?

Their voices are shriller now, more hectoring. Our social democrats do not like questioning. Populist is the greatest insult for these people and if the people cannot be guided then they must be coerced. Legally of course, where they cannot afford a voice. It's almost enough to make you want to join Fianna Fáil, the republican party, with a small r.

Their voices dominate the media also. This the major weapon of our new colonists. The leader of the pack is, of course, M. D. Higgins, socialist by kind permission, intellectual defender of the working-class. The tragedy for all of us who desire change is that Mr. Higgins is precisely the same as those he has condemned most virulently. After all he's in coalition with them. Fortunately, the self-important arrogance which seems to inhere in academics protects him very nicely from perceiving this.

Hypocrite also in his desire to portray himself as a defender of the weak and underprivileged. Only in the abstract, Michael, only if you can be their guide, or perhaps celebrate the vibrancy of the lives of this exotic species in the drawing rooms of literary societies. But meet them? No, our friend will be happier in the Department of Arts, Culture and the Gaeltacht than Social Welfare, the drawing-rooms of An Taisce than the dole office.

STANDARDS   11/2//93

The standard of political life in this state today is so low. I don't mind the chancers. What I detest are those people always meandering about low standards in high places, demagogues masquerading as reformers. The Labour party are the masters of this politics of begrudgery. All this has led to a collapse of trust and respect between politicians and the electorate.

Each despises the other equally. Politicians speak of the gobshite vote as being the most important one. They despise it but they also fear it. Ability alone does not convince the gobshite voter. You must weave pretty stories, nice pictures, you must woo rather than convince.

We have deserved our leaders, our golden circles. Politicians may fear today's voter but that fear will only lead them to deceive us. If we expect too much from them, if we apply impossible standards viz. Albert and the "crap" incident, shock, horror, etc., etc., that process intensifies.

We, in short, bear responsibility for the weak demagogues which rule this state today. We ourselves, sinn féin, have created the problems which are corroding our state and the soap opera political system which pretends to solve them.

ESCAPE FROM A.I.D.S.   12/2/93

Am still trying to adjust to the freedom from that old shadow, the terror, haunting, laughing, invading, now suddenly gone, dissipated like a cloud in air. One fear is that I will become casual, contemptuous in my freedom. At the moment all I feel is gratitude and relief and an intense desire to achieve something valuable out of my life, not to live for self alone. Will that change? Will I return to casual selfishness again?

I feel a deep regret that I was not more honest with my girlfriend. That would not have happened if I were a better person than I am. But this hate is a pointless indulgence for someone who loves self-hate as much as I do. Too many lives in Ireland are blighted by guilt and its attractive sisters.

It was late when it was done but at least it was done. Love is the unveiling of lies, defences, self-conceits. If lovers knew the tangled nightmares of their partners' minds at the start of a relationship it would be still-born. My girlfriend has told me things that have shocked me also. The A.I.D.S. thing was not told because it was not the time to tell it.

I have learnt so much from this, not only of my weaknesses, but also my strength and my girlfriend's strength also. Above all, I have learnt not to be so harshly critical of others. I have not earned the right to become the great moraliser yet. Something not always the case with many other of our great moralisers.

CHANGES   14/2/93

Meet a friend of mine today. Haven't seen him in a long time and we are both initially wary. He is doing well at work. I am pleased at that. I was envious at first. That shocked me. Dear, kind, generous me, wanting everyone else to fail like me. Finding it difficult to accept the success of others that I knew. The oldest human greed, wanting to drag everyone down to your own patch of the gutter.

Didn't contact him for two months. Eventually it came around. Hence the meeting today. It is so sad. Every day I learn something more of the darkness hidden inside of me. He's doing well at the job. Still managing to remain witty and detached, he has managed to avoid centring his life and worth around the sale of fire hydrants. Still hasn't bought into the lie . . . yet.

I hope he remains that way, remains witty and irreverent, doesn't join the rest of the living dead. But already I sense a nascent self-importance. I hope I am wrong for if it is true then our friendship will die, slowly but inevitably. That will be sad, not tragic, just disappointing.

QUESTIONS   16/2/93

What is a job? What is work? What are these things these strange clock-work people do in their half lives spent in offices, trains and cars, that small rabbit world, home, office, home, the suit and briefcase, the only heraldry of their lives. And why can't I get a life like that, why can I not succeed in trapping myself into that bubble world we are all taught to dive towards.

Watching them all I feel so distant/alienated from these strange small people and their obsessions. Often I feel ashamed that I too cannot make that leap. I want to play too.

Yet part of me knows I do not want this world. Life is too passing, sweet, to spend always tomorrow and tomorrow as a cottier to the capitalist, job, car, mortgage, video, Club 30-35 holiday, the marketing man's sucker. What sort of life is built around such inanimate things? What mind covets them? The only reason I want a job is for self-respect? I could not respect myself if I only lived my life for those valueless things, if I became like the rabbits on the same bus for 40 years. I'm different and it's time I stopped battling it.

But the cold voice whispers another story also. Why should you believe that you are special, that your voice alone possesses truth. Egotist. Perhaps you are not so great after all. Perhaps you are a greater failure than you have ever thought yourself to be. Your unemployment is merely the badge of this. Your alienation merely a rhetorical camouflage.

After these highflown thoughts I am faced with more practical disasters when I find that my signing-on card has gone missing. Of course the inevitable response – panic. Am I in really big trouble? Is this the end? Go down inventing profuse and unreal apologies. Am lucky as the officer gives me a replacement without fuss or drama. The other officer, the bad cop, would have rounded up a search party, implicitly castigating me for my carelessness, and would have asked me had I actually looked for it. This is because, God bless her, she lives under the permanent belief that everyone on the dole spends whole days slobbed out in front of the television drinking yellowpack lager and eating yellowpack crisp sandwiches. Eventually, after much gesticulation and sighing she would have issued me with a replacement but only after another severe buffeting of my well-frayed pride.

It's amazing the minor little things you get so upset about after being too long on the dole. You get so highly strung, like a dog in a high rise estate, ready to snap. If I'm not careful I'll end up like the heroine in one of Jane Austen's novels . . . ready to faint at a moment's notice. Just give me the cue. Perhaps like the backbenchers of the F.F. party I am just socially dysfunctional . . .

HEALTH CENTRE MANIA   17/2/93

More excitement in the Health Centre today. Our gurriers are divided into two, those who are stupid and dangerous and those who are merely stupid. One of the latter is in flying form today. Twenty-four, he is already the acknowledged father of three children with three separate mothers under the age of eighteen. If after he dies he is reincarnated as a department of agriculture bull he will do the country some service.

A friend of mine once stayed . . . briefly. . . in the same house as him. Apparently he used to sing Chiwaddy waddy in the kitchen every morning. Better still, each night he could be heard giving instructions on the optimum sexual position to a giggling girlfriend. Yes, she's that stupid. He's certainly that stupid.

Today by mischance two of the mothers of his children are in the same Centre. Others might be embarrassed by this but not the stud. Our hero enjoys himself standing outside with the present Lolita making faces at the first girlfriend's child which he has long abandoned. The child, of course, starts screaming for its father. Touching in a perverse way. Give the child another ten years and it will despise him.

Our gurrier keeps this up for an hour. He is encouraged by the new girlfriend, who inspired by a dull mixture of spite, jealousy and a need for security, doesn't realise that she soon will be in the same position as the girl inside.

The ex inside has to contend with her child screaming, the rest of us glaring, and the other children outside encouraging. Eventually the child's cries subside into a tired whine as the others tire of the sport, bored with her embarrassment. It was a strange sight, petty, spiteful, almost funny in a cold farcical way. It was a scene like a modern version of hell, beyond even Sartre, the child, the girl-friend, the fool and all of the cycle inevitably recurring. The embarrassment, the stupidity, the humiliation.

FIRST INSURANCE INTERVIEW   20/2/93

An interview selling insurance. I must have an honest face. The thought worries me. How am I fooling these people or are they just thick? Go to the interview wearing a suit. Takes me forty-five minutes to master the tie. I won-der do they still sell those little Holy Communion ties, the ones with the perma-nent knot and a little elastic band around the neck to keep it in place. I don't mind looking cheap for convenience. Story of modern Ireland, I suppose.

Victory complete I head to Dublin like a lion. The insincerity is palpable, as expected . . . I mean, who really, I mean really, who wants to sell Life Assur-ance? I do. Badly, of course. The sole goal and objective my life has been building towards. The interview actually goes well. He impresses me, lets me know there's no easy money, mate, but that it's bloody hard work. This guy appears half-honest. I agree to a second interview. This might actually be worth a shot.

S.E.S. SCHEMES AND FAMINE RELIEF   22/2/93

Pass yet another S.E.S. scheme today. The country is fit to burst with these recently. Groups of old men dodder around the place with half empty wheel-barrows picking fitfully at weeds and nettles, half empty coke cans, cider bot-tles, the town's rubbish. Is this a vision of the future?

This is Ireland's biggest growth industry today, worse even than the public works in the famine, pointless jobs going nowhere, doing nothing, hiding the truth. Everything there is useless, embarrassing, even the organiser, loud and enthusiastic like an overgrown boy scout leader, his children too old to enjoy these stupid games.

They are re-hanging flower-baskets now. This is the new big idea. The tour-ists will flock to see all the hanging flower baskets. We will be known from now on as Ireland of the thousand flower baskets as distinct from Ireland of the thousand welcomes. Nothing but bloody baskets and nothing about the bloody basket cases who govern us, the ones who devise schemes about hanging flower baskets as a response to mass unemployment.

Is this a nation's future? That is truly shocking.

UNHEALTHINESS AND THE DOLE   23/2/93

Have felt increasingly unhealthy recently; very tired and sleepy with a strange nausea. I feel as though I could sleep twenty hours a day and still be tired. Bed is more interesting than the real world, sleep an avoidance tactic to escape the void of another empty day spent trying to kill time.

It is the lack of anything to do which is the killer. That is the real prison cell, the real punishment of unemployment. The looking and the wondering at all those other people who manage to be useful, the wondering what is wrong with you, where is the fault in you. Are they all looking and judging you? And what is worst is that you are imprisoned yet you are innocent.

It is this self-hatred and doubt, this life without purpose or challenge that is causing me to feel so unhealthy. My girlfriend is calling it depression but I think that is a bit of an overreaction. I think I'll have my nervous breakdown next year. I prefer to see it as just being in bad form. Please God get me a job soon. She has suggested a novena. I'm too cynical these days to pray sincerely. Anyway I don't believe in praying for material things. I'm starting to revise that view however.

PLANS FOR INSURANCE JOB . . .   24/2/93

Shook myself today. That mythical lethargic pity is too easy. Make plans for the new insurance job. New suit and clothes, briefcase for porno mags, new car. It's wonderful to possess a purpose in life again even if it is only based on a nod and wink. I feel so little confidence in me and this job. I must give it everything, break down everything through hard work. This cannot be allowed fail. It is my last chance. With luck, just a small bit; please God it will. I will eat glass to ensure that it will. The prospect of work feels strange, new and almost wonderful.

TRAINS   25/2/93

Even on trains now I see the first breakdown, that utter absence of cohesion or unity. A couple sit in beside me. Young, happy, going out for the first year. They are both sharp and intelligent yet they will never quite make it. They caress, arms, legs touching casually yet aware, and liking that awareness, liking contact, the essence of living. A yuppie sits in beside me. She is not arrogant, yet I see them stiffening, feel the discomfort of the three. It is as if a dog has invaded another's territory. Hackles rise.

She leaves two stations later to join friends she has met. Relieved. When she goes the bitching starts. Close to hate. Spoiling the previous happiness I had seen. I look around. Aware. Everywhere are tight little groups, the difference in status palpable, obvious in the way they dress but most clearly in their attitude, some groups comfortable, free at ease, the rest either sullen or manic and the tension there, living, vibrant.

SELF-EMPLOYMENT THE ONLY OPTION   26/2/93

My life is hovering around nothing these dog days. I know that when I get work self-respect and all the old things of my past life will return. Even my relationship with my girlfriend. That has changed subtly . . . it seems only the last few days . . . but it has changed for the worse. This job has almost acquired mythical qualities at this stage. An ordinary job but holding the status of a talisman . . . or a placebo.

In many ways it conforms to a belief of mine in earlier darker days. It is much the same as being self-employed. This is the only option for so many of us these days given the death of the permanent, secure executive job out there waiting for us. The absence of those jobs is a hard blow for those of us educated solely to serve others, not to create wealth ourselves.

That is no longer an option. But what to do? What brilliant idea which will create millions and earn a profile in the business section of *The Irish Times*. I have frantically chased alternatives, paper recycling, bookstores, all recipes for poverty. Always giving up in disgust with my own limitations. Perhaps this job will solve my problems.

FINAL INSURANCE INTERVIEW   27/2/93

Had final insurance interview today. Quite dubious about the whole thing. I pepper him with questions trying to find him out. I am impressed by his answers. Am quite shocked to find that I want this job out of choice rather than desperation. His honesty impresses me. This could be it I think as visions of forty grand a year float sweetly around my head.

The interview continues brilliantly, even when he switches to questioning me. Smile at all the anticipated questions, the attempts to disconcert me, to put me under pressure. Particularly pleasurable is the close questioning on a sales prospectus they handed me last week. That anticipated also. He is impressed. I am impressed. We're all impressed, a happy scene all round.

C'mon, C'mon you bastard, just give me the fucking job. My mind is racing like a trapped rat. This is easy . . . sucker. We are just at the point of acceptance, of asking when do I start. Then the trap-door opens and the noose brushes against my face.

"And what type of car do you drive?" So casual but it is the beginning of the messy end.

"Em, Am, Er," I begin to sound like Bertie Ahern on a bad day. Eventually like the defendant I mutter, "None".

I almost feel sorry for him, for the intensity of his anguish as his face drops. Oh, oh, obviously no car equals no job. Now this is what I call gridlock. Maybe the government could provide me with a car out of the eight billion. Five grand for one job. It's a better rate than the I.D.A. The interview peters out to a desultory end. Ridiculous, pointless questions and requests like, "Can I get my hands on a car over three weeks?" Well, I can save out of my £56 a week. As Mr. Micawber might say, "Car £2,000, Insurance £2,000, Income £3,000, Result – Misery." Me asking will you give me a chance anyway. Begging again. We separate rapidly, falsely promising to contact each other if we can find a solution to the problem.

Time, I think, for another bout of self-pity about the injustices which dog my life. What hurts the most is that I really had that job. Now it is back to normality. An end to dreams . . . again, or is it back to dreams.

PRAYERS AND FAVOURS   28/2//93

Have eventually been coerced into contacting my local T.D. to see if he can get me a job. This is both pointless and embarrassing. Pointless because the days when a T.D. could pull a stroke to get a job for a constituent are well gone. Too few jobs and too many requests. You have to be at least a cabinet minister to do that nowadays. My poor T.D. If he was to satisfy all the requests to get X, Y and Z a job he would probably reduce the unemployment figures by five thousand at least. In fact, you could probably make a very good civil service exam question out of it, something on the lines of, "If there are X numbers of T.D.s, Y numbers of jobs and Z numbers of people asking X for Y, please answer the following:

i) what percentage of Zs will get jobs?

ii) how many of Y will have to be created to satisfy Z?

iii) what is the likelihood of enough of Ys being created to satisfy Z?

iv) how many of X will lose their seats because of their failure to provide Y for Z?

(100 marcanna)

This is embarrassing for me. It implies that I am a bit of a gobshite, not quite able for the real world, not able to make it on my own steam. It also goes against what I have always railed against, pull clientalism, the mammies and daddies syndrome. So much for my principled opposition to that! I also feel that my independence, something I have always been so proud of, has been compromised subtly but irrevocably. I will always be under a compliment to this man from now on.

He is affable, but distant. We shake hands when I arrive; shake hands when I leave. Somehow I feel that nothing has been achieved except that my status as supplicant is clear. Maybe he'll get me a job in the county council. My aspirations are not very high these days.

On the way home I hear a tuneful little ditty. It goes something like this:

If you want to stay with me,
Then you've got to get a Jay. . .OOO... Beee,
If you want to stay with meee,
Then you've got to pay the rent.

Cheery really.

At home the girlfriend suggests a novena. Wasn't there once a time when qualifications were enough to get you a job. . . Now you have to attend three times a week, first Mondays and Fridays and that's just constituency clinics. Then there's the religious ceremonies. It appears that the new Ireland is no different than the old. Now as then, it is still prayers and favours that get jobs, T.D.s rather than C.V.s.

MARCH

SLEEPING IN LATE   1/3/93

Slept in late again today. This is a bad suss. It's the first sign of a loss of pride, a sloppy self-indulgent indiscipline. It all depresses me, turns me narky and unpleasant. It also causes me to question myself again. Am I really just a lazy failure? Perhaps I really just need a kick up the arse, all the other old clichés. Despite all this I can no more break the habit than build myself a new life as the books say. My girlfriend is wary lately. She's feeling the irrational backlash of my irrational situation.

Go out walking this afternoon. Something spoils the view. There he is . . . wanker . . . .walking around with a ramrod back. Our Napoleon of the canal banks. His subjects bow respectfully, then swim off quacking. I have seen him at public meetings. Arrogant, incapable of meeting or accepting dissent. One of our liberal democrats, busy saving the underclass again.

The workers follow respectfully, agreeing, laughing at his stupidity behind his back. A career as a sociology lecturer does not qualify you as a buildings engineer. But there is no dissent here. Disagree, however logical the reason and he hates.

It is amazing. People have always believed building sites to be the worst places to work in. Yet I remember them with affection. If you worked hard you were rewarded, unless you were a fool. But talking to the lads on the scheme, if you work hard here, or show initiative then you are seen as a threat, different, undefeated.

So he stalks his little kingdom. Behind the workers watch anxiously. S.E.S. workers, they should be grateful for any job, our new serf class.

LOGIC IN THE WELFARE DEPARTMENT   3/3/93

Michael Woods announces a new scheme to help the unemployed manage their budget, "in an improved fashion". No, it's not a reversal of the dirty dozen or an increase of welfare payments. The latter would be illogical. Increasing welfare allowances to give one million of our people a better quality of life. Madness! As Garrett Fitzgerald once said "It might be all very well in practice but will it work in theory?"

Back to the good doctor of tomatoes. Michael has apparently set up this little press release . . . sorry scheme, whereby £200,000 is to be spent on advising the unemployed how to escape from the debts the Minister's policies has forced them to incur. Clever Minister!

NOVEL   6/3/93

For me at least the stagnancy of life on the dole is hardly tranquil . . . Thank God! or more accurately the novel which has harassed away another week. Have written seventy-five pages, incorporating lust, intrigue, sex, violence, politics, all of the above enhanced by a moral dimension, of course. I have no time for these people writing masterpieces who crawl along at the rate of one page a day and are so overcome by the brilliance of their exertions they have to rest four hours to recover from five minutes of writing. Fortunately I am never awed to such an extent by the brilliance of my output. Anyway, I am a literary Calvinist. Novels and poetry are only produced through blood and tears.

I know all of this is a gamble, possibly a waste of time but in my view it is worth it. Cliché but you do only live once and most of us are even stymied in this. Besides, honestly, I have few other options in this wonderful state outside of becoming a best-selling author. So let's not overemphasise my courage in this matter. Give me the safe option and I would grasp it. Dreamers carry a government safety warning, but even if I fail, at least I will have made the effort. I can at least be proud of that.

SEAMUS   8/3/93

The local barman is getting very twitchy lately, jumping whenever the door opens. I ask him gently has an arms deal with the I.R.A. gone sour. I want to drink my pints in peace and not be interrupted by terrified squeals as the boys get the pneumatic drill and concrete mixer ready.

It is, alas, nothing as exciting as that. Instead our poor barman is going insane. "It's the bores", he gibbers as the glass he is holding bounces off the counter. "I can take the long hours, the fights, the low pay and abuse but the bores." I calm him down, patting his head and soothing him.

It is true really. When you meet a pub-bore you can generally despatch him in fifteen minutes or leave. But imagine your situation as a barman, trapped behind the counter day after day, year after year, decade after decade, listening to the man who remembers the great storm in '58, or who knows precisely how the country can be saved but is too shy to confide it to a grateful nation, or worst of all the man who will tell you a funny one. It's a wonder they don't poison the drink.

I leave. His piteous eyes follow and the guilt washes over me in great waves. I have left another poor fellow traveller to sink in the hollow seas of the wit and wisdom of our fellow man. Poor man. I can see his arm waving as he ducks under the great sea of knowledge, the third time.

SHE THINKS I EXIST FOR HER   11/3/93

Tension is growing between us. Unspoken. Because I am unemployed she seems to think I should be available to her at every time of the day and for every crisis. The fact that I am working hard at my novel appears to be an irrelevancy. That shows how much she thinks of that. This, of course, is doing my confidence a world of good.

The attitude is not always that open, but implicitly I sense it, lying beneath the surface, an ever-present undercurrent, fraying invisibly. Her unspoken command:

"You're doing nothing useful, you can be there for me whenever I want you". This used to be the centuries old cry of women. That is now my status in the relationship.

ALIENATION FROM MY GIRLFRIEND WORSENS   12/3/93

Go out with girlfriend. Meet another student. They blab and blab on and on and bloody on about work problems, challenges etc., etc. I am filled with a dull boredom not unrelated to envy. On and on the conversation goes. What have I to talk about? The half-finished chapter seventeen of the great unpublished European novel. Yawn/snicker, "Oh, well done, good boy", or "Boiled the tea-towels today, gosh they were in an awful mess". "Yes," yawn.

A hesitant polite inquiry as to whether I'm working breaks the isolation momentarily. But there is a short answer to that and I am soon back in the isolation ward playing gooseberry. Going home I get my revenge by studiously ignoring her. A Pyrrhic victory but mine own. We sleep with our backs to each other that night. Fuck her.

BENEFITS OF THE DOLE   14/3/93

Life on the dole is not entirely a sombre existence of quiet despair. We do sometimes enjoy life despite our best efforts and the intentions of the government. You cannot punish yourself forever because you're unemployed. You can't make a talisman, an icon out of work.

Today I take off with my girlfriend enjoying the potentiality of unfettered time. We spend the day together, a rarer thing recently, breathing in the presence of each other like the start, enjoying the laughter, slagging, kissing, love. All I have ever wanted from life ultimately is happiness. That is synonymous with love. I have been fortunate enough to have achieved both.

We end the day refreshed. I realise with a little shock that it is the first day of any value that I/we have spent in a long time.

HIERARCHIES   15/3/93

Even amongst the unemployed there exist hierarchies. There are three grades. Of highest repute are the master unemployed. These have been fiddling the system for years. They are not on the dole. They are on the scratcher. The scratcher is a grant by the state which supplements the real money earned in the black economy. It is a handy little bonus and a justifiable reward for a hard week's work. These people swagger into the office on signing day with the quiet content felt only by those who are ripping the state off good.

Most of the rest are mere journeymen unemployed. Like an erring husband they still feel at home in the exchange if rarely comfortable. For these the dole represents the major part of their income, therefore they are more *au fait* with their rights than the rest of us. They get on best with the Social Welfare Officers. They know the rules of the game, when to cheat, when to lie, and when the truth is necessary.

If the Welfare Officers dislike the arrogance of the master-unemployed they positively detest the naiveté of the lowest rung of the aristocracy, the newly unemployed, the apprentices. We are to be tamed, and fast, lest we acquire the tricks of the masters. We, of course, acquiesce in this, slinking into the office ashamed and already beaten. Our foolish questions irritate and annoy. I, of course, belong to this category though I am progressing and hope for promotion soon.

Of course, the clearest example of my gormlessness was my decision to sign on in my local office. There are hierarchies of dole offices also and mine is amongst the worst. The knowing ones told me, raising their eyes to the heavens,

"You're not signing on there – go to Head Office like a good lad". But I actually believed the system was fair. That, and I was full of pride – two fatal flaws. I said to them:

"I've earned my money here, this is my home town, I'm entitled to this and I'm damned if I'm going to shift for these people", and so I continued my march towards Armageddon and the experienced ones sighed knowledgeably, awed at my courage.

THE BLACK DOG   16/3/93

Am seized with what Churchill called "the familiar black dog of depression" though he had more cause for its visits than I. Get up late again. Wander desultorily around for ten to fifteen minutes. Don't wash or shave. There's no reason to. Look at myself in the mirror. Can only feel nausea and disgust at what a slob I've become. Big, fat lazy face from comfort eating, sloppy clothes, a shapeless middle-aged spread. Lazy red eyes from oversleeping. Jesus! I've become disgusting in the last month. Look at that scruff on your face. You're not even man enough to grow a beard. The smell of stale sweat hints, jostling for attention with the dirty room and the fur on my tongue. Rouse yourself, you lazy bastard.

Go out the front gate. No letters . . . again. They must be able to see me. Again that hidden subtle ache bites. The whole world appears fresh this morning. Everyone busy, purposeful except me. Again the same old thoughts intrude. Hated, unsolicited, like a catechism, knowing question and answer by heart. The same theme. Why am I so fuckin' useless. Spare us a job buddy. Pathetic.

This is indeed an empty form of living. Trail inside and settle down to write. Fill the gap. Hide the vacuum. But I know it will take little to distract me and that if that little is not available, I will manufacture it. It will be a fruitless day. Is that dream running on empty too?

WHEN IN ROME   18/3/93

It is indeed wonderful how unemployment has improved my personality. Before I was cynical and self-centred. Now I am a new man, empathising, sympathising, suffering with fierce indignation every blow felt by any disadvantaged group, but in particular the homeless and the unemployed. Before, these were abstract groups, social problems or concepts. Now, of course, they are my friends and I feel their every blow personally.

I wonder whenever . . . let's get real here . . . if ever I get a job will my concern be as acute, but my old friend Thomas whispers, "No". Once I escape from this there ain't no coming back. That's why there's no cohesion amongst the unemployed, no lobby group amongst the social partners or in Europe. No candidate running for election on an unemployment ticket will ever succeed. There's no unity in this squabbling mass, no bonding as a group, for to do so is to admit defeat, to admit the perpetuity of our situation.

GENEROSITY   20/3/93

Examples of the progressive nature of your welfare state abound like rabbits in the spring. Read today of someone being forced out of their family home by the Department of Social Welfare. Are those last two words correct? He was two stamps short of the correct number to qualify for benefit. As a result he was forced to apply for assistance and received the princely sum of £2.80 a week. Eventually he left home to qualify for full assistance. I thought it was only the British who used to do that in the bad old days?

RATIOS   22/3/93

Read that a new factory starting off in Cork advertised two hundred vacancies. They received ten thousand replies. That's odds of fifty to one. Comforting that. At least with a lotto ticket you have a nine to one chance. Perhaps the lads in the bookies aren't so foolish after all?

BRING BACK DAT PEN   23/3/93

Welfare Officers seem to love the petty gesture, the footnote of their importance. Some are fine but others cannot survive the day without spreading the load of their misery. Embarrassing and humiliating you is a positive pleasure. "Bring back dat pen" is the most popular and well-known one. Another high point, however, is when someone arrives late. Profuse apologies are, of course, required, plenty of sorrow and promises that it won't happen again, sor; just like the good old days under the Brits.

What they don't realise is that people do not sleep in until 2 p.m. just for pleasure. Well, most people don't, and certainly not if they're in bed alone.

Often it's the first sign of that greatest enemy of the unemployed, depression. Setting the alarm for 2 p.m. becomes the norm because there really is nothing to face or live for. It happens when you're finally depressed and beaten, when you want to escape but cannot afford drugs. And that, of course, is the precise moment when the smart ass in the dole office decides to piss on you.

It happened even to me recently. I signed my name in the wrong place. Stupid but I suppose if I wasn't stupid I wouldn't be here.

"It's in the wrong place", she hisses. Ooops, a mortal sin. She looks at me as though I had forged something. I reach out to cross it out. It seems logical for it is only a matter of an inch.

"You can't do that", she screams, "it's against regulations".

At this stage I'm being looked at and it's embarrassing. I ask why. The response is an order.

"Go back and get a replacement". I look along the queue. If I do as she says I'll be an hour in this hell. Mutiny strikes and I ask her to be reasonable.

"That will take all day", I whine. It's a poor mutiny, rapidly beaten, as her eyes narrow suspiciously.

"Why, are you going somewhere?" she snaps, this time loudly with the anticipation of battle to brighten the dull afternoon. The queue mutters at the delay and I realise I am beaten.

"Naw", I mutter, then pout my lips and move silently away past the bored faces. My mind throbs with the one word, "Bitch". I return. Her eyes roll towards the heavens at the sight of this rebellious native. She takes the slip gingerly, her distaste emphasised, then gracelessly throws out the money. I take it, feeling cheap and dirty, the way they like us. I take it all without a murmur, like the stupid, beaten fool that I am.

SHE THINKS I EXIST FOR HER AGAIN!!? 24/3/93

More complaints against my girlfriend. I am fed up at her constant treatment of my unemployment as a holiday for both of us. I hate these lazy mornings where neither of us get up until 10 or 11. I feel tense and irritated for the rest of those days, as much at myself as her for my complete lack of self-discipline or control. But she doesn't help or, worse still, does she care so long as she gets her own sweet way.

Our sex life acts as a metaphor to all this. Always and always she wants more and more, insatiable in the demand of her own desires. I am turned off by it all, the smell, the sweat, the rancidity. All I want is to be left alone in my own little island.

I think things would be better if I didn't feel so profoundly ambivalent about me. I cringe when she calls me her man. How can I be that when I can't even cut it in the jobs' market, can't keep myself, let alone her. A man in the bedroom, a lamb everywhere else. Our relationship is a fake, a fraud, a mirage. Wait until she outgrows this infatuation, when she will see that I am not a man but a failure. Until then, every time she tells me how wonderful I am, every time she wants me I cringe . . . because I know it is false, an illusion. Nothing more.

"Talk to me", she says. I can no more talk to her than I can make love to her. Not until I sort out my own demons. Then I can come to her.

I need a psychiatrist. They don't provide those on the Medical Card. The unemployed have no reason to be mentally ill. All they do is sit around all day and do nothing. Like the fucking polar bears in Dublin Zoo. Perhaps I could get myself a cage. Compete with the seals. There could be the possibility of an I.D.A. grant. Only the rich deserve to have psychiatric problems, not poor overwrought imposed-upon me!

MORE WANKERS   25/3/93

Any work yet? Wanker. Laugh. Give them the usual old shite. Don't let them see how much it hurts. No, I'm still on holidays, the government's paying it in recognition of all my services to the state. Haw haw, shure isn't it well for you. I smile and move on before I burst him. Now it's an old woman. I can't burst her. "Any luck yet?" A short answer but I should know by now that there is no escape. "Isn't it terrible?" Yeah, Blah Blah Blah, Yeah Yeah Yeah. "And you with all your qualifications. Aw, something will turn up." Yes, probably my stomach. But I don't say that. Still a coward at heart, and happy that way.

Return home and take it all out on the landlord's cats. Am chasing these cats out of boredom. Neither they nor I have had so much exercise in years. A sad sight. Puffing cats and puffing twenty-four year old. The landlord wonders why the cats are so nervous these days. I chuckle silently. Seriously though, I wonder what I will be like as a parent. With the cats I alternate between extravagant kindness and trying to kill them. The latter is facilitated by the fact that one of the cats resembles someone I detest. Is this not redolent of Edgar Allan Poe?

Will my children turn out to be as psychotic as the cats? Will I end up like the character in the Poe story, walling up cats and landlord in a frenzied rage. These are the things which concern me these long dole days. Already my landlord is beginning to look at me with a new caution. Has he copped my deepest plans?

SUICIDE A VIABLE OPTION   26/3/93
Sounds like a bit of an over-reaction to the events and fears of this week. There again, logic and myself are more distant relations than at happier times of my life. It could yet be seen as a noble and heroic gesture to draw attention to the plight of the unemployed. Our attempts at political demonstrations are so boring and conventional. Strikes, overlong press releases, marches to tunes from the sixties. Hard to imagine Larry Gogan overthrowing the institutions of the state unless we forced our leaders to listen to blanket repeats. In India they practice self-immolation. Imagine that in O'Connell Street. An attention grabber I do think.

IRONY OF MICHAEL WOODS AS DEFENDER
OF THE FAMILY   27/3/93
Superman isn't in it with Michael when it comes to defending the family. Must be a kind of side-effect of all those tomatoes, some form of neo-Kryptonite applicable only to protection of the family and press releases. I wonder does this *soi disant* guardian of state against the frankenstein of divorce (more and more Irish politics resembles a game of Dungeons and Dragons) recognise the irony of his position. One of the greatest destroyers of the family is the present welfare system which is pushing more and more people out of the family home because the only way people can get the full dole is to move into squalid little bedsits. And then the Minister cries about the breakdown of community and the family unit. Someone should teach these guys the laws of cause and effect.

It can be argued that if people don't qualify for full dole whilst living at home then there must be enough money in the home to support them. Not with our qualification levels. Families cannot afford to have grown adults in the home contributing nothing. Not only is it financially destructive, it is also psychologically destructive for the dependent, in ways quite comparable to prison.

It is a foolish policy which breaks up families and communities to create large welfare ghettoes. We are living in a society where a sense of community, of connection is being lost. The result has been a colder and more dangerous society. It's not going to get any better whilst the present anomaly continues unnoticed by politicians capable only of understanding economic issues.

Is this not sad? Community, family, the self-respect of our people are all valuable things. We should protect them . . . This, however, is apparently not recognised by our defender of the constitution, too busy issuing press releases on how he has saved the half-pennies and the pence.

SOMEONE GOES BERSERK IN THE DOLE OFFICE II   28/3/93
Great word that . . . berserk . . . glamourous like. Generally the Dole Office is boring enough. You don't really hang around it for kicks. There is the occasional ruckus but generally we are too polite a race to keep it up. This is the countryside, not like Dublin or London. There are standards to be maintained and no-one is going to shame themselves by screaming out their family problems to the public and a cynical Dole Officer.

We have a bit of drama however, today. . . hurrah . . . as someone else suffers a bout of temporary insanity. A familiar litany.

"They're all scum." Yeah.

"Throw them out of their fuckin' state cars." Yeah.

"They've betrayed us all." Yeah.

"Let's storm Dáil Eireann." Em.

Can you hold on for half an hour? I've a pint on across the road.

The speech contains any number of very commendable sentiments. These raise a faint cheer but more suited to Dáil Eireann than the Labour Exchange. Significantly the speech only begins after he receives his Dole money.

He departs disconcerted by the silence disrupted only by the odd surreptitious chuckle. Nowhere worse than dole queues for cynicism and indifference. Not that the speech was very rousing anyway. All old stuff, old hat. Yeah sure, let's march on the Dáil, 1916 and all that. They're all bastards, Gee, you're kidding. Most of us are embarrassed rather than amused. What causes someone to completely forego their dignity, and more importantly ours, for he is saying what is bubbling below the surface of this queue every day. But they want it said with more dignity.

He was probably normal once. Who do you blame? His own weaknesses, the system, the bastards behind the desk, politicians, society, western capitalism. Probably all and probably none. Ultimately the responsibility is his whether we like it or not. No-one can organise their life around scapegoats. Life on the dole is not sweet but you do not have to surrender yourself as completely as that man this afternoon. You do not have to abnegate yourself to that level as a protest. His departure sours the afternoon for all of us. Are we not just as petty?

S.E.S. VISION OF THE FUTURE   29/3/93
  Go into an S.E.S. scheme today checking the suss. Look at those tired defeated people and just want to go away. A man approaches me with a sideways action as though fearing physical assault. He is forty, his face empty . . . No other word can describe it. Empty. I look around in faint disgust hoping I will never be like that. Of that I can no longer be so certain. Sometimes that fear drives me crazy. That is why I hate them so much. They are my Dorian Grey.
  It is a place like a frightening dream; to be left quick. They move slowly, prisoners of war defeated by their own deep inadequacies, unprepared for this new society. Working in a job that's a joke, a pretence, dreaming that their lives still possess some tincture of worth, but knowing. Is that me also?
  Most of them know they will never work again. You can see it in their pleading eyes, "Buddy, please give me a job". The place itself mirrors its inhabitants, dusty, unkempt, a forgotten corner of an indifferent world.
  I feel as though I have trodden on my future gravestone. I avoid those gentle questioning eyes, seeing in those orbs a world, a future that is grey; an eternal middle age of tomorrow and tomorrow, I will seize the day. But tomorrow never comes. I leave briskly, returning to that streaming sunlight. It seems colder now.

CRYING   30/3/93
  Relations are cold between me and the girlfriend. She told my father I had been crying over being on the dole. Depressed, yes, but more worthy subjects exist for tears. Any crying that I do will be inside where they can remain hidden, secret. But on this she pre-empts me, as she is so good at doing, by telling me this is precisely where I have been crying.
  The impotence, the drinking, the distance, the self-hate, even the fishing trip where you became hysterical because it wouldn't stop raining. Your hysteria there wasn't because of the rain, it was the frustration of feeling denied in every aspect of life, particularly employment. All of that was you crying within. So don't tell me you haven't cried about it all.

She loves being certain about me but God I love her. The old Irish proverb, the worst tears are those not cried at all, is very true. I've shed a bellyful of those. But to tell my father that ! That's almost a betrayal. I will not let him see me when I am weak or defenceless.

CIVIL SERVICE/SELF SERVICE   31/3/93
Results of Civil Service test arrive today. Yahoo, secure employment at last. God, I crave the lifebuoy of work, safety. I am out of that tradition that seeks the security of the permanent job, the kiss of respectability. My hands shake. Christ, I am actually nervous. This could be it. This could be my ticket out. Don't mind that crap about the public service. I'm in this for self-service, mortgages, the car, incremental promotion and pay rises, etc.

The disappointment is bitter. Good but not good enough. These words will be engraved on my tomb. Perhaps they were engraved on me at birth. The story of my life. This is a bad blow, another banker gone. That was a job I believed to be in my hands and I blew it. I won't get that many opportunities. I go around in a daze for the rest of the day.

I refrain from telling my girlfriend on the phone. Naw, nuthing yet. My voice hides nothing. She senses something wrong in my voice, an all too familiar, too boring flatness. Are you okay? Yeah, fine, fuck off. I would prefer to tell her this to her face. The week will be spoilt by this. I was sure I'd qualify. So was everyone else who knew me. What little demon is ruling my life ensuring I will be the only failure of my contemporaries. There goes my last reason for optimism.

APRIL

PARENTAL PRESSURE AND VOLUNTARY WORK 1/4/93

Pressure from home worsening. I don't care about my father. He's just a sulky old bollocks. The Irish begrudger. He was the first. I hate the concern it causes my mother. God love her, she's swallowed all the old myths, that if you work hard and are dedicated then the rewards will come. It's not like that anymore, Mam.

I hate the way her voice quivers with a nervous concern every time when she says,

"Any work yet?" It's as though I've betrayed her. I hate that concern. It traps. I don't want people to care. I want to be left alone with this thing, to become anonymous, living in flatland. Then, there is no shame or hurt. I want to go away somewhere, and lock myself into a room with a catflap for food, better still I'll bring in thirty-one cans of tuna fish and dispense with the flap. Maybe it will all look better when I come back out.

She asks me will I do voluntary work. Noooo thanks. If anybody wants me to work for them they can have the decency to pay me. If all of us on the dole start to do voluntary work there is no greater certainty but that we will be exploited. Already this is happening.

I have heard many horror stories about these S.E.S. schemes. Apparently they are a bit like the First World War. Keep your head down or you'll be shot. One of the problems appears to be that most of them are run by lunatics. There is only one type of employer worse than the church, or even a hung-over Donegal subcontractor on Cricklewood Broadway. That type of employer is the socially concerned one.

S.E.S. schemes are riddled with these. You know the type, Vice P.R.O.s of residents associations, Tidy Towns groups, community councillors, all busy saving us and the world whether we want it or not. The sort of people committees were invented for.

And because they are saving you, they have no respect for you. Therefore they can never be wrong, and if you are right it is because you are difficult and obstructive. We are the victims. We are therefore incapable of independent action or thought, and if we attempt this, then obviously we are still dysfunctional. So we must be taught, reformatted and above all patronised. Therefore, anyone who retains independence, ambition, or self-respect, is difficult. I have seen several people destroyed by these schemes.

Our S.E.S. organisers are the ironic inheritors of the concept of Tory paternalism, ironic because most of them would call themselves Social Democrats. But, now that they are in power, social democracy has evolved into paternalism of the worst type, needing victims to save. That is the essence of paternalism/ Social Democracy. They cannot exist without the presence of slaves.

And these are the people charged with fostering, facilitating, enhancing, empowering, blah, blah, blah, self-respect, independence, worth amongst the long-term unemployed. These people are dangerous. They control and destroy lives as a hobby, out of boredom and arrogance. They are Ireland's version of Orwell's *1984*.

UNEMPLOYED – ARE WE USELESS LUMPS?   2/4/93

Read a severely critical article today on unemployed husbands and boy-friends. Apparently we are all carping moaners who should get off our arses and do a bit of work. This is true. After all *Bella* or whatever the magazine was, is famed for its sociological expertise and for its carefully constructed articles. No-one more capable of writing about an underclass than a highly paid and successful journalist in a Wapping apartment.

Nevertheless, I read the article carefully to see if I fit any of the stereotypes. Like everything else in these sensationalist articles, "Are you a potential rapist", blah, blah, blah, there are elements of myself in all of the portraits, particularly the self-pity and the whingeing. It's rather frightening when you seek to find mirrors of yourself amongst the failures of society.

However, I am not totally without redemption. I don't force my harassed lover to make love to me in the morning time when she's rushing to work instead of calming my beating libido until evening. Neither do I sit in a pub boozing her money away all day. Nor do I think any jobs outside of whoring beneath my dignity. Anything will do. Anything! I'll even clean house, cook the dinner. Whatever it takes, I'm a good little boy. Anyway, after reading *Bella* it is comforting to know one is only a partial, as distinct from a total arse-hole?

RENT ALLOWANCE REFORM YIPPEE!!!!! . . .   3/4/93

Even small releases are welcome now. Of course, the latest development is so logical it's only surprising that it hasn't taken longer to implement. From now on instead of queueing two hours every week in that furnace, rent allowances are to be posted out. The system displays humanity and imagination! What is wrong? Is the revolution at hand?

As ever there is a sting in the tail. The rent is to be paid a month in arrears. No chance of our Social Welfare friends being caught out. That is all very well if you are lucky enough to own that protected species, a reasonable landlord. If you don't then our caring system has only one answer, tough. Keep the faith lads. It really does say something about the quality of one's life however, when the ending of a two hour queue is a contender for highlight of the month. Honestly ... without carping ....

DICKS ...   4/4/93

Heard Dick Spring on T.V. He really is so pathetic. All the clichés of the clown as Yeats would say. See the Banquo's ghost of his scriptwriter in every statement which he pretends is his own. Change?! The only change the Labour party wants is at National Collection day and of course the few crumbs from our friends in Europe for all the camp followers being employed as co-ordinators, facilitators, programme managers, secretaries and car-drivers. Yes, vote Labour for a real response to unemployment.

P.F.O.s HAMMER SELF-BELIEF   6/4/93

It's amazing just how bad for morale all these repeated refusals really are. Over one hundred at this stage and still they come thick and fast. One hundred slaps in the face, each hammering your self-belief further into the dust. And then inevitably and so expectedly, the reaction sets in.

First you wonder are you as talented and as bright as you once (it seems a long time ago now) thought you were, as everyone told you you were. Past tense now. Then you start to scapegoat, "It's all pull, yeah". Then your pride all shot to pieces, the begging letters start. The old confidence, I believe I have the necessary qualifications to make a success of this post, etc. etc., has been dissipated.

Apply for another job today using my new-found humility. The whole tone is pleading. Please give me a job. Look, I know I'm not very bright. I only have an M.A. but I'll work hard, I will, I will and you needn't pay me too much, in fact don't worry about that. Oh and also I'm sorry if I'm over-qualified but don't hold it against me. That is its entire undercurrent. That's the way it's gone now. Perhaps as well as a psychiatrist I need assertiveness training.

POINTLESSNESS OF APPLYING FOR WORK 7/4/93

Still applying, a triumph of pointless optimism over realism and instinct. Five more job applications today. Waste of time. All I'll get are five more refusals if I'm privileged enough for them to write back to me. It's hard to know what to do, what jobs to look for. I don't want to teach. The prospect sickens me, working in a job I don't want with children who wish I wasn't there. Not that there's anything going in my line or any line. Loads of sales jobs, coincidentally from the same companies which advertised last month. They must be doing well. Yeah! Fifty grand a year mate, easy . . .and we're giving it to you. My dear, what lovely people! Any of the good jobs want car-owners which rules me out for somewhat obvious reasons.

Open *The Irish Times* today. Jobs galore! the headline screams. Okay, the exclamation mark is an exaggeration. So too, however, is the headline. Three whole pages to do the three hundred thousand of us, one page per hundred thousand. The miracle of the loaves and fishes isn't in it. Scan the pages with the usual sick feeling. See three jobs I may be vaguely qualified for. Yeah, me and 3,000 others. Begin to write desultorily. It's worse to be in competition with 3,000 than 300,000. Ironical that.

SEPARATION FROM GIRLFRIEND 8/4/93

I'm hurting her. I can see it in her eyes. Jesus! I love them, their colour and their depth, their life; so unlike the dead eyes I see around me, mine own amongst them. They are unhappy recently. I'm hurting her with my "distance". She is pleading to be allowed share the pain, to talk about it.

Poor Catherine, so far off the beaten track. Talking about "it" is the last thing I would ever want to do. Bury it, hide, sublimate, avoid, those are my only tactics, my sole ambition with this thing.

How can I let her in? There's nothing to be let into, just a hollow feeling, an empty space, a hunger. Absence. How can you share that? You can't – don't. You just will it to go away, to cease cankering your life. Even things unrelated, love, family, religion, are decayed by that hollow, gnawing emptiness.

I know I am not unique in this. There are thousands suffering like me. But it is unique to me, it is my pain, and I am not able to intellectualise it like those editorials in the *Economist*. It is as though I am the only one.

FIRST DRAFT OF NOVEL COMPLETED   9/4/93

Complete first draft of novel today. "Is this not good?" to quote another famous dreamer, Graham Taylor. Part of me is proud, the other part wonders just what am I at. This is a joke, the chances of success nil. I hear the sweet voice of my father mumbling, "You'd be better off looking for a job than that shite".

My girlfriend says she is delighted, says she believes in me. Do I not doubt that, to again paraphrase Graham Taylor? Maybe I'm paranoid, but I sense an undercurrent in her views, not a million miles removed from my father, or indeed her father. They don't seem to realise that I am looking for work, desperately seeking work. The book is a dream, offering transient purpose. I know enough about how dreams can betray you not to invest everything in it.

If she believes in the novel why does she distract me so easily from it? Why does she dismiss my protestations when I want to work, and she wants to go out or just talk or mess. If I believe in it why do I let her win so easily? It has become yet another silent battle-ground.

I must retain faith in myself and the novel. It has taken an enormous amount of self-belief and self-respect to go this far. It is at present the only promise in my life. If it fails the cost will be high. Sometimes I wonder is it better to cherish our dreams inside and not risk them in the cold air of reality. But then if that were true, my fat father would be right.

JOB INTERVIEW   10/4/93

What is that word "interview"? I had almost forgotten what it means. Endure one today, more farce than trial. Selling insurance. To paraphrase Groucho Marx, "Who'd want a job that would want me". A lovely man, very plausible. The interviewer. Twenty-five grand a year, he enthuses. I am his mate. I smile cheesily, embarrassed by the lies. Twenty-five big ones, easy, and he has chosen me. . . Me!

I enquire about the salary and the first clouds enter the horizon, darkening the sunny fields of our relationship.

"Em, well, er", is this man related to Bertie Ahern? Eventually like truth in a good movie it all comes out. There is none.

"It's all . . . em . . . based on commission". I smile, attempting archness. He turns all emotional now.

"You're the life blood of our organisation. Without sales, without you, we cannot survive." Yeah, like the infantry in W.W.1. A life insurance salesman trying to sell me life, a job, oh, oh. He coos:

"Are you interested?" I lie. Car? I lie again, name the most expensive model. Gosh! these interviews are fun.

We arrange a time for the second interview, to have another little chat. I grin crookedly, arranging practising for my putative job. Of course, Tony. No problem, Tony. Fuck off, Tony. I hope he doesn't wait for me. I hope I don't spoil his faith in human nature. There again, fuck him, he's wasted my afternoon, I might as well waste his. All in the name of equity of course.

CHANGES   11/4/93

Try to get my girlfriend to lay off . . . again. Even her love sickens me now. You're brilliant, you're intelligent, giving, profound, deep. I smile feebly, my mind cursing this silly woman so divorced from reality. Yeah, yeah, yeah.

Jesus, it's great to be such a fine human being. Amazing with all this brilliance that I'm still unemployed. I should be hiring security to drive away wankers begging at the door, their heels dragging in the ground crying:

"Please, Seán, join us".

"No, us".

"Me, Me, Me". But I wave them away with lordly disdain.

She's cloying me with her love, need? worry, faith. I just want her to fuck off. I hate being worried over. It makes me feel guilty, fretful . . .It implies responsibility on my part. All I want is to be left alone, with my self-pity and my hatred, to cope with this thing - condition, me, myself alone.

She can't understand, poor cow, for all her insight. I don't want help, Christ. I don't want sympathy, but nothing I say works. If I tell her to back off she comes back twice as strong. She asks me to tell her what is wrong. But that is just the point. That I don't want to. It's too personal, too inside of me and until she recognises this, any conversation between us is a joke, another excuse for Mother Theresa stuff.

BITTERNESS   12/4/93

Feel bitter against my girlfriend now. That's a first. It catches me by surprise. I didn't think things had bitten that deep, that this would happen. She's so safe, nice, secure and comfortable. Sometimes I am just waiting for the summons, "Get out Seán, you don't fit into this new life". She's incapable of knowing what I am going through. Just the sympathy, the same pointless, stupid, fucking sympathy.

"I understand".

"No, you don't. Fuck off."

I am much rougher with everything lately. Sex, playful slaps and punches connecting more solidly than they really should. Nothing obvious, even to me, but there. I hadn't realised the subtle release of frustration until now.

Everything is so easy for her. God! Is this me, indulging in the loser's whine? I indulge. Last year I spent a lot of time helping her, time I could have spent on myself. Now this year she's A okay, I'm in the shit and she's useless to me. I don't like this self-centred pettiness, bubbling through like damp in a rotting house. But I can't stop the envious thoughts that she's done better out of all this than I have.

Later on my mood is not improved by the landlord. He slumps dejectedly into his chair. "Another boring day", he chimes, almost cheerily. Two seconds later the voice again, "Lord I'm bored". I begin to feel an anxious guilt. What should I do? Tap-dance, strip or something? Five seconds later a trilogy, "Aw God I'm bored, I'm bored, I'm fuckin' bored". I reach for the hatchet. Life is bad enough without some old bollocks repeating its tuneless melody, telling me what I already know. He'd better watch himself or I'll kill the cats.

BEGGING LETTER REJECTED   13/4/93

Received reply from another begging letter I sent for that job two weeks ago. Today I get the inevitable response. Needless to say they thank me very much for my interest but ultimately it's yet another curt dismissal for a job I am actually over-qualified for. The committee, however, feels that I do not possess the necessary qualifications. Nice touch that. Hiding behind the committee. I emerge from the house breathing fire and brimstone, my girlfriend's pleas for sanity and control unavailing. I'll murder them. I ring and my voice is as sweet and as pure as a Bord Fáilte ad.

The voice on the other side is arrogant and self-righteous. Good, an old battle axe. This will enhance the pleasure. I enquire about the job.

"It's filled," she snaps. I respond with the correct degree of humility,

"I know, I'd just like to inquire as to why I didn't get it in case I apply for a similar job elsewhere."

A sigh and a loud tut prologues the slap of the phone, then a series of scratching noises as she conducts a desultory search. A grunt announces the return.

"Well?"

If I get any sweeter I'll be reincarnated as a sugar cube.

"Dunno", she snaps, "we get a lot of applications".

"What?" I rasp. Obviously my asperity shows. The change disorientates her.

"Oh yeah," she says, fumbling for an excuse, "you're over-qualified." Wow! My voice returns to its former sweetness, lulling her suspicions.

"Thank you very much," I smile verbally, "can I ask you a favour?"

Great, this is the moment I've been waiting for, at last in my hands. I delay, savouring the moment, the release. God, it's almost like a climax. I take a deep breath, then release it all,

"Yes", she asks, mixing charity with impatience. My voice is humble now.

"Could you please stuff your job up your hole".

"What?".

I repeat the request with pleasure, adding in "snotty old bitch" for emphasis. I am rewarded with the phone slamming down. Well, I suppose this means they won't be sending me any more application forms.

I haven't achieved anything of value outside of spoiling some old bag's afternoon but God! I feel better. My girlfriend carries herself with an air of cold disgust for the rest of the day but what care I? I feel free for the first time in months. I told 'em! Yes, I know she's right. Yes, I know they're right. Yeah, Yeah, Yeah. I know I'm wrong but I don't care. It was worth it just for the sharp intake of breath, then SLAM!

FINDING OUT   14/4/93

It is strange reading through these pages how much darkness I find. Scary really. The diary, a poor man's psychiatrist.

What is quite disturbing is my attitude towards Catherine. There appear to be so many hidden tensions. Reading this you would think I hated her, yet there is so much of joy and fun in the relationship, that I/we take for granted, yet cherish too.

Still I feel a subtle change in the relationship, a shift, barely noticeable, but there. It is as though the pressure towards transcendence has eased. We are more companionable now, calmer. We still love each other but we are less in love. Is that wrong? Catherine, are we going to become just ordinary now. Is that our settlement, the final chapter of our love, becoming ordinary. It is easier really. But that is not enough sustenance for us, love?

I certainly would not like these pages to stand testament to my virility. I seem to be similar to one of those Victorian wives, lying back and thinking of baking powder. I have my share of passion also. I've had testimonials. It is, I think, because we are so close, that when separation occurs these pages become so bleak, so bitter, foolishly so.

BERNHARD LANGER 15/4//93
Bernhard Langer romps home at 25/1 to win U.S. Masters. I thrill with every blow, live, love and suffer with him. He is my friend. At the end of it all he is fine whilst my head throbs with a pounding headache with the tension of it all. The little things which pass for excitement when you're on the dole and all of this for a quid each way.

By the time I meet the lads this has swollen to a tenner and I am rich. No sense in spoiling a good story with the truth. Not that it would have mattered even I won £350. My debts, thanks to the Social Welfare Department would easily swallow that. It would be nice, a treat, some day to actually own your own money rather than having some bank greedily expropriating every free penny beyond survival. That, however, is even the cry of the successful in our society, thanks to the genius of our marketing men.

STRUGGLE WITH DRINK 16/4/93
Just when you think it's easy it rears its head again, just when you think you may have won. Tonight I feel so low, so very, very low. Find myself in a pub. Wanting. I feel curiously light-headed. Sweating. A soft tremble of desire sweeps over me. God, I want it. The black pint fixates me. This will cure everything. The white collar promises freedom, and I feel a deep nostalgia for the lovely dark forgetfulness, the escape, from the real me. The peaty scent.

I speak. Wait. Promise. Promise. Nearly. First gulp – Second – Ahhh! No. Leave – break away, panic. If I lose to this once, I cannot return. Losing would be a final surrender. I have promised finality in that break. To go back on the beer, admit the monster again is to accept failure, is to prepare the ground for the next failure and the next; to return to where I was before. I leave feeling it has only been a temporary victory.

ACADEMIC SNOBBERY, WORK AND
A GAY GERRY COLLINS?   17/4/93

It's amazing how invisible yet thorough the process of moving to one class occurs in college. It's true that no matter what your status is, once you go through those gates you become a member of the middle classes. Congratulations! It doesn't matter if you're dressed like a yob, drink from a mug or eat chicken with your hands. You are doomed never to be a man of the people, never again to be Jim Mitchell.

I saw that clearly the other Wednesday reading the jobs advertisements. Security posts going in a local factory. Passed on without even thinking. It only struck me ten minutes later. Last week I applied with a touching eagerness for a teaching job that would only pay me one hundred pounds a week. Now here I am sailing by and refusing with my nose in the air a permanent job.

Why? Because I am a graduate and known in my area as one. I am therefore embarrassed at the idea of walking around a factory in my local area wearing a peaked cap and uniform. This, despite the fact that some of my best friends are security officers. I would be seen as having failed. As being incapable of making the leap. What are the implications there for my attitudes towards my friends? A sort of hidden condescension.

It's the same with the insurance job. A sort of half-assed embarrassment about working in the insurance industry. Not quite us, M'Lud. Apply for the security job anyway. There is surely some status in being a valet to a multinational. Any job in a storm, given the present economic climate. Don't get it of course. Don't even make interview. That does a lot for my confidence. The tone of the letter is almost apologetic, adding to my embarrassment. Don't feel sorry for me mate, that's my girlfriend's task. Just give me a job. Any fucking job. . . anywhere.

Later that evening R.T.E. announces it's comedy season for the rest of the year. The star performer is Gerry Collins appearing once weekly on *Questions and Answers*. The highlight of the first programme is Gerry attempting to articulate the F.F. position on homosexual law reform.

Gerry is not happy. This sort of earthy sensuality, the whole question of gay erotica appears foreign to Gerry's life experience. It's difficult enough for the F.F. mind set, of which Gerry represents the apogée, to answer a straight question let alone one on homosexuality. To my mind Gerry has always belonged to the realm of angels dancing on pins. Certainly as he squirms on the T.V. set tonight he looks as if he's hopping around on something unpleasant and sharp.

Poor Gerry. That's what you get for trying not to burst open the party. It's all right Gerry. Punishments over now. Nobody really cares about homosexual law reform, you don't have to contort yourself anymore. Honest. It's too painful for you and it's too funny for us the viewers.

SOCIAL WELFARE OFFICER KNOWS MY FILE
WITHOUT LOOKING   18/4/93

Another workless week. The Social Welfare Officer picks out my file without even looking. My God, I've become a regular here almost without even noticing. I never expected, never wanted this to happen. This is a slow turgid nightmare come true. I leave, feeling only an all too familiar emptiness. No longer desolate or angry, almost content with defeat. Like an old dog, comfortable in what I know.

So . . . it has come to this now; social casualty, long-term unemployed, statistic. This is my new trinity. All that optimism, that vigour defeated, dissipated like a coward's life. All my academic successes an illusion, a false joke. Nothing but lies.

FREEDOM/VISIT TO CARLOW   19/4/93

Life is what you make of it, even at the bottom. Seize the day and all that. There is freedom even on the dole, not freedom in terms of money or choice but of time, to do whatever you want in a given week with just the exception of fifteen minutes to register the badge of your slavery. I am taking advantage of that freedom much more regularly lately, trying to enjoy myself. Sometimes I wonder if this is a sign of surrender, an attempt to normalise a way of life that is completely at odds with everything that will bring me long-term happiness. Have I quisling-like accepted the occupation of this alien condition?

The day, however, drives away these dark thoughts, replacing them with a vague and thoughtless feeling of content. I thumb my way towards my destination, an adventurer, a pioneer discovering new territories. It is all fantasy of course. Poverty ultimately gives you no real freedom, that is its essence, why the dole is punitive, but I enjoy the myth whilst it lasts.

A car pulls up and I know by the make that he is a character. Inside I reinvent myself, telling him I am an author in between books, travelling through. He looks at me half impressed, half envious. A good life, he probes, and I give him my best shot at a Mona Lisa smile, feed the myth. Stop in Carlow and treat myself to a greasy dinner. I love the ordinariness of these places, the cook looking worse than the food. Later arrive at destination feeling liberated by the change of scene, the sense of a day grabbed from the mundane.

WHY COALITION IS WORKING   20/4/93

Well, that's enough about me. On to national politics and the death of egotism. After all, the nation remains shocked about the great betrayal. Which one I hear you ask: 1014, 1798, 1848, 1916 plus, etc., etc. None of these, you fools. Of course, and a nation smacks its head in real or feigned disgust, the F.F./Labour coalition.

The harmony of this alliance should shock nobody except seasoned observers of the political scene. All this surprise is based on two fundamental misapprehensions. First F.F. and Labour's economic policy is compatible rather than contradictory. F.F. supports economic nationalism, Labour state socialism. Both our emperors wear the same clothes. In fact as the 1983-87 coalition indicated, the differences between F.G. and Labour cut far deeper. F.F. and Labour however, both support high levels of state borrowing and intervention in the economy, the latter not always because of the highest motives. Both perceive the private sector with a mixture of distaste and mistrust. F.F. under Haughey moved away from that position, and many others, but now, bless 'em, they're returning to their own unique version of normality.

The second and perhaps more critical misapprehension is this belief that F.F. is a conservative party, particularly on social issues. This is untrue. F.F. is first and foremost a populist party. That is the rock it stands upon. F.F. in fact abhor the tag of conservatism.

What this means in practice is that now that the agenda of Social Democracy has become accepted by the peasants, F.F. has few problems with divorce, the legalization of homosexuality (with the exception of a few headbangers in the senate and on the back-benches) and of course, the Labour party, particularly if there is eight billion quid in the pigsty.

In fact, the coalition of F.F./Labour is a far more natural alignment than that which has gone before. The bitter reflection of one F.G. T.D. that it was F.G. who were in government the last time but it was Labour which doubled the national debt indicates the bitter legacy of that failed experiment.

KNOWLEDGE IS TRUTH: TRUTH BEAUTY   21/4/93

The local alcoholic approaches again. This is like something out of Flann O'Brien or perhaps its nihilism is more suited to Beckett, Sartre, even Gerry Ryan. He, the alco, is in aphoristic form tonight. Gems such as "You'll always be clean if you wash yourself" proliferate. Yes, indeed, a glittering array of *bon mots*, many of them floating on the drink. We nod our heads sagely, encouraging him on to even greater heights of discovery. Sarky, cynical humour, but then it is the Irish way. We love our fools.

He says, "I love my mammy" full of sincerity, drunken but real. I no longer feel like laughing. We are in the presence of tragedy now. Those vacant eyes frighten. Two black holes devoid of everything, of all meaning, a skull's eyes set incongruously in this empty grinning face. He probably does love her. He knows he's drinking himself to death. Can't stop, don't really want to now. It's the first time I've really looked into the eyes of someone who's given up on life.

The eyes are the key, mirroring the soul, the void lurking behind these cold black depths, reflecting the black indifference of the drink he consumes, craving, the only passion left to him. I shiver as though someone has trodden on my grave, sensing a shadow of the past; a mirror revealing the future? Somewhere in these anonymous estates a mother is crying tonight.

DEPRESSION AND LOVE SONGS   22/4/93

Must be seriously depressed. Am crying at love songs today. "Why are you leaving me?" "How can we be lovers if we can't be friends," etc., etc. What frightens me is that I am genuinely crying and not just at the literary content of the lyrics. I suppose that's what failing to gain a career in the insurance industry does to you.

Later, I go into Moore Street. It restores me somewhat, so full of life and vitality, in comparison to the dull-eyed slaves of the multi-nationals, Dunnes Stores and Quinnsworth, with their mass-produced goods for a mass-produced society, controlled by smart bastards of marketing men out to screw you with a smile.

No surprise that the system hates and opposes Moore Street and its independent traders just as it hates and opposes any display of independence. That's why it fought so hard for licensing. Anything to collar individuality, to have the bureaucrats control all. The same with the rod licence. Really, what they would most like to do is turn Moore Street into an interpretative centre and open it with a sweet speech by M.D. Higgins. That's why they love the tourist industry. It fosters the service mentality.

DEATH OF A LOCAL ALCOHOLIC 27/4/93

Local alcoholic got killed last night. Weaving his way home the same as ever then smack! . . . all the lights went out. I wonder where he is now, heaven or hell, or just as confused as usual.

Actually, I do feel quite sad about it all but then in our uniquely Irish/masculine way we always hide from sadness and tragedy in humour and the absurd. Very deep and perceptive me. The town will be emptier without him and his mad ways, emptier than if someone important from the chamber of commerce died. He was the happiest and most harmless of men. The only heart he broke was his mother's, sitting up waiting and often crying for him every night. If all of us hurt as few . . .

It's hard to know whether he ever really lived. His childhood was brutish in a way that is rare today, thank God. He spent most of his life in an alcoholic stupor. That which wasn't spent that way was not very pleasant. Opportunities are few for those who cannot read or write. Given the totality of it all he is perhaps better off dead.

What will be his epitaph? How can there be one?

REASONS FOR UNEMPLOYMENT 28 /4/93

Watching all these new housing estates being built provides a rationale for why there is so much unemployment. Ten men building forty houses and all the profits going to one. Forty men spread over ten miles of road. Twenty years ago those projects would have employed thousands. And still our politicians are stuck in a time warp. Feed the construction industry, build roads, houses that will employ the people.

But even if it did, what will all these people do when the roads and the houses are built? What will we do when the Euro money runs out and all we will have is a thousand miles of roads leading to nowhere and carrying nothing. An empty testament to our politicians' folly.

All this is doing at the moment is creating money for a select few, the landlords and the subcontractors. At least I suppose the houses will be put to some use being leased out to the unemployed at exorbitant rates, subsidised by the Eastern Health Board. The same process is going on in white collar industry but less obviously. And all this is of course progress and competition, the greatest White Elephants the Irish state has been able to conjure.

In so many ways we are still colonised. It is frightening, Ireland 1894, Ireland © 1994, nothing has changed. Frightening really. Then political life was centred around the acquisition of things from Britain, subsidies, independence, education, a Congested Districts Board. Now it is Europe. Only the location is changed.

This is evident even in our Industrial Policy. We attract huge multi-nationals over from America. The Minister smiles as he cuts the ribbon. Five hundred new jobs. But we have not created those jobs ourselves. They have been given to us. Yes there are five hundred jobs but if those jobs go we will not be able to replace them ourselves because we do not know how to do this. Still cottiers. We can work and work well for others but we cannot create for ourselves.

Then we wonder why entrepreneurial skills are so low in the country. The I.D.A. will never create an indigenous industrial base, because like Ireland, it depends. F.A.S. will never solve the unemployment crisis because it is the I.D.A.'s mirror image. Teaching entrepreneurial skills in school will never succeed because they are being taught by people who know nothing about these strange foreign things. Solutions? I can offer none for I have been brought up in the same world.

Bring back the Brits . . . Fuck it, bring back the Romans.

STRENGTH   29/4/93

Lots of self-pity recently. That I do not like. It's so easy to drift into, like sleeping late and just as comforting. Just let go, it's easy. Poor me.

Nothing about how lucky I am. Lucky first of all because I'm educated and still have prospects. Lucky also because I can analyse what is happening, break it down, understand it, not become yet another mute passive victim. Lucky also because I have the novel. That gives me purpose and pride, also fear, terror, anxiety, frustration, sometimes self-disgust at my dreaming, but then everything in life is a double-edged sword. I have a girlfriend who loves me so much I feel guilty. Is that good? I am not starving nor poor, at least not in the real sense of the word.

Most of all I'm tough. You need that on the dole, to be a battler, an obstinate bastard. Often your worst enemy is yourself, the fifth column, snapping at faith and self-belief, the flowers of the human spirit.

I have been lucky in that regard. I'm used to struggle, to crises. I know in my heart and soul, this is another phase, another test I am going through. I will survive this one too, if I am strong enough. St. Paul has a marvellous quote in the Bible "You must endure pain to understand the fullness of joy". I heard that when I was in love and its truth grabbed my heart for my life had been empty a long time prior to that, and the impact of that love was all the greater for that. This also will be the case here.

VALUE   30/4/93

There is a darkness hanging over me recently that I do not like; a quiet impulse towards self-destruction, hidden but deeply present. I try to escape this today, visiting a famous ruin. That is the sole benefit of the dole, the freedom, the escape from control, from time that it offers. Even that, however, has its strings, few of them hidden.

I feel free outside, free from the grey city, tomb to a million unknown workers. The ruin is vibrant with life, the air bracing and clear, piercing, cleansing. A fevered sun bathes the surrounding countryside in a strange supernatural glow, the colour of an artist's dream. The skeletal walls are all that survive, silence now where people once loved, fought, generated, led the same commonplace lives we do. The stone is grey now. Once it too had its colour washed crimson in blood.

I leave transformed, feeling there has been some unspoken value in this day. We are so insignificant, our dreams, terror, fears, desires as insubstantial as the ghostly voices whispering in the wind, flickering through the quiet ruins. I leave in love with the place, its history, its grandeur, its fall, glad to have spent a day discovering something of value, something reminiscent of grandeur in this devalued society; my devalued life.

MAY

DEFEAT   1/5/93

Madness, this is madness. At it again, tempting, persuading, that damned voice. It caresses, promises, sinuous, whispering, "Let it go, release your true self," and then most insistently, "She'll never know." Just once for old times sake. Do it.

I get the bus out of town. I feel part of a dream as though this is not me. I cannot drink here. Too many people know me. The word would spread, reaching the wrong ears, "He's on the batter again", and then they'd all be in to watch the performance. Well, the latter is perhaps an overestimation of my fame, but not by much. And, of course, add to that the mystique which accrues to anyone who goes off the beer in Irish society, the excitement when that person falls, proving the eternal truths about human nature.

Enter a pub, anywhere, somewhere. Home . . . again. Self-respect, love for my girlfriend, freedom from drink. All these very distant and irrelevant. Something belonging to hope, the past . . . that's all over now.

The pint is harsh and sweet. I feel a fierce hunger in my gut. Order another and another. Gulp them down. Feel the first stages of repletion and with it thought, order, logic, the reduction of need. The want is duller now, still tugging but less imperative. My head begins to spin and with that the first feelings of nausea, panic. What am I doing here? I feel myself being drawn back into an old familiar dark nightmare. Suddenly I leave, seeking home and the solace of sleep, fearful of what I may become if I stay in that warm place.

AFTERMATH   2/5/93

Woke with a familiar ache today. The old pang of self-hatred strong and throbbing. I feel a pain I thought I had forgotten. Get up. What is it the tramp in Beckett says, "Can't go on. Must go on. Can't go on. I'll go on". Will I?

The unfamiliarity of the beer in my system leaves me feeling sick and heavy-headed until noon. There can be no doubt but that alcohol is a poison. But I am poisoned mentally rather than physically. Am I facing this struggle forever? Perhaps in this dispirited morning I have learnt the emptiness of what I have . . . had rejected? Perhaps the worst is now over? Why all these question marks?

PEOPLE YOU HATE   3/5/93

When you're down they swarm around you sensing your weakness like flies in shit. This morning one attaches himself to me. In my present state it will take me at least a week to recover. He is a big fat toss-pot who has recently completed a course in college on Community Youth Work, gays, lesbians, tinkers, that sort of thing. . . sorry if I've offended anyone, used the wrong words. Again sorry. Nothing can put a bigger smile on this man's face than someone in despair, someone he can counsel and help. Thanks for the thought, but please fuck off.

He's working with young offenders at the moment. Loves them. They're characters, as only rapists, thieves and muggers can be. His admiration is false. I detest this sort of self-absorption when someone who perceives himself as an outcast from society identifies with other social outcasts out of a sort of personal narcissism. If they are like him, they are okay.

He possesses all the jargon. Social conditioning, facilitators, empowerment; wearing the correct language like a political grunge fashion statement. And the tragedy is, these people will get jobs, insinuating and sliming themselves into posts and interviews with the politically correct nods and winks of a new generation; more disingenuous than the old republican rhetoric.

He, of course, asks the dreaded question and my heart sinks, knowing the inevitable outcome. "Nothing", I reply bluntly and watch in silent misery as his face contorts into a mixture of shock, horror and consolation. "Really". *Am I now to be consoled by this!*

"Nothing", he repeats. "Aw, you're joking. Go on, you're such a laugh". But eventually I convince him and then the terror of the stock phrases.

"That's terrible". Yes.

"Poor you." Yeah.

"Such a waste of talent". Yah. The mock friendly voice washes over me like the contents of a sewer.

"I blame society etc., etc. Someone should really do something, gobble, gobble, gobble."

I close my eyes imagining a lump of timber. Right between the eyes. Yeah lovely. A lump hammer in the chops. I open my eyes at the sudden quiet and I smile my first happy smile of the week. It works, as convinced he had consoled me, the bore begins to amble pointlessly away. However, God and the fates have reserved one final humiliation. He turns sharply towards me and as his face clouds over I see with a growing disquiet the beginnings of a profound statement and some good advice.

"You know", he smiles brightly, "you should do my course". The abyss is near.

IT'S OKAY LADS   4/5/93
   More politicians again.

"We really must do something about the cancer of unemployment eating away at our young".

"What! Jesus! I've got cancer eating away at me. Where? How long?"

"It's okay, it's okay son, only a bad metaphor". And still they continue, and still and still and still. Tax breaks, Employers' P.R.S.I., Culliton, Moriarity, Sherlock Holmes, F.A.S. etc., etc.; blah, blah, blah. Aw lads, give us a fuckin break. Awright. Okay, okay, okay. We surrender. We know you care. It's not your fault and you can't do anything about it. You haven't made it worse and your haven't made it better. Just irrelevant really.

Just spare us the god-awful drivel about S.E.S. schemes or F.A.S. courses creating employment. F.A.S. courses only create employees, not employers. We already have enough of the former. We don't need to train our workforce anymore. They're the most over-trained in Europe. All together lads, "We need to create EMPLOYERS". That's it, shout it, particularly the ERS bit. And if you can't do that, please don't feed us drivel or insult our intelligence about the need for more training. Tell the truth lads. It'll get you votes. Honest.

Mind you, that analysis may not be correct. The only politician to speak the truth about this whole unemployment thing was, strangely enough, Brian Lenihan. Maybe he got confused. "Emigrate", he said, "we're a small island. There's too many of us on it to be supported". He, of course, got crucified by all the political sores, the meeja and a public unused to a diet of logic. There can be no doubt about it, we elect the politicians we deserve. They're as honest as we are.

CONFERENCE ON UNEMPLOYMENT   5/5/93
   Attend . . . Please! . . . Am dragged into a Young F.G. conference on unemployment. Do I look unemployed or needy? I should have combed my hair this morning. Knew it. Well? What a bore! God, I sound like a socialite describing a bad party. What did I expect? Excitement? Thoughtful analysis? Relevance? Innovative and challenging thoughts and ideas. Well, that's what the literature said.

Instead we get Richard Bruton, more self-important and patronising than usual, and Monica! So thrilled and breathless just to be there!!! The Y.F.G. speaker and the person from the I.N.O.U. are just plain embarrassing. Where do these people get their ideas? Are these our future leaders!?

Both yap away without any knowledge or depth about the scourge of unemployment . . . sigh . . . its destructive effect on the human psyche . . . sigh . . . the need for alternative solutions. And then the solutions and we are into the valley of death or Slattery's Fusiliers. A national minimum wage, job share, training . . . again . . . paternity leave. . . twenty hour week. All fail to recognise fundamental truths.

We are not living in Utopia. Things such as twenty hour weeks, job share etc. will not work. They will not work because people and society are greedy. There is no getting around this fundamental selfishness. What we have we keep and we want more. That is what feeds capitalism, what feeds all economic growth.

No amount of dickering with hours or minimum wages or training will alter the basic problem, which is, surprise, surprise, that we have too few jobs to go around. All that job-share will do is share the poverty. But then this is the essence of adolescent politics, grandiose and unworkable solutions.

The only good speaker was Sean Barrett who told it as it was. No frills or promises or crap . . . sorry Albert! We have, are and will make a mess of our economy. The eight billion will not solve anything. Unemployment is here to stay and we might as well become used to it. Twenty hour weeks don't earn forty hour wages. All we can do to create employment is to produce and sell more goods. It is as simple and as real as that. That's why Sean Barrett isn't in politics.

ORNAMENTS   6/5/93

We are the useless. Unqualified for anything. Just a social decoration. Ornaments and not even pretty. Experts in our own limited field, wasted on anything else, except perhaps public administration. That tends to prove the point. What use would I be to the nation in a highly-paid position of service to the people. How would I add to the sum of human happiness? How many jobs would I create? A deadweight, part of the golden fable, the boy done well, safe job sucking the tax-payer, and complaining about the level of taxation in the state.

Meet three fellow M.A.s today. All of us on the dole. Shocking isn't it. Undeserved? Not really. All of us probing gently. Any work yet? Half relieved with the chorus of "Nos". Will we ever work? Regardless of the truth of my analysis of our social use I feel betrayed by the promises, the expectations, the wasted effort for a piece of paper, a handful of dust. Do well in college, young fella and you'll be sure of a job. Yeah and Bollocks to you too!

MORE TENSION WITH GIRLFRIEND   7/5/93
Go shopping with girlfriend today. She buys a suit for me. This is excruciating. I feel like a whore, toyboy. What would my father think of this? I have no real choice. I don't have the money but I need a suit for interviews. More charity. I try to resist but are my protestations really sincere? Are they just an elaborate pretence.

My girlfriend cannot understand my attitude and there is again tension between us. Am I a bastard for accepting this charity, or am I an even bigger bastard for resisting it, for accepting it so churlishly? Is she wrong for trying to create me in her own image, irrespective of how I feel? These are the questions which occupy the problem pages of the women's magazines but they are serious to me. If the relationship turns sour then this will be a prime source of bitterness on both sides.

But the present is the imperative and I concede gracelessly, well aware that the only suit I can afford to buy is one that would shrink in the rain. How have I ended up in this cheap polyester world, where everything you buy is disposable?

RELIGIOUS DEMENTIA   8/5/93
The country continues to hurtle towards collective insanity. I blame the government. At present a madwoman, (at least I suspect it is a woman – they are generally more prone to this sort of religious dementia. Ooops! Sorry feminists) is putting up a series of crude posters all over the country, all on abortion. "Government Policy 1993, Save the hare but MURDER the little child", or "Beware Freemasonry Abortion sponsors". Someone should tell this woman that she is doing the work of Bored (sic) Fáilte no little harm. There they are, promoting Ireland to the Americans as a safe tranquil haven and the first thing they see on arrival is that Ireland has as many nut-cases as home.

This sort of thing is half funny. Funny in the pointlessness of it all, in the stupidity of the message, the thought of some little old lady climbing up poles in the darkest hours of night. Let me assure you dear, if the Irish government is active in anything it is not the procurement of abortions but in the avoidance of the whole issue. Such is also the case in hare-coursing though I doubt this is the woman's primary concern.

Ultimately this sort of unpleasant madness is not funny. Its prevalence in Ireland today signifies some level of social breakdown. The posters are the most extreme manifestation but it is present much more quietly in many others. And that, unlike the madwoman alone on her ladder at night, is dangerous. It implies a failure of society and of government. It will only result in alienation and marginalisation. The consequences of this will not be good for Ireland.

END OF NIXER   9/5/93

The end of my nixer came last week. I am nervous as to the consequences of this. It has given the week some focus, given me the feeling/illusion of being useful in some way. The extra money was nice too, though most of it went on debts, compliments of your friendly local office. Consequently I do not look on my actions as fraudulent or illegal but as a form of repayment. It was also nice, just sometimes, to take the girlfriend out to a cinema (afternoon rates of course), burgers 'n' chips. Discos are still out. I'm lucky that like myself she is not materialistic. Other women would not put up with this. Her mother, for example, and boy does she make this clear.

It's not just the absence of money that will damage us. It is the whole atmosphere of grubbiness and cheapness it fosters. There is such a total absence of security, of promise in my life at the moment, it has paralysed everything, will, confidence, ambition. That may yet destroy me and with this us, as effectively as the absence of money to go into discos. For the first time in my life I am afraid of the future. That is bad, the beginnings of the final signs of defeat? . . .

PERCEPTIONS   13/5/93

It is good to see the tourists again. Particularly those from places like Germany, Holland, Britain, serious advanced countries. They cannot cope with the unique madness of an Irish pub. For all their gormlessness American tourists are more clued in. They have a sufficiency of space cadets at home to recognise the more exotic foreign species.

Am sitting beside two serious Dutch tourists on my left and one of the local headcases on my right. Playing God, but do not ask me which ones are the sheep and which ones are the goats. The headcase is in good old form, babbling away whilst the tourists watch. Eventually as I knew would happen, one of them speaks.

"Who is that?"

I wonder what story to make up, leprechaun catcher suffering an outbreak of guilt, or the local raindance co-ordinator but the headcase solves the problem for me as he begins to shout and gesticulate angrily at the far wall. I see he's wearing a tie and inspiration strikes.

"Oh him, he's the local T.D., look, he's wearing a tie".

They look seriously, then return to the fray again as the decibel level rises. Understandable really, the fir bolgs have just entered the room.

"But why is he shouting?"

"Oh, he's just practising for his speech in the Dáil tomorrow."

Our Dutch visitors ponder and leave, obviously impressed by this experiment in socio-political street democracy. Our reputation must be high in Europe. Meanwhile our national leader has just rushed out the door. The Black and Tans must be due soon.

GO OFF CIGARETTES   16/5/93

I feel the quiet pride of a priest's mother on ordination day. At last I have broken the greatest oppressor of my health. Two days off now and still my resolve remains unshaken. I bask in the vast superiority I feel towards my fellow men, looking with an unspoken arrogance at the weak and fallible, those who have only succeeded through the use of nicotine patches. I am beyond such weakness. I am immortal . . . or is that immoral?

SNOBBERY OF ACADEMIA RE INSURANCE JOB   17/5/93

There is no doubt that I am a product of my society, poor defenceless little moi! Nowhere is that clearer than in my attitude to the insurance job, this illogical embarrassment about a career in life assurance. It is this attitude which is shafting the country, this deference to the professions, the aristocracy of Irish labour, and like all aristocracies, parasites on wealth creation. It is so typical of this bankrupt republic that we look down on jobs in the assurance industry which actually generate wealth through creating capital, venerating instead our civil servants and teachers. Looking at the patrimony these have created, particularly the latter, it appears in the cold light of day that such respect is somewhat misplaced.

IMPOTENCE AND THE DOLE 18/5/93

I never thought I'd see the day. Now I am truly aware of my mortality. It's even funny in a tragi-comic sort of way. I have lost all interest in sex. If this is the case with all unemployed men then the roles are well and truly reversed.

Now I know how women feel when they just lie under a man wishing for it to be over. Now. Soon. Please. Anxious enquiries. "Are you okay?" "Yeah". Her eyes betray her. Don't stop now, you fucker.

I don't say anything. I don't want to hurt her. She takes rejection badly. But this sort of thing cannot be continued either, this sexual resentment and not talking, feeding into everything else.

She asks again. I hold back a yawn, hope my erection survives, answer again "Yeah" in a tone that hints desperately I'd really rather be doing anything else. But very deaf sometimes is my girlfriend.

I know part of the problem is based around self-esteem. It's like before only so much more ordinary, not a hint of danger or heroism. This endless round of rejections has sapped my virility. How can I be a man when, like a child, I cannot fend for myself, dependent on the charity of others . . . useful people.

Disgust is also hampering my performance. Disgust at my obesity – all that comfort eating. I cannot connect with anybody, certainly not at the intimate level that involves sexual contact. It's a farce now, a habit.

It ends in the expected disaster. The usual concern and sympathy but do I detect a frayed edge in it this time? A note of "not again". I don't care. All I want is the release of sleep, of nothingness from this sweaty boredom, this bedroom of decayed dreams.

COUNT NUMBER AND COST OF APPLICATIONS 19/5/93

Decide for amusement to count the number of refusals. Impressed, reaching towards the two hundred mark now. That's out of those who replied, about two-thirds. That means three hundred applications. I should go and get my own post office. Perhaps I could create a job for myself applying for work. It's not as mad as it first seems.

It's an expensive process. Each application costs me roughly a pound. At the present rate after a year I will have spent about six hundred pounds on applications. That's a lot out of a basic income of £3,500. I wouldn't mind but according to the experts I'm cheap-skating. No gold leaf margins, no fax machine in the home to just pop it all off. No offers to work for free during the first six months. Mr. Gradgrind won't be pleased.

What is just as sickening is that employers expect all of this. How important do these people think they are? How do these people expect us to have the money? Or is the pursuit of a job only the preserve of the moneyed classes now? The same as university education in our democracy.

RELIGION GONE ALSO   20/5/93

Religion is also gone. It is not that I don't want to believe in God anymore, or blame him for my condition like a politician who has failed to deliver. It is instead an extension of everything else within myself. I am too dead inside, too low to love or worship anymore. If I cannot love people or myself can I love a God dependant on those qualities. Yet I still cling on, still observe the formalities, rituals, rites. Why? Because I know the sour emptiness of atheism too well. Faith gives us something to aspire towards, a sort of security, a sense of roots or purpose. For that reason it is valuable, a thing worth fighting to retain.

It is the absence of so much of these in my life that has left me unable to worship. Everything is habit now, Mass, love, laughter, sex, life, all debased into repetition, all engaged in out of the absence of alternatives, to kill time. In that dead world what is easier than to lapse away from everything, to slide into that cocoon world, house, T.V., dole office, bed, pub, sex. To become totally alienated from the outside world, lest its judgements hurt you anymore.

Marx once said that the mass poverty and alienation caused by capitalism would bring it down. Today it appears more correct to state that the greatest consequence of unrestrained capitalism is unemployment. If anything is going to destroy capitalism, this will be the catalyst.

It will not happen. Capitalism is too close to the heart of human darkness to be ever overthrown. My strongest critique of Marxism is centred around its attitude toward religion. Religion may have been the opium of the lower orders but that was no bad thing. Looking at what we have replaced it with today, our new opiates, heroin, greed, SKY multi-channel, Tallaght shopping centre, consumerism, coke and porn, Super Mario and the Nintendo generation. Marx would have been more correct to see religion as an ally not an opponent. They are both equally at odds with this shadow world.

TAX AMNESTY   21/5/93

Government announces a tax amnesty. Ah good, an overdue reduction in the tax burden of the long-suffering P.A.Y.E. worker, less income tax for the struggling small businessman. "What a good government is this", you cry with a sweet innocence long absent from Western society. Erm, well, am, hem, nooo, not exactly as such. "Oh?" Yes, actually it's for the bollocks who hasn't paid any tax for years. As a reward for his intelligence he is getting away with paying 15% of his unpaid taxes, this to be assessed by himself. You know the type, the poor pressurized chap that has a Merc, and that's the car the wife drives for the shopping, and a five storey Dallas-style ranch containing just a hint of the Acropolis in its design. The fellow that sends his kids to college on the grant. Poor chap. "No indoor sauna and swimming pool this year, had to pay my taxes".

Now this sort of thing is not only mad, indeed I wouldn't mind if it was only that, but it is also dangerous. The state, law and order, democracy, are centred around the belief that all citizens are equal. In short that justice will be given to all. Tamper with this and you create a fissure in society; you remove not only all faith in the political system but more seriously you destroy the incentive to obey the law, to respect the institutions of the state.

This is the first step towards social breakdown and the declivity arches steeply from there. If a substantial body of society withdraw their support from the state, even if that rejection is silent, taking the invisible forms of alienation, withdrawal and apathy, then the social compact is broken. The ultimate consequence of this will be the creation of a quiet civil war, but one just as vicious and destructive as our last one. We are succeeding in creating a two track society, one where the state is seen as an alien and enemy force favouring only some sections of society. That is some achievement since independence, the building of our own slums, the fostering of our own native ascendancy, our own Irish born colonisers.

We, in Ireland, have not yet reached the levels of America but that is only because we do not have an ethnic minority problem. The process is, however, accelerating. More and more people are withdrawing from the political process. Some, but only some, of the more energetic are looking towards the community to provide leadership, pride, direction. Too many, however, are retreating into the narcissism of self in a selfish society. This withdrawal is not only political. The black economy flourishes to the beat of political apathy. In this world everything from education to sex is there to be exploited and acquired, honesty is a farce, the law a joke, politicians despised as liars for a particular class.

The joke, however, may yet turn sour. It is after all just a short step from alienation to social disobedience. After this week, the unemployed, those who are struggling, the honest and the disempowered, those on hospital waiting lists, owe no allegiance to this state. There will be no revolution but there will be a gradual withdrawal of consent, of participation until suddenly our legislators wake up and it looks like a flood tide.

Then we will see the politicians in all their hues from liberals to my favourites, the hang 'em high brigades throwing shapes and asking why. And then, of course, we will have government commissions and reports set up. But that's a different and just as pointless story. At least they will create employment.

ONE MAN'S MEAT ANOTHER MAN'S MUTTON   22/5/93

Was I too harsh on the state the other day? For what do I see but that the unemployed are to get their own amnesty. My conscience, (What?) whispers to me to do the decent thing. I consider it but wait, what's this small piece of print at the bottom. Aha! would you believe it, those unemployed who have fiddled the dole, "Shame, boo, hiss," they don't have to pay back 15% of the proceeds like the rich multinationals. Instead we have to pay the full whack, 100%. Mustn't have paid enough into the party coffers. Still it's nice to be clear about whose side the government is on.

It's typical really. Ivan Yates put up a brilliant performance against the amnesty. It would almost restore your faith in democracy, . . . almost . . . until you find out that it was a performance and that Yates himself has advocated a similar scheme, indeed excoriated the government for its failure to implement such a good idea. Such news can only restore one's faith in Irish democracy to its previous levels.

CAREER ASPIRATIONS   23/5/93

Look through jobs section of *Irish Independent* . . . abloodygain. Chief Executive of the I.R.A. . . . oops . . . sorry I.D.A. Oh God, no I wouldn't be able for the responsibility, the future economic health of Ireland, no I couldn't follow such illustrious footsteps, I couldn't possibly waste that much money for so little gain. I wouldn't be able to. Hmmm, Health Board Nurse to exceedingly dangerous psychiatric patients; own V.H.I. scheme . . . Dentist's Assistant, Petrol Pump Assistant, Undertaker's Assistant, No. No No . . . Too overqualified for all these, I'm afraid. How sad. Oh well, there is no alternative.

Dear Ruairí,

With reference to the post of I.D.A. Chief Executive advertised *Irish Independent* please find enclosed C.V. and reference in application for the post of Industrial Supremo.

Most of the C.V. is imaginary and the references appear to have been composed whilst under the influence of hallucogenic drugs but being a politician this will not worry you. Anyway it indicates the sort of entrepreneurial spirit we wish to cultivate in this country.

Indeed many's the time when pissed I have written up mock I.D.A. brochures instead of the usual activities, just for a break. As you will see, these bear a shocking resemblance to passages in the Programme for a Partnership Government. I'm sure it will please you to know both of us are thinking on similar lines.

Ruairí, isn't it good to know we have such a "pool of talent" in this country that almost anyone can write an I.D.A. brochure. Finally my most important qualification is that I have always voted Labour even when 'twas neither popular nor profitable. That certainly isn't the case now Ruairí, is it?

Yours, with affectionate contempt.

Enough of this low humour.

GIRLFRIEND OVERDUE   24/5/93

Noticed a difference in my girlfriend yesterday when she was laughing. Something incorrect, not quite connecting. She tells me she's overdue. My answer is almost, "So what?" I'm so used to it at this stage. But this is cruel. Pregnancy is something that terrifies her. It would be intensely destructive to her life, her career and her family. And it is something which in so many ways will only affect her. It is as separate a matter for her as A.I.D.S. and the dole are for me and one in which I can do as little for her as she can for me.

Pregnancy is the recurring nightmare of our relationship, a constant dragging fear and one which we are not grown up enough to deal with. This is particularly the case given that our relationship and finances are so rocky. I really feel that if the latter were solved, the former would not be a problem but until that occurs I feel so much self-hate and guilt over my lack of financial stability that it is poisoning the relationship. If you hate yourself then you can never really love someone else.

My greatest fear is that Catherine will become pregnant when I am out of love with her and quietly considering dropping her. From that perspective her announcement could hardly come at a better time. Irony. Irony. That is the night-mare scenario and given the insane practical jokes of this world, the most likely. Of course my ego does not permit me to consider that they might be hers also. And all the time in the background I hear the ghost of my Victorian grandfather or more accurately my father whispering spitefully, "Improvident fool". How can I contend with that statement. I have always been a grasshopper rather than an ant and he, cowed by centuries of oppression, by his own fears, has always been the latter. And he has always hated me for that rebellion.

ENVY   25/5/93
Another friend gets a job. Bastard connections. Yeah. The small nasty thoughts bite and I wallow in them. He is no longer one of us, he is one of them now. . . the employed. I have only noticed this envy growing and feeding re-cently. It has probably been there a while. This is a bad sign. Envy is for losers.

Even my girlfriend is getting it now. "You have things easy, rich parents, car, job, etc. etc.", as if everybody should be living on the poverty line like poor little meeee.

If I want the truth I would admit she has not had it easy but I don't want that. I want to scapegoat, lash out, avoid blame. I want to believe the myth of poor little me, to believe that everyone and everything is against me, that the others are all lucky bastards . . . yeah!

FRENCH TARMACKERS   26/5/93
They are tarring the road today. A foreign machine. Costs over £600,000 and does ten kilometres a day, I am told with some awe. The workers are French. They strip to the waist even though it is a cold day. Small tough men, their sinewy muscularity makes the rest of us look as soft and fat as we are. A motley crew watches silently. Ours is a quiet town. Anything for excitement.

Our Irish council workers bask in the attention, unused to such fame. The French dismiss it with nonchalant indifference. They have seen a thousand such towns at this stage and are used to the crowds. Nevertheless it must be nice to be passing superstars in a thousand small villages. A girl in every pothole.

All the technical work is done by the French, the tarmac laying, levelling, rolling. The Irish workers direct the traffic. Inspired by the unwonted crowds they play shamelessly to the gallery. They sweep their arms vigorously at prams, their elaborate gestures and mysterious circles rivalling an Italian traffic policeman and utterly mystifying several drivers.

I leave the workers, cornerboys, old men, dogs, gurriers, and women. Smiling. Welcome to Europe.

INTO THE BREACH ONCE MORE . . .   30/5/93

Have just spent a wretched night with the cream of Labour Youth. Why do I continue this quest for participation in the democratic process? Some blind faith, some relic of childhood innocence . . . some hope. Labour, a middle class party interested only in liberal issues. When they talk to the working classes they are only capable of talking down to them. It's not their fault, like horses, it's in the blood, the breeding.

This is the essence of social democracy as practised by Labour. Setting little hurdles for the lower orders to jump over, then clapping with enthusiastic benevolence when they succeed. Unpopular meeting and converting popular culture.

That describes the night's chatter. They're all lovely little boys (some token girls), all dying to "save the world and make it a better place", to quote Michael Jackson. Just like their parents. Somehow little boys, I don't think it's going to work.

I listen in awe to their confident solutions to the problems that affect Irish society. Their chief concern is, of course, taxation. They want to reform this, primarily to help the poor, to get them off welfare. The latter idea is particularly popular, for the sake of the unemployed of course! Nothing to do with the fact that this will reduce the level of taxation they pay.

I feel very distant from the confident certainty of these people. Am embarrassed when asked what do I do for a living, muttering half-assed replies. Unemployment is such a visceral thing, cutting and disempowering at every level.

These experts have no cognisance of the realities of what they talk so glibly about, in particular unemployment, on which I pride myself in having some expertise. Would I not be the same if my life had not taken such a savagely unexpected turn? Probably . . . but self-pity does not allow such awkward questions. All I know is that I am not of the same party as these young unimaginative people.

At least there is one bright spot with the news that the Rovers have avoided relegation after a thrilling 0-0 draw with Bray Wanderers. Okay, okay, I exaggerate but at the end of this year I'll grasp at any straws that are going.

ARTS OFFICER . . . NOT LIKELY   31/5/93

Receive forms in post today for job as Arts Officer. Guess what, they want me to own a car. So much for the Minister's belief in cultural-democracy. Non-car owners need not apply. Is this a conspiracy theory or is it just that everyone in Ireland except me owns a car. Literacy skills used to be the key to work, now it is technology. Without a car or computer skills you are as illiterate as that cottier a hundred years ago.

It's probably as well I didn't apply since I know who's going to get the job in Waterford. A right snot. Daughter of a prominent local businessman who contributes discreetly to the correct party. His daughter is equally politically correct, going to the right college, acquiring the right accent to mix with the right people in the right pubs. The centre of the social centre so to speak. Her opinions are as correct as everything else, neither of the right or left but of course the centre. Her whole persona speaks of the message that the world was made for me, my very being, a little flower to gladden it, the role and purpose of my existence, to brighten the lives of the ordinary.

She will fit in perfectly with the other upholders of unpopular culture, with their petty little poetry circles, drama and operatic groups, little self-contained cultural islands, well-defended from the masses. They will love her because she is one of them. They will love her because they do not want difference. They believe themselves and their small universe as perfect and complete. What they want are little replicas of themselves. They will get that with her.

That is another secret of success in the Irish job market. Becoming one of them. Fitting in. Smart boy wanted . . . No Independence or Originality . . . Please . . . be it Arts Officer, Teacher, Social Worker, A.I.D.S. Counsellor or Civil Servant. The right noises, the correct echoes to the correct people, the sexy language of wink and nod. I can't buy that (hero that I am). I wish sometimes that I could, that I wasn't so fucking socially dysfunctional but it would cut away the central part of me to change that . . . to enter, at last, polite society, to lose forever the joys of rebellious self-importance.

JUNE

ESCAPE   1/6/93

Leave all that bitchiness today. We are so fortunate to live near the countryside. Nature is the only release from this tepid emptiness. There is a freedom
there, a vitality which drives away self-pity, relegates what seems to be important to its proper role. The sky is heavy today but even that enhances the heavy
scent of the pollen, the rank sensual aura of the grass growing on the fertile soil
hidden coyly below.

I feel the fertility, sensing God flirting in the grass, unlike that other place,
the grey barren streets of the rushing city. I do not find God or life in that place
only dead people with dead dreams. In the countryside He is there in the yielding grass, the sun dappled trees, the clear river and above all in my lover's eyes
reflecting, living all that beauty. I could live on the dole in the countryside.
There you can create your own freedom, your own escape. In the city I would
just curl up and die like an old rubber doll cast aside on the indifferent bonfire.

THE RETURN   2/6/93

Back to reality today, back with a vengeance. Anxiously yet half cynically
scan the pages. Only three pages of jobs . . . again. That's bad. Difficult to find
anything that suits me. That's too regular a complaint for my liking. I've been
on the dole for dangerously long now. My central problem is that my degree is
so general that it qualifies me for everything and for nothing. That wasn't so
bad a few years ago when employers were willing to take a chance.

Now the bastards have it easy, can afford to be choosy and boy do they love
it. Now they want specialisation, people trained specifically to their needs, nar-
row little bastards who want nothing more out of life than the joy of being a
Dunnes Stores manager. Anything else is dross to their piggy little eyes. The
Arts degree in this world is a six course meal. They want Burger-King instead.
Must, however, keep going just like the tramps. Look like them nowadays.
Surrendering to doubt is the final acceptance of failure.

FRENCH JOB MARKET   3/6/93

Read article in the paper about the French job market. Apparently the big
problem there is breaking into it. Most of the jobs advertised there involve

150

switching from one job to another. That seems to be the major Irish problem also. Every second job is seeking people with two to three years' experience. This is locking the rest of us out, fostering a graduate underclass.

Sometimes I think I'll end up like Yosser Hughes in Boys from the Black Stuff, begging for jobs, saying "Go on, I can do that" and headbutting recruitment office executives after each inevitable refusal.

Some of them probably deserve that. The arrogance of employers in Ireland today has become breath-taking, more and more similar to the landed classes of yore. One of them was on the radio the other day, demanding that we should work for free for a year before being employed, to show our enthusiasm. What we see there is the growing stratification of opportunity. Only those who can afford to work for free will be awarded jobs. I wonder what socio-economic group they come from. Just like the myth of third level education, all of us are equal but some are more equal than others, whilst our government squealers nod approvingly.

What will be the response of our graduates to these demands for free labour? It would, I think, be idealistic to expect stern and upright resistance, that our cowboy employers will be told where to go. We have come a long way from the idealism of the early twentieth century. Education emasculates now instead of liberating or teaching independence and self-respect. We are taught to crawl so as to acquire the designer clothes. Enough. I think it can be said that the response of most of our graduates and future leaders will be to beg nicely for the jobs.

HOME LIFE   4/6/93

This is the fourth week in a row I have gone home. It's time to give it a break. The tension is unbearable, between my mother worrying and my dear pleasant father sitting there glowering. He spoke to me today.

My God! it lives.

Note the date in a diary when it spoke. Commemorate it every year in a simple ceremony, possibly in the Mansion House with the Taoiseach and a few friends. Admittedly it was only a mumble, something on the lines of,

"Whenareyegoingto get a JOBandstopfuckingaround"

"Pardon?"

Same conglomeration of mumbles.

Eventually I translate the mess. I mean how do you respond to this shite?

"Well eckshually Daddums, I'm a male prostitute in the Phoenix Park but as it doesn't suit me for tax reasons and because of the negative publicity I might incur to advertise this, I claim to be on the dole as a cover".

"Oh, that's all right so, just so long as you're working". Hugs 'n' kisses all round.

"Son, I love you",

"Poppa, I love you too", as family reconcile. An unlikely scenario I think.

Back to reality. I mutter and walk out. Not so loudly, just enough for him not to hear the words clearly but guess the emotions. Yes, indeed, nothing like good ole fashioned father, Irish style father-son bonding. Whatever happened to it? I wonder will Daniel O'Donnell issue a song about it?

ENVY   5/6/93

It is so fucking hard not to be bitter sometimes. So much in this country depends on pull and connections. That's all very well if you're born into the right class but if not, tough. The words "and son" over a thousand businesses mark the graveyards of a thousand dreams. This outburst is stimulated by the fact that my girlfriend has been offered four jobs without interview.

It somehow spoils the phone call, the old rant bubbling below the surface.

"It's okay for you and your Daddy and your connections. It's people like you that make sure I haven't a job". But, of course, nothing is said and she remains surprised and hurt at my coldness over her good news.

It's not her fault, this sort of occurrence. Favouritism is endemic in the Irish culture and if I was in the inside lane I would use it also. But fuck her, if she's going to get it that easy on the jobs front I'll spoil her pleasure emotionally. Unfair, but what do I care. I'm not getting it easy. Let's level out the field of unhappiness. Much loved and used territory.

YOUNG LOVE   6/6/93

I see a young couple on the bus today, in that separate world, that place we experience so rarely; just an inch beyond the real. Ordinary kids, they are special today, their eyes shining with a rare lustre.

I smile, half cynicism, half nostalgia. They may yet have a bellyful of each other. Are they fooling themselves? Reality is too hard a taskmaster for those of us who will spend our lives in buses. Let them have their wonder. I wish them well.

TRICKS OF THE WELFARE OFFICE II 7/6/93

I see the welfare state is going theological now. In the old days before Vatican II the Catholic Church believed in a place called limbo where all unbaptized children went. It was a grey amoebic place where nothing happened or existed. Now the Welfare Office has created its own limbo. Anyone leaving school no longer exists for three months. Until then they cannot sign on. Even if they are unemployed they're not unemployed . . . if you know what I mean????? Oh well, it will save a few quid.

Logically, of course, that also means that anyone who gains employment in the first three months after leaving school will not have to pay tax or P.R.S.I. "Em no, not exactly". Surprise!! After all, it is only the unemployed who do not exist under this partnership government, partners with the employers, the trade unions and no-one else.

WHORE I 8/6/93

Go into Dublin today for cheap tobacco. Walk back along the canal. Save the bus fare, save everything. The city is hot and clammy, the sun beating off the soiled concrete. I smell the sour taste of myself rising beneath my clothes. I should really have washed myself.

A whore stands out from the wall sunbathing. She is dressed in a low cut top, black mini-skirt, red shoes glittering against the bare legs.

I sense the hardness, half shocked at the arousal, the wanting. It is a hard lust, as cold as the pinched face of the whore. She's not even attractive, not more than 17 and already she's shrivelled and broken.

I want her because of that, not because she's sexually attractive, but because she's easy, because I feel the same, cheap and used. This is my new level, a sordid ride in a dirty alleyway, the client, the john, the whore, anonymous triology in a soiled city.

Part of me says, "What about my girlfriend?" She's a long way away. Desire drives conscience away. I approach her, wondering, I want this. I want cheap. I am cheap. We are together. How many men had she known? I am another one. Anonymous. The way I want to be.

My girlfriend. Fuck her, she's going to leave me anyway for some nice little middle-class banker with her nice little job and their nice little home. Deep pile carpets and video players. Fuck her. She's got it easy.

Approach her. Go on, Seán, a little excitement. Trembling, half with shock, half with desire. The voice shocks me:

"Want biz love?"

The voice is a contradiction, beaten yet coarse and defiant, shattering the reverie of self-pity. Do I want to throw everything away for the emptiness of that voice, the cold smile signifying recognition of another client, a user. Am I that low yet? I smile sadly and pass on.

Only later do I realise the full arrogance of my self-pity. The two of us the same? I would make a poor whore with my cloistered life. A few months on the dole and running to fat on it. Have I been raped, abused, made feel like a piece of dirt by a thousand men, H.I.V. positive? Am I a victim on the same level as her? Come off it, lover boy.

ALTERNATIVES TO TRAIN SPOTTING . . .   9/6/93

Am in a sour cynical frame of mind today. After yesterday it's no wonder. Indulge in one of my newest pastimes which I use to pad out the time in my leisured existence, that of seeing which of the old perverts are reading H & E. It also helps to deflect my mind from considering my own newly acquired habits.

A new challenger has, however, recently arrived in the perverts stake. Certain pages of an increasingly popular magazine are now totally dedicated to the treatment of stress and football injuries. A favourite sport of mine recently is to creep up beside some engrossed old boy, cough, snicker and see how high he jumps. It's good exercise for them.

THE LIE OF PROGRESS   10/6/93

Walk around the town today. Housing estates are full of cars, cars belonging to people who used to work. Not anymore. The streets are full of people with nothing to do and nowhere to go. Aimless, like the characters in *Invasion of the Bodysnatchers*. It's a strange country. Half its people are on the dole not including those in pre-retirement schemes and S.E.S schemes, the rest are working one hundred hours a week to try and snatch a crust or what they define as a crust. That's progress?

What are we doing in Ireland today? Why? This thing we call progress slowly killing three hundred thousand people, another million on the poverty line, the remainder just empty, acquisitive savages and like savages, always living for the moment, obsessed only by the transient, the bright beads of the laughing marketing men. SKY T.V. the flashing mirror lulling a generation into stupor. New whiskey for new Indians.

So little has really changed. We eat better, live longer, have new past-times. More of us are educated. A.I.D.S. is the new killer instead of syphilis but what else? Our William Martin Murphys are still here and there are no Larkins or Connollys, just a series of hollow copy cats.

We're lucky to have a job, they tell us. Tax us and we relocate Asia, Eastern Europe, Japan. Relocate, the synonym for lockout. We are all still slaves, driven and controlled by strange new gods, growth, social mobility, the market, G.N.P. Understand that language and you rule.

The rest of us are just things; commodities, target groups and audiences. Marx is dead, but capitalism and its effects are still thriving. The ordinary possess more but still possess nothing, no freedom, no lives outside their master's offices or the dole for those who fail Quality Control. Was Orwell correct? Are we too controlled to recognise this? Has 1984 happened without us knowing? Who is our Napoleon the pig? Who is his junior partner? Who is Napoleon's Squealer?

MORRISON VISA   11/6/93
Read today of abuses of the Morrison visa, of people taking up offers even though they have absolutely no intention of working or settling in America. This is, of course, at the expense of emigrants over there years, or the unemployed here who really need those visas. I know two prime examples myself, both employed, both users. They are using the visa for a cheap holiday.

This is a symbol of the new Ireland, our new ethos. Take the visa, take two jobs, three, plenty of overtime and Fuck the rest. Vote the Labour party for divorce and contraception. Don't worry about economic redistribution. The P.E.S.P. shows theirs is a choosy pluralism. Pay the middle income voters, they're the only ones that vote. Let them grab everything and Fuck the rest and Fuck the consequences. Our new Ireland, finally part of Europe.

LETTER FROM GIRLFRIEND? HOW WEAK IS LOVE?   12/6/93
Another letter from girlfriend. Keeps on calling me "Baby". My heart leaps at her handwriting. It indicates something of the past survives for you but cannot pretend these things. Jesus, how I wish she would stop calling me "Baby". It's cloying and embarrassing. She is coming down for a week, to save me no doubt.

The events of the past months have weakened our love, I think, irrevocably. Distances have been created, great barren patches of silence over which neither partner can travel to reach the other. Sometimes recently I wonder are we just chasing memories, trying to give the past a false rebirth. Once either partner goes through experiences they cannot relate to the other, then the relationship is dying.

I still love her but I feel more cynical about it now. Those first years when we were so close were in some way false. That was a level of connection that will never be replicated. Too fragile and too beautiful. The world is always too harsh for that to survive. Or do we make it that way . . . . running from beauty out of fear. Seeking the normal.

HOME AND AWAY   13/6/93

Am still doubting my love for girlfriend. Watch *Home and Away*, the sure sign of a man with little excitement in his life. Amazed again by how life imitates art . . . sort of. Greg is considering dumping Bobby. He also is unemployed. Is there a pattern here?

RETURN OF THE MAJOR   15/6/93

Weak fallible man. Everything Nell McCafferty, everything that good woman says about you is true. Am back on the cigarettes and no longer an example to society. Why? Boredom, perversity, a fundamental dislike of being congratulated too long and too often as being an example to the community, were dominant factors.

Anyway, am hooked again and am disgusted with myself as is mother, father, girlfriend, community etc., etc. Yeah, Yeah, Yeah . . . okay . . . okay . . .I'm sorry I've let you all down. Jeez, I feel like Tom Sawyer or Just William. . . . Oops, showing my age there. Okay, Bart Simpson, the victim of a harsh excessively demanding world always wrong even when right. Only the dole office really understands. Thank you, lads, for your existence.

ENVY   16/6/93

Out for a meal with Cathy tonight. She paid . . . of course. In celebration of the new job. Not a success. I am cold and bitter. Envious begrudger. She has a job only two months after qualification and here am I almost a year down the line and still nothing and she thinks . . . still! . . . that I'm cleverer and more qualified than her. Fool!

I feel very depressed about the future. You can't get a home or marry or have kids if you are on the dole. Not in the real world anyway. Jesus, I can't even get it up at the moment I'm so depressed. Jeez, a *man* of 24 and he can't even get his dick to work. Poor lamb. But seriously, what can I offer her in the future? House husband, an emotional prostitute. I'll give you sex and emotional security if you feed me.

I'm a traditionalist. A man who cannot feed his woman and children cannot respect himself. House husband would kill my pride, turn me cynical and defeated, the way I am now. I am not a Neanderthal in all this. I have no problem in sharing housework, cooking, cleaning etc. I would never believe in ending any woman's career by imprisoning her to the home but I need to be at least an equal in any relationship. I need to play the role of breadwinner too.

This is bred into, is natural to all men. Take it away from us and you take away something of our species' essence. Even in nature it is women who rear their young, men who forage for sustenance. No amount of social theory can defeat instinct or deal with the consequences of the negation of that instinct. We might be better than the animals but we are still cut from the same cloth. Unemployment has negated my sexuality. It is that which has led to my impotence. Only in Hulk Hogan's *Mr. Nanny* are men really happy to be house husbands.

LIVING IN THE SHADOW OF WOMEN   17/6/93

The prospect of spending my days living in the shadow of my girlfriend fills me with numb terror. This is not the way it was supposed to be. There can be no continuation of the relationship if one partner possesses no self-respect. Implicit in the relationship up to recently is the belief that we will marry, have kids, she'll stay at home, for a while anyway, and I will support the family. Clichéd, I know, definitely sexually incorrect, but we are all allowed our perversions, even a traditional old style relationship.

That expectation has now been eroded and with its decline has come a slow but cumulative erosion of us. She will not want to marry me as a dependant and I will not want it myself. This is not supposed to be happening. Sometimes it feels as though everything is collapsing around me, future, career, self-respect, relationships, marriage, children, everything, even love tainted and corroded by this thing, this condition called unemployment.

It is in many ways a lesson. What I am facing are the same restrictions which have imprisoned women for centuries. It is made all the worse by the fact that this is happening to *meee*. And there was a time when I would have imposed just such limitations so casually on my own girlfriend . . . without thought . . . like all tyrants, even benevolent ones.

ROSCOMMON, A RED LIGHT DISTRICT   18/6/93

I read in the *Sunday World* that prostitutes are planning to set up brothels on river boats in Albert Reynold's constituency. Somehow I don't think An Taisce envisaged this when they said we should follow the Dutch model in how we market our canals. Boyle, the Amsterdam of the West, does have a certain *je ne sais quoi*. This is decentralisation of a kind Albert was not expecting.

It should not be knocked. Oops, bad pun there. I mean think of the tourist potential, more Gardai, building on our reputation as the biggest and the cutest whores in Europe, the sale of boats to them by the O.P.W., and probably a few quid on the side for all those boring canal restoration societies in return for keeping the locks open for those late night visitors.

The job potential, Albert, and more jobs for women than men, redressing the gender inequality in our labour force. Think, Albert, of all those waiting female voters. Yes, already I can see An Taoiseach's dream that Ireland become the Asia of Western Europe coming true, though it might resemble a slightly different part of Asia to the one he had in mind.

WEEK OF PASSION   19/6/93

Disastrous week so far. Last night typified everything. Any closeness between us is fragile and ephemeral, always waiting to be punctured by the icy floes of my pain, hurt and indifference. She is petulant now because I have failed to live up to expectations, because I have been cranky and depressed. That was typified by tonight.

To be dumped by my girlfriend for the weekly chat show is not good for my delicate little male ego. I am left sitting on my own; she flirts incessantly with a group of rich tourists. God, this is death. One barman turns the T.V. off. I silently celebrate whilst the mob bays for its return. As in all things in Ireland today the mob wins. I continue to fume silently amongst the dentures, songs and poems.

Eventually . . . eventually it is all over and we go home. Silently. No holding hands tonight. She knows she has done something wrong. But I, of course, self-righteous, say nothing. Again. I am becoming more and more like my father. We will sleep with our backs to each other tonight . . . again.

DISAPPOINTMENT   20/6/93

We part puzzled and disappointed after an unfulfilling and disjointed week. I have written little about it. In truth there was nothing positive to write about. Where the fuck are we?

So much is wrong between us but, this curse of Irish men, I am incapable of articulating it. I feel the relationship is static, no, stagnant is more apt. She's getting more out of it than I am. I feel used as though I am just a toy she uses to calm herself, a cheap psychiatrist, useful for sex, whether I want it or not.

She seems incapable of understanding the depth of my depression, the fact that I don't want sex because I no longer feel like a man. She is always on top now. It's handier, I don't have to pretend a passion I have forgotten. Not that she would notice.

What if she gets pregnant? How will I support it . . . her. That would be a fine mess to add to the others. Some man, unable to feed my own child. My father would love that. Correct again.

Still I can't talk, too churned up inside with hurt, anger, hate, fear, mostly depression, sapping, destroying . . . too churned up to articulate this mess. We are going to have to change or break. If it is the latter then the hurt will be bad for we have travelled a long distance and the fall will be steep. I wonder if either of us have reached this point?

How true is this self-pitiful wail that I am being used? How much of a user am I, afraid of facing a world without her to depend upon, and that dependence to cry about? Am I just playing "cute hoor", saying nothing, in order to keep what is rapidly becoming nothing. Perhaps best to say nothing. It may cure itself. Anyway no-one dies or drowns in stagnant water, they just wither away. Why should we be so arrogant as to believe ourselves different.

LAST VISIT?   21/6/93

My girlfriend is gone. I won't see her for three months, she says. Do I really care? She does. Will our relationship survive? I feel a strange sense of indifference towards things I previously found vitally important. How long before she feels the same? Is it starting already with this deliberate separation?

But, of course, I placated her. Of course, I love you/miss you/will work out, blah, blah, blah. I don't believe those words anymore, not fully anyway. That time when I really meant them seems so far distant now. That is the quiet despair of unemployment. The boredom, the sense of uselessness wraps itself around your life. Totally. Life becomes a series of habitual acts, lived without passion or purpose. And when that atrophy sets in, everything splinters, even love.

The voices whisper inside of you, take it out on her. She's going to dump you anyway, go out with that nice middle-class boy she was always destined for. You will become an exotic memory. Dump her and prove your fears. I don't however. Is that because of cynicism or some memory of what was once there, some lingering faith or hope that we or I can return to what once existed. I will be easy on myself for once and claim the latter.

ONLY OUR RIVERS RUN FREE   23/6/93

Certain moments in all our lives, moments of epiphany, realization, knowledge, impact more deeply than the more common flux of normality. They possess a depth and value which mark them out as landmarks. Often they are the most poignant ones, a failed love affair, that first recognition of hurt, or sin, or evil; revealing and frightening. Thank God they are generally rare.

The night started off the same as usual, listening to a crap local band. Boredom, like classical music, has its tranquillity.

One of them began to sing and the voice for once possessed emotion rather than habit. It hung quivering in air, connecting and revealing, a man revealing in song his hidden heart,

A land that has never known freedom
And only our rivers run free
– allowing you to see into the centre of his life. He also has never known freedom except perhaps in song. Married young, wife, children, running to fat, he has spent his life, rat in a box, driving machinery, always others constructing the pattern of his life with their time-sheets, running, always running, the only lightness of being he has ever known are those tantalizing notes, hanging, teasing in the air in their perfect inaccessibility.

Then the dole and the knowledge gnawing that he was different, no, better than this, that it all could have been different. Time is laughing at him now. Its chuckles echo spitefully in the interior of his mind, the laughter of a beautiful spoilt child. Too late, too late, it chimes. Perhaps it was always so.

He takes another gulp from his pint. You can see the great lustre of self- pity glittering in his eyes. You empathise, then draw back fearfully. Is that a ghost or a mirror? Is this the future you have laid out for yourself. You race from the thought. But not fast enough.

NEED FOR A SENSE OF HUMOUR   25/6/93
Why do I joke so much in these pages? Primarily as a defence. My sanity would break if I thought my present situation was logical or deserved, as distinct from being the consequence of a particularly cruel series of practical jokes by cosmic forces. Anyway, this is a country of so many savage ironies your sanity would buckle if you couldn't laugh coldly at it all. And I don't think they provide top quality psychiatrists on the medical card.

These thoughts are partly inspired by yet another fascinating debate by self-important social critics on the Work-fare/Learn-fare issue. A pointless discussion really. Work-fare is the preserve of minds who believe the country is full of fat loungers on the dole. A nation of Stanley Ogdens for those who remember earlier episodes of *Coronation Street*. Unfortunately, in these politically correct times, they cannot say this; hence the concept of Work-fare.

Learn-fare is the product of the other side, of nice little middle class people who acquired a social conscience when young through watching *Little House on the Prairie*. The further education provided by subsequent Michael Landon programmes has led these to conclude that as the unemployed are terminally stupid they will only ever get a job if they are educated to become like us.

Both utterly miss the central point that unemployment is caused by too few jobs for too many people. The only way to actually solve the problem is to create loads of jobs. Anything else is a farce and a disguise to mask our powerlessness in this issue. But, of course, we cannot say that, hence the farce that I am laughing at.

The other central reason why I joke so much is that I am too frightened to look too closely at the nature of the pain of my situation. I am like the stereotype of my country taking refuge in manic laughter to avoid the horrible tedium of reality.

PAINTERS IN DUBLIN   26/6/93

In Dublin today, swarmed by the usual tight-lipped sweaty crowds imprisoned in suits, their tension and their pressure sweating through the strait-jack-
ets of collars and cheap ties. And I want to be part of this? Some of me says yes,
the remainder equivocates, questions. Questioning; the method of my doom,
just like the cat.

Down a side street a group of brilliantly white-overalled painters work. They
make a vivid contrast to the surly crowds, the colours of their trade, not the
black briefcase, but mysterious, oriental; ochre, magenta, crimson, their over-
alls stained a rainbow of colour unlike the monochrome suits. They chat away
enjoying the rare sun. They look so free, escapees from the rest of the trapped
city, their shafts of wit and sly humour giving them an individuality, a lightness
of being not shared by the rest of us melting in the tight heat.

Yet I know that what I have described is not completely true. Winter will
come and then the others will be safe whilst the painters silently freeze in the
sullen cold. It is the painters who will be broken first.

It's like the old fable of the ant and the grasshopper. The grasshopper cel-
ebrates summer but in that celebration forgets to store up for the winter and
dies. The others around me are like the ants burrowing, ferreting, looking to
screw and deceive in the name of ambition and security, fighting and squabbling until they die. They live longer but never live. I don't want that. To die
without ever having lived. I would choose the grasshopper as my reincarnation.
They, at least, can celebrate.

WHORE II   27/6/93

I meet her again. Accidently, of course. The sexuality is as blatant as before.
Be truthful, Seán, these meetings are no longer accidental. Something is tugging at the core of me, a lack of self-respect, an aching hatred, submerging
what I had become. The woman, she is not real, not flesh. She is a metaphor, a
symbol of something inside me. If that is not too pretentious. If I go with her I
touch bottom. Become as cheap and as empty as I feel, as my world, as the
whore's world.

In this empty city why should I care. I who feel so separate from all connections, friends, family, girlfriend. Why should I care about detection, I who count,
matter for so little. Why worry about hurting Catherine? She has gone now,

busy in her new little world, car, job, prospective mortgage, partners who possess three suits, can buy her flowers, dinners, the valuable things from which I am so abstracted.

I want the whore almost for the excitement, the rebelliousness of the act, the denial of being good. A darker part lusts having power over another, or more accurately the imposition of that power. I have money. She wants it. She is going to have to pay the price.

The heat of the city mirrors the heat of the moment, the desire. To profane everything, to prove nothing is valuable because if that is so, then nothing has been lost. Sex, love, life itself, all these were precious. Now there is nothing except the woman and myself leering with a self-pitiful hunger, everything else dust and lies.

Yet I don't. Some last memory of love, self-respect, pride, hope . . . or was it just self-preservation, respectability, and I leave sneaking down side-alleys to avoid detection.

I phone Catherine later that evening.

"A quiet week, you know yourself", half wanting, half not wanting detection but I can play the role of considerate boyfriend too well by this stage. Later on I watch *Home and Away*. . . again. The theme is that of an unfaithful lover in a previously blissful relationship. I realise sadly that I can never boo the baddie in these programmes again, and muse ironically on the truth that life does indeed imitate art.

THE CHURCH AND UNEMPLOYMENT   28/6/93

Bishops issue a pastoral on unemployment. Truly this country is changing. The church acquiring a social conscience. Well, I suppose someone's got to do it; the politicians and the media are not interested.

The pamphlet is particularly concerned about the consequences of unemployment, in particular the creation of a weak civic culture, the effects of large scale alienation and the collapse of the social compact. Ooops! is that a hidden agenda I see lurking there? Come out, come out wherever you are, lurking there in the bushes! For what will the collapse of this civic culture lead to? Threats to property, law and order, the decline of, . . . again . . . crime, the decline of the family . . . again . . . and of course with that divorce, abortion, contraception and loadsa pre-marital sex . . . again!

Well, thanks for your concern, Your Lordships.

Why not join Fine Gael?

That piece of bile was easy . . . Too easy. I should not be so critical of these concerned old men. This sort of anti-clericalism is intellectually lazy and really a little outdated. All these battles have already been fought and as usual nobody has really won. Most of the church people attacking unemployment, particularly those connected with the C.M.R.S., are more knowledgeable and sincere than our politicians, particularly those in the party of change who use attacks on the church in the same way as George Bush uses foreign policy, to divert attention from domestic failures.

The insincerity of the political debate about unemployment is typified by the P.D. claim, not hotly contested by the government, that increased Social Welfare payments are bankrupting the country. In fact, figures released by the C.M.R.S. indicate that a lower percentage of G.N.P. is spent on Social Welfare today than in 1986 despite the fact that the numbers of unemployed has risen. What does that imply? Why do I not expect headlines on this one? Is that a discontented P.D. T.D. I hear muttering about the desirability that priests keep out of politics. Do I not love this?

So, if the government is spending less on Social Welfare, who gains? The education system? The health system? Worthy causes, the Kilkenny football team, Shamrock Rovers. Actually it is the . . . erm . . . top ten percent . . . you know the people Mary Harney prays for every morning. These poor struggling people with their three jobs. Why are there so many people unemployed, Mary?

Isn't it comforting to know that this top ten per cent that we worry about every day have seen their salaries rise at twice the rate of Social Welfare. Isn't it comforting to know that there is a just society out there after all, and that we can all sleep comfortably in our beds tonight.

FAILURE TO GET JOB – JOKE   29/6/93

My failure to get a job has become a joke at this stage. That is the only way I can deal with the present situation. Any other response and I would go mad. All around me people with fewer qualifications, people I know objectively to be less talented than I, are falling into jobs. They may not be great jobs but they qualify for the title.

It is some reversal. In college I was looked up to and respected by these people. In college I was a leader, an organiser. I sound like Charlie Haughey in his dotage, remembering the old days. Now I am not even a footsoldier let alone a leader. I don't envy those who are getting jobs. Liar! G'luck to them and all that, but what is so wrong with me?

It's the employers I hate. The rise in unemployment has made them arrogant and complacent. That sickens me. Met a friend yesterday still fuming after a three hour interview for a job. Three interviewers. One of them finally asked her with the arrogant little half smile so beloved of these people, did she not think she was under-qualified in her subject and that she was really wasting her time here. The girl in question has an M.A. The under-qualified one I mean.

This is what I mean about employers becoming more and more arrogant, illogically so. But the best part has yet to come. The whole paraphernalia was all set up for a job, three hours long, worth £45 a week, spread over three days. And these people seriously expected prospective employees to make themselves unemployable, to go through this shite for that. Of course the ad for the job never said anything about it only being worth £45 a week. That way you get more interviewees, a longer power-play. Yet they had at least fifty employees fighting for that job. Its probably an aphrodisiac for some of these people. And then the government claims we need more training schemes!

I would really like to meet these self-important wankers. In my present mind-set which is negative, I would probably end up in court as a result of such a meeting, or in care if I had a 'right-on' sympathetic judge. First I would, depending on sex, tell them where to stick their job. Then I would trash the place and violently assault them. That, of course, would make me unemployable. These nasty little middle-class bastards have long memories, particularly if they are socialists, and someone dents their importance. They cherish that like a new form of virginity.

There again, given my defeated state of mind I might just accept all that shit, plead for the job, squirm and bow. I hope, for my self-respect, I have not yet sunk that low. I'm not sure, however, whether or not I can honestly answer that question. Anger, after all, is the only weapon of the disempowered and the one used most effectively by their rulers to defeat them by showing that they are behaving unreasonably. And our employers are acting reasonably. It's a sellers' market for jobs at the moment and boy, are they using that to the hilt.

INFIDELITY   30/6/93

Everything is tawdry tonight. Go out to the pub still feeling the cheapness of the other day flowing in me. In the bar I chat up someone I know. She is drunk. Tús maith, leath na hoibre (sic), as they say in my native tongue. We get on famously and as the night wears on all that stuff about Catherine and me being like swans mating for life seems very distant. She'll reject me anyway when she sees how useless I am, sees the real me. Self-pity demands that I get my retaliation in first. Anyway, nothing is valuable in my world anymore. I am too cheap to deserve that now.

As she becomes drunk we touch more frequently. Just a one night stand to break the boredom would be nice. There would be nothing more than that for us. She leans into me. I can smell the cheap perfume. Yes, we're away. She asks me how is Catherine. Drat. I feign a non-committal response implying imminent break-up of our previously blissful relationship. She looks at my owlishly for a moment, then draws me close again. This is it. Her lips tease as she whispers and I resist the temptation to kiss her now, enjoying the moment, the proximity of sex.

"I think yourself and Catherine are a beautiful couple. It's great to see real love in this world".

I draw back and smile weakly. Damn.

"Thank you," I murmur.

Defeated I make my excuses and leave. Outside I am seized with a choking laughter. Life can be so insane.

JULY

IRONIES

The insanity continues. The very next day after my planned night of passion
I receive a letter from my girlfriend informing me with delight that she is coming down this week-end. This after the last week is not good. I feel a half-
hearted and guilty enthusiasm. I do not want this.

In the space of three short months everything in our relationship has been
terrifyingly reversed. I feel her concern as intrusion, her love as perverse and
stupid, her needs as imprisoning. Everything is so cold between us now . . . on
my side at least. I even resent my continued need for her as something wrong. I
am not worthy. I will drag her down. And I resent that realisation. Desiring the
whore was in some way an objectification of these conflictual emotions, a justification of my unworthiness.

All of this is happening so fast. I am in a river, out of control and drowning.
Cannot, not able, to stop, look, choose. Sometimes for just one moment I stop
and say, "Jesus, what the fuck is happening?" and then I am dragged back into
the maelstrom again. Blind.

I need distance to find and understand myself, control the situation and this
thing eating away inside of me. I need to stop, regroup, redefine and begin
again. I cannot do that in her cloying presence, demanding, urging, filling the
centre, leaving nothing for me. My need for space, her need for connection
with its genesis in the former. Something must break soon. She tells me she has
had a period. That shadow is at least lifted for both of us now. But how strong is
a relationship if the prospect of creating life holds terrors for both partners?
How real is the connection or is it just habit?

COPS, SHOULD I JOIN?

Someone today suggests I should join the cops. That would be brilliant. A
case of the fox amongst the geese. I demur. Ballymun, O'Connell Street, Oliver
Bond flats. Courage, like charity, has never been a defining factor of my life.

He smiles at my refusal, pointing out that I can transfer into the clerical staff
after three years. He is an Executive Officer in the uncivil service. I doubt he
had to spend three years chasing joyriders and drug-dealers in Coolock, though
God knows, I have done enough of the latter in recent years. Somehow I think

that if I want a career as a clerical officer I will do a F.A.S. course rather than join the Gardai.

It is only later that I realise with some relief that not only do I suffer from a courage deficit but that as I am vertically challenged I can never ever become a guard. I give up the idea of a career as a legendary crime-fighter with a quiet, studied regret.

GOLF AND CRICKET   3/7/93

It is amazing the lengths you go to in order to pass the time on the dole. Recently I've started playing golf again. The U.S. Open is on this week and I'm in with a very good chance with my tempestuous swaggering game. A poor opening round is followed up with rounds of 67 and 69, to leave me right up there with Payne Stewart and Lee Janzen in the final round. Being behind suits me. I like to make a charge through the field on the final day.

The course is a difficult one. The front garden and the patch of sand outside the house acts as greens. The shrubs are trees, the stream a water hazard. Don't use clubs, just flick a stone with my fingers. Dunked the stone/ball in the water hazard twice in my opening round of 74. I know I look a little mad throwing stones, gesticulating and waving my arms angrily at a bad shot, but it all gets so engrossing in a life short of high tension.

There is also the thrill of flirting with danger. Have already almost hit an old lady and, more seriously, a local gurrier with hook shots whilst I score a direct hit on a low passing terrier with a slice. Fortunately it merely growls menacingly before continuing on its pugnacious way. Mass times are to be avoided. Too many people holding you up, some of them even laughing at you as you take a shot. These spectators have no consideration. My neighbours just avoid me. They just think I'm insane. Thank God my poor parents are not around to see the downfall of their loved son and expected stalwart of their old age.

Later that night I am triumphant. A birdie on the eighteenth green results in a final round of 68 to beat Janzen by one shot. Have won £300,000. Shall I tell the dole office? I decide against it, preferring to maintain my privacy as against the pressures of fame. Besides, I hear the exchange rate for Monopoly currency is not good. My girlfriend, who will be down tomorrow, congratulates me profusely on my win. Asks is it my first Major. Is that a tone of irony I detect in her voice? She had better watch out. I am an international golf star now and can have my pick of women. Even air-hostesses!

TOUCHING BOTTOM   4/7/93

I go into a Dublin sex shop today. Why? I don't know. Boredom. Nothing else to do. Curiosity? Or something uglier. I need a change. Something to spice up my love-life. Ideas. The shop is bright and cheery, a world of shiny packages and grinning plastic, like a child's toy shop. Only the customers and staff give it the expected seediness.

I am a bit shocked at it all. Blow up women pouting eternally, a sheep for a touch of humour, black leather skirts, huge dildos and vibrators built in the image of what men think women want, when they want "it" and a funny look-ing thing reminiscent of a bicycle pump, attached to a stethoscope, attached to a loo plunger, which is supposed to simulate a blow job. It looks chancy.

It is the porn mags which give the game away, which allow the visitor to peek into the soul of what is here. Drugged faces, bodies strung up and in pain. Empty holes like the sheep, the blow up dolls, the core, what is living, hol-lowed away. A part of me is screaming to go. But despite all of my scruples I muffle conscience as effectively as ever. I purchase and go half-laughing at the stupidity of it all but is that laughter another mask like the "looking in love with a Catherine that I no longer *deeply* want"? Is it a pretence, a cloak?

At home I read. Wanting. The number tempts but I do not yet. Remember-ing the other funny little men there. I am one with them now. No, I am not! Why? You want to be. Don't you? I begin to caress. Lazily, cynically. There's nothing else to do. Do you want to touch bottom, just once, "to dance with the devil in the blue moonlight". Just for kicks.

BITTER-SWEET   5/7/93

We meet. Shocked. I had not expected this. Guilty – furtive man after yesterday. Again I feel the bitter-sweet thrill as her car pulls up. The familiar sound of the clutch dying, sun-roof up, the glance and that half-hesitant smile that I love .. do I, and if so, why is that sweetness mingled with the word bitter. She walks towards me and we hug strongly. Yet her eyes are different, as though a cloud has suddenly formed over a blue sea suddenly turning it to a scowling grey. We kiss and it is strange … awkward and funny as though both of us have recoiled on impact, I remembering the whore, Judas, unable to kiss fully.

We spend the day rushing, running stupidly from place to place, driving in the car where there can be no talk except foolish fickle things – weather, who we have met, jokes, serious things avoided as though there is a centre of broken glass, glittering, attracting, but we are afraid to walk over it lest it cut and maim. The day dwindles away, food, cinema, the pub. We look lovely there. Almost as if we are in love. But is that all we are at? Looking nice. Looking as though we are in love. Sex is almost conventional, expected, a nice way to round off the day. I am soft with her tonight, soft because I want her to feel cherished, to heal this cold sadness between us, or is it just in egoistical me?

COLD   6/7/93
Watching her the next day I feel only surprise. She seems plain this morn- ing. Offering nothing I have not already experienced. I have not felt this cold before. She wakes and I recoil. Her breath is sour. I remember a time when I did not notice these things.

Waking she kisses me at first gently then hungrily, her lips sucking as though trying to draw something, some poison out of me. Sometimes in these last months her need has frightened me. Yet I have felt so distant, as though her desire is trying to capture a part of me that is gone, that is memory. I am unenthusiastic. It is too early for this sort of stuff. She senses, stopping. Her eyes are vulnerable yet cold. Cynicism is hiding there, using uncertainty as a camouflage. Cynical bastard, Seán. The voice is soft.

"What would you like most in bed?"

Suprised I temporise, pretending disinterest, confusion. What does she know? What does she suspect? Innocent voice.

"What do you mean?" yet secretly a cold part of me is interested. Knowing the potential of the offer. She senses my interest. It would be hard not to. Her eyes glitter with a shine totally separate from anything I have seen there before.

"Go on, whatever you want baby."

Images flickering. The room is dull. All the better to hide. Remembering the hot city. That afternoon. The whore. Cathy. Which do I want? Remem- bering the book. Hidden quickly beneath the mattress at the sound of her car. The images merge again. I see her, Cathy, magically transformed, now the woman in the street, wanting it, wanting anybody, the three of us, unified. I whisper, Yes, recoil waiting for disgust, but there is none.

"I'd like that too."

What's the catch? I look at her closely. There is none. Then lust takes over and we smile with the cold knowingness of childhood bullies. Connecting. Each as sensual, as cheap in our desires. Nothing special anymore. The bottom is reached. Both hard now. Seeking new experiences. The old ones are dull, not providing kicks anymore. Image and reality meet, threshing. It is quick. A squeal. Finished. We lie back, unable to talk. But her eyes still glisten, opaque in the dark room. Her lips curl.

"Would you still like it? After that? Three of us?"

She whispers, voice and words arousing. I purr, Yeah. I enter again, surprised at a virility I thought lost. She sighs, voice rising. I watch her below. She is gone. Indifferent. I am just the conductor of her release. Thing. Method. Cold voyeur. Watching her groan in her separate world, our separate worlds.

Afterwards,

"Do you know how we can do it?"

"Yes", I hiss.

"OK, when?"

"Soon, you're coming down next weekend?" I ask anxiously.

But she is silent, asleep. I watch. Sated. Now I can allow myself the luxury of guilt. Her breathing is soft. Face unlined. Look around the room which has seen so much passion.

She is murmuring, her eyes open. Whispers my name. Sadness just for a moment then she turns. I realise with shock that she is almost a stranger to me. I cannot sleep. The air is stuffy, sour. Later she wakes. We sleep together again. Moving with habitual grace. Yeah. Another command performance. The hat-trick. I murmur the usual,

"Thanks, are you OK?"

"Yeah".

"I love you".

"Yeah".

She is tired now, chasing sleep. Her eyes close. I lie back. What to say. There is nothing. Only sex chasing away tedium. But that is over now. I want a bath. Dirty. Outside the wind kicks up a clatter of leaves. It is dusk. The noise irritates. Talk to her. Why? What is there to say anymore? Nothing, just a habitual familiar squeeze. Looking.

Is this the same room as the beginning? No, it is a wilderness. She sleeps now. We are finished for today. She will leave tomorrow. Welcome to our separate worlds.

METAPHORS 7/7/93

She leaves. I wave stupidly. Inadequate. She is gone now. Now there is nothing. Only a distance as the car cuts further into Ireland, into some mysterious place where I can never see her.

The cat running stupidly across the road. Too desperate, too committed to draw back. Caught by an indifferent car it leaps one, two, three, its body jerking as if trying to claw back a life, a spirit that is already gone.

It ceases. I walk over casually but its eyes already have the glassy spite of death. I look at it briefly then toss the inert form into the cold ditch.

A metaphor for us.

I am alone now. The room is empty, yet heavy with the scent of smoke, of sex. I know what I will do. Disgusted yet excited and wanting. The vision dominates, prostitute, Cathy, desire, all coalescing and unifying, feeding this terrible empty hunger, a hunger that is born in hell.

I go hard, knowing what I will do. Unzip. Slowly my hands move down. Sensuous sound of clothes hitting the floor. Stroking then clenching the other hand thrusts harder and harder and my eyes are filled with the vision until there is nothing but my hands stroking and thrusting, nothing, only the desolate vision, then a shudder, calm, I have come.

All gone now. All calm. Released and with that release in the twilight I see now what I, we, us, have become. I have almost, out of boredom, become one of those small men in the van . . . cruising . . . I have quite casually destroyed something that had a touch of God in it.

I feel only disgust, disgust not born out of conventional morality but disgust born out of the knowing of the value of the human spirit, the knowing about love, and the knowing of how awful an act it is to debase and corrupt these things. What are we now after this weekend of wanking where we did not talk or love once? The whole thing has horrified and shocked me. This crouched debasing of the spirit, the loss of self, of individuality, of the sense of being special, that is not us.

It is now.

I am bouncing around on the rocks and I have brought her there for company. Oh! my love I am sorry for what I have done, for what we have become. I need to talk, need to ring her, need to start to re-build, create again. But I do not even know her address, her 'phone. I need, want for her to ring to let her know that in my heart love is here that it is true. Christ! Oh please! To grow, to change, to escape from what we, no! what I have become. My love, I am sorry.

She does not ring. I go out. Return, there is nowhere to go.

TALENT IN THE COMMUNITY/THE NEED FOR A NEW
DEFINITION OF UNEMPLOYMENT   8/7/93

The amount of wasted talent in this community continues to amaze and half anger me. We have created the framework of the perfect employee. Of course, one of the central features of this construction is conformity. One has to be mass produced, preferably by an R.T.C. The marketing graduate, the vision of our new educators.

The community I live in is full of people possessing a special brilliance either in music or art or drama. None of them are employed. They are too different, too independent of the rat-race, the little rats scurrying around in their cars with their sour little dreams. The others may be more talented but they are too intelligent, independent, too different for the liking of our employers, the biggest rats.

More bloody whining. I hear the chorus. Why don't they utilise these talents, take risks, perform. The reason is simple. The system, the famous system operates most efficiently in its blind brilliance to effectively neutralise their talents.

Take the example of two musicians I know. First of all they are informed that their talent is relatively minor, not as important or valuable for the greater happiness of all as word processing or computer programming. There are no grants available for them, no information packs. Their confidence and self-worth is damaged. They become cynical about their talents.

If they survive this process there is then another problem. They're unemployed and have families. If they begin gigging, income will be scarce for the first six months. Anything they earn will be deducted from their dole with no account taken of travelling expenses, the cost of musical instruments etc. In short, every possible trouble will be taken, out of pure stupidity allied to incomprehension, to hinder their progress. It takes enormous will and perseverance to defeat that sort of thing and this is something most people do not possess.

This applies not only to musicians and artists but indeed to all small businesses. They will be either hampered or patronised. People are not encouraged to dream in this country, but always and always, be it in politics or sport or economics to play both ends against the middle, to be always sucking the hind tit, seeking the safe job, the grant. And then we wonder why we have so few small businesses and why our entrepreneurial skills are so low. Until we create a culture which encourages independence and the taking of risk, then it will always be so.

Am nervy, jumpy this evening. She did not ring yesterday. She normally does. Why has she not? Is she okay and why this terrible sudden gush of sadness as though something awful has happened? Oh, my love, please ring. Please do not leave.

This is foolish.

NEPOTISM   9/7/93
Friend at job interview today heard the interviewees talking later in the pub. One of them said he believed boys from Clongowes and the other private schools are much more suited for the job. That's encouraging. I was kind of hoping they would be focussing on exam results, irrelevant stuff like that. And just when you think you are being paranoid about the entire system being against you. And who said you were being paranoid. Of course. Someone who is employed.

I keep telling myself that this sort of thing is not going to force me to emigrate. This place, the plain unadventurous countryside, tugs at your soul in a way that no other place can. I have too many connections here now to emigrate. If I were to leave now I would never come back. I would have nothing left to return to. Have I anything to stay for now? Unemployment has already come close to killing my relationship with Catherine. If that has fully died, then I probably will leave. What will be left to stay for?

Things are no different abroad anyway. The same values that I hate so profoundly are even more powerful there. We are merely copying them. I would be running from the periphery of something right into its centre. There is nowhere to run to anyway.

They are streaming back from England, America, Europe. And if they're returning here things must be pretty horrific because they are not good here. Unfortunate really, to be at your prime during one of those times in human history like the Depression. One hundred years from now people will look back and say, "Thank God I wasn't around in Ireland in the 1990s".

Emigrate? In so many ways I already have.

RESTORATION OF LOVE   10/7/93

All things may yet be restored. I say this without sarcasm or irony, thank God. It is time to talk now, to recreate those nights at the beginning when we talked rather than slept. I cannot say everything yet. I am not capable of too much truth yet; as much for her sake as mine. At least we now know how far we have slipped and how much I need, want to travel that road again, to begin the slow process of rebuilding, redefining.

Why did I not tell her? It was the same as with the A.I.D.S. test. I hoped that if I buried it, the thing would dissipate, and when it didn't, it grew too big, swallowing and swallowing, taking, until there was none of me in us. That was when she got frightened, then came the cloying and the possessiveness, then finally the boredom, the habit. She will leave me, she will hurt me, if this is not stopped. Something in my egotism I had not comprehended the possibility of.

I am stronger now. Firmer in my love. I believe there is so much that is unique in Catherine that I had blinded myself in my egotism and self-pity. The look in her eyes prior to love-making, the grace and poise, voice, eyes, that fullness that comes only with depth. Things common to every couple but unique to us. She obsesses me, devours. I am truly glad of that brilliance in these cold times.

The realization that I do not have her new phone number or address filled me with a cold shock. Nor did she give it to me. Is that how far we had gone?! Was that weekend a test? If so, we did not do very well.

ENDINGS   11/7/93

Receive a letter from girlfriend today. My heart does its usual bittersweet, half dance of joy. Afterwards I am NOT angry. For have I not betrayed her in a thousand little ways in the last months. I can only feel a gentle sorrow at her discovery of the transience of even that which is closest, that which we believe will last forever. I had already known the truth of the story of Bedes sparrow. Now she also knows that truth.

She has shifted someone and expects me to be angry. How can I be? I know so much, I am only saddened at her realisation that the first part of our relationship is over, that the total innocence and faith on both sides?

She asks should we separate for a while. How do I answer that? How can I fight for something that I have thrown away? Have I the right?

LOVERS ON CANAL   14/7/93

I have been trying to forget you, love, trying to forget, escape, blame. The last would be the easiest but we, who gave so much, oh, is that past tense now, we were not made for bitterness, for hate. In some ways I would prefer if I had never known you for when you are dead there is no pain. But now there is and I must deal with it . . . alone. After all, you can hardly help me with this night-mare, dear. It is not always as simple as this, love, is it? Pain and logic are hardly best friends. The squealing pig doesn't think about Plato.

Go into Dublin today. The train moves slowly along the canal, flowering in summer. Two lovers lie there and the pain snaps between my heart and gut, sharp as a broken guitar string. They are full. I am dead in this carriage, as imprisoned as they are free.

He lifts her head and kisses with the gentle arrogance held only by those who possess. I had that once. Now I have only the emptiness, the humility of those who have nothing.

I remember that. Those past scenes biting. The grass, her scent, eyes, neck imprisoning me brilliantly. Memories, the curse of those who have lost. No comfort in those dreams. Only the gnawing pain. Oh, I am desolate, desolate, the memories, lovers, haunting, laughing. The train glides past slowly and I feel as though I am in hell looking at a re-run of a previous time.

Where are you now, love? Are you crying somewhere too, separate now, already consigning me to a past, a mistake to be forgotten? An example. Per-haps you are relieved. Ha! Ha!

So now, my love, you have left me for ever. And what can I do to stop you. Bitch . . . and are you not right.

CONSCRIPTION   15/7/93

Yes indeed; conscription, that's what's needed. That and cutting nettles in graveyards will solve everything. Thanks lads and no thanks. The last time we introduced conscription into Ireland we had a war of independence and a civil war. Still, I suppose a war would help pick up the construction trade, E.C. re-lief, U.N. aid. Perhaps not such a bad idea after all. But come off it lads, we couldn't even implement a rod licence here let alone large scale conscription.

STRAWBERRIES 16/7/93

All my arrogant self-centredness is well gone now, Catherine. I buy straw-berries and cream today but they taste dead in your absence love. There is no point in this mourning any longer though. Anything after you is second best and my sorrow is that I became second best for you, for what could I offer but a life of lies and self-pity.

We must, however, like the tramps, go on. That is what Mary Harney would say anyway. Oh, I would tell a million lies to get that fabulous love back, build a thousand illusions, but what would they be only lies and we need, deserve more sustenance than that, love. Can I offer you more than that? I no longer know. Goodbye my love, my Catherine.

FATHER'S WEEK 17/7/93

Letter from home today. When am I coming home again. This on top of heartbreak, not likely. A week at home looking after my father is no joy to either of us. The last time was no different to the time before and the time before that. Why do we always lose ourselves in these separate places, always bickering over inconsequentialities, avoiding the main issues.

Things are too far gone for truth or release. He has never forgiven me for not taking that safe job in the civil service. Two different worlds. Why at eighteen should I have locked myself in the same trap that he did? Why should I have accepted comfortable mediocrity as the pinnacle of success just because he never even achieved that? He could not understand life is for living.

Since that time, no surrender, never any praise or affection, not that there ever was. The legacy of that is present even today with my girlfriend, past girlfriend, Ha! Ha!

There are thousands of people like me today in Irish society. People whose greatest ambition is never to become like their fathers. That is some legacy, some testament to the nature of father/sibling relationships in Ireland. He's get-ting crabby in his old age, "mumble, grumble, rumble". Now I know why mid-dle-aged Irish women look so disheartened. It's not the menopause; it's seeing their husbands transforming into what their fathers were, and the prospect of no escape. Ever.

DISAPPEARANCE 18/7/93

She is gone now. The house like a tomb possesses only memories. All that love, that giving, pain, terror, love, joy, all only remind now, sepia photographs of the mind. The phone does not ring, will never ring, except with pointless people, people I do not want to know. There will be no more letters, except perhaps for a fickle postcard or two. Everything is gone now, that voice, kisses, warmth, fun, connection.

Oh, I know I will recover; build, start again, find someone new, all that stuff, but that is all so very, very far away. I need a fucking self-help book, you know the sort of thing, or perhaps I should buy some of that bottled stuff to help me pull the birds like they promise in the back of the *News of the World*. Mind you, knowing my luck they'd probably send the wrong bottle and I'd end up trapped in the house with a thousand dogs outside barking.

Nothing now only the silence. The silence haunts like that damned ringing phone that breaks my sleep. Her voice, kisses, warmth are only memories to taunt. I am alone in my room now, alone in this mild suburban estate. I think I will purchase a shotgun and shoot out all the double-glazed windows. Joke!

SIGNING OFF 19/7/93

Am looking forward to signing off the dole. That's it, bye now, see you next year. Strange, the little, parochial ambitions we develop after a year on the dole. Now an S.E.S. scheme is achievement, liberty, freedom, escape, a small restoration of pride. It's good to know you're good enough for something, even a scheme which is a government dodge, a ploy to mask the real level of unemployment.

I will, however, be a little more cautious signing off this time. Do everything by the book. The last two times I was arrogant; didn't even bother signing off. Fuck 'em, I wont be back here again. This time I'm not arrogant. Life is not unfolding out for me like the red carpet I expected it to be. At this stage my confidence in me is shot, gone, slowly dissipated with the clinical cold efficiency of failure. Maybe I won't be back here in this sullen office, this grey world. Probably I will. But for the moment adieu and farewell to the paint blisters.

GENDER CHANGES   20/7/93

Unemployment connects at every level. Some are obvious, poverty, crime etc. Others are hidden, more subtle. Gender roles represent one of the latter. The new society is more tailored towards the needs and aspirations of woman particularly in the world of work. In offices the word-processor and computerised technology is now king. Many of the old male employment stereotypes, heavy industry, the building trade, the county council, are vanishing. In the more progressive industries and the professions, teaching, tourism, textiles, offices, the role of women has become primary, rather than secondary.

This should not be seen as a social evil. But it is attended by consequences we must recognise. For women the change is a liberation and a deserved one. But for men in an age of mass unemployment the change is dangerously threatening to their self-esteem. The shattering of the old stereotype of male breadwinner, female home-maker threatens perceptions of the male role, suggesting that in an age of mass unemployment men are pretty useless.

Lest this raise yet another cheap laugh from Nell McCafferty it should be pointed out that this possesses serious consequences for both men and women. Apart from destroying the self-worth of almost an entire generation of men it will also lead to increased irresponsibility. For if we are worthless, and under many of the old assumptions we are, then why be responsible? Furthermore, people who are unemployed more or less permanently are often left in a state of perpetual adolescence. Work inculcates responsibility and discipline. The absence of work for entire sections of our society can only attenuate those traits.

This loss of self-worth will also lead to increased broken marriages, illhealth, violence and alcoholism. People denied a sense of worth, of purpose, will not foster a healthy society. They possess no incentive to do so. Nor indeed will their children if they are denied any positive male role models.

We must recognise that changes in gender roles cuts both ways. We have encouraged women to get into the workforce. We now need to similarly extend the role of men, particularly in the area of child-rearing. Prior to the 70s, women generally could only achieve self-worth and value from their work in the home. Most men, even today, are incapable of this, see child-rearing as a loss of identity and value. These beliefs, these socialising forces need to be challenged. Men need to be informed that the position of home-maker possesses as much value as the world of work and that men are equally suited to the challenge, that both sexes possess equal responsibility for the rearing of children. These represent difficult tasks and are just a little bit more important than the battle between church and state.

I would represent an excellent example of the difficulty of this task. It would be nice if I could possess sufficient maturity to apply this analysis to my own life. But pub philosophers/politicians have never been as mature in their own lives as on paper.

JOIN S.A.S. 21/7/93

Join S.A.S. scheme today. Bid farewell to weeping family, friends, etc.etc. I wonder what the job will be. Kuwait, Bosnia, Iran. Why did they pick me given my lack of combat experience, except inside the pub on a Friday evening, or a bit of rabbit shooting. Nothing however on the line of what the S.A.S. require. Perhaps I was hired for my brilliant strategic mind.

Imagine my horror therefore, reader, when after all the tears, the nostalgia and going-way parties, my shocked horror when I realise that I have misread the forms and I am in fact on an S.O.S. (otherwise known as S.E.S.) scheme. For the uninitiated S.O.S. means same old shite as being on the dole. You do nothing all day, then go home and pretend you've worked. Same money and status as the dole. The job reminds me in its uselessness of prison labour or the work-house, the uselessness of the work a gentle punishment.

The discerning reader may detect a slight tone of cynicism in the aforementioned remarks. What can you expect? The Please Fuck Off letter has become the centre of my world. Allow me a small piece of bile please.

These S.E.S. schemes are a metaphor for everything, for the scrag end of a century no-one has really very much liked. This has been a decade of grey, like those sepia films of America in the Depression or Ireland under De Valera. A noisy gimcrack of a society that has lost courage and cohesion, the welfare generation. This is Independence?

We all know, too well, that there is no Utopia outside waiting for us. The iron of cynicism/respectability is branded too deep. Utopia in Ireland is now a sex shop.

DUBLIN 6.15 a.m. SUNDAY MORNING 23/7/93

There is nothing worse in this earthly world, in this God awful country than walking the streets of Dublin broken-hearted at 6.15 a.m. It is almost funny, so pathetic, so clichéd is it all, only I am in it. Music comes from one window, Jimmy Hendrix, the dregs of another fickle party, the last endings.

The street mirrors it all. At one end a newly-killed dog glistens, bored by its death, at the other a spatter of puke, of broken glass. I am the only living thing on this road surveying the devastation of another Saturday night, surveying the devastation of another relationship. Oh poor me. I am the only one to have suffered in the world. But there is no escape here in irony. The cuts are too deep for this.

I know I possess the self-importance held only by those who have lost love. I know I will get better. I know it happens everyone. I know we are not unique I know – I know I must snap out of it. I know, I know, I know. Alright, I fucking know I've had the benefit of a university education. I know all this stuff but its unique to me, its happening to me. This is ugly. It is wrong.

DREAMS   24/7/93

It is almost two weeks now. Two weeks of silence where nothing lives. Connection is gone. Only the abscess of absence. All that is lost now. The woman that was weaved into my soul – gone, kissing some other man. Alien. Heartbroken but needing the sustenance of even the brief love of Saturday night cattle-marts. Better than I can give.

I am a parody these dog days, frantic and false, all smiles and pretence and then somebody notices, catches you unaware – how do you deal with that, how do you escape when the mask drops?

The pain frightens me, visceral, physical, facing every day heavy in sleep and pain, a bruised heart. I am now, I think, coming out of shock, beginning to ferret around, to see how I will survive.

At least now I know how the *amour courtois* poets felt. I do not sleep, do not eat, disgusted with that body which has been rejected so deservedly, disgusted with my failures which made it so easy, so right to toss me aside. That is all gone now, all only a bubble, a dream taunting in its inaccessibility. Who are you kissing now, love? And can I no longer possess that which I once most fully had, most fully wanted . . . want?

The phone is ringing. Night. I jump, scrabble frantically, then waken. It is silent. I realise laughing cynically that it is a dream. Silence. This is the third time now. I turn again into the silence of sleep, that silence which is killing me.

S.E.S. RESPONSE   25/7/93

Tell one of the boys about the S.E.S. scheme. His response is a mixture of pity and contempt. I'm getting a lot more of that these days, or is it just my over imaginative paranoid imagination coming to the fore. Most people are probably just indifferent. It is the sympathetic ones that kill me. Each sympathetic glance and I feel I have let another good person down.

The wanker drones on. Consoles me as though I had endured the death of a close family member. Shockin'. Yeah. the country is on its knees. Yeah. Fine young man like you. These schemes are useless. Thanks. I agree with him totally. I just wish he would go away and tell it to somebody else.

What he doesn't realise is that it gives me something to do, the pretence of value, use, purpose, release from the emptiness that is stifling. More importantly my benefit has run out. I don't fancy the prospect of depending on the charity of the Social Welfare Department as distinct from that which is mine by legal right. I remember that last time too well. I'm not taking that chance again. So it's off again to the S.A.S. Oops, Sorry, S.O.S. Scheme.

DESIRE FOR MONEY   26/7/93

Have never felt such a strong desire for money as today. Perhaps this is linked to the fact that I will be no better off on the S.E.S. scheme than when I was on the dole. This despite the fact that I will be working twenty hours a week. This is the nature of our generous government. As a result of joining this scheme I will lose my rent allowance and Medical Card. After those deductions I am making a net profit of £3 for twenty hours. Clever government!

I have never really possessed any money. I scrimped and saved my way through college never possessing the same freedom from fear about money the others had. And now this. Okay. I have never starved, but I would really like the little luxuries that money brings. Just for a little while. Comfort, security, above all an escape from the state of mind that grows in you like a cancer when you are always on the breadline, always looking for the cheapest foods, clothes, restaurants. Worrying if your girl wants an expensive present and grudging her everything. Everything in life always cheap, second hand, always second best. I don't want that.

WALKING 27/7/93

The tension of it all, the oppressiveness is unbearable. Alone, waiting, worst of all hoping, and laughing at that. Those two weeks of silence, of nothing, I do not want to live those again.

I have blanked my mind during those dead days trying to worry about important things, society, the state of the country, etc. etc. but still the bastard thoughts and memories keep interfering. In this tomb, the phone never rings except to mock with absence. I go out this evening, walking, looking at trees, pot-holes, tarmac, anything to distract, escape, release. End this foolish pointless thinking and nostalgia.

There is a big match tonight and the whole country is cheering. I do not want this, do not want a nation celebrating whilst I nurse my private heartbreak. Selfish me.

And in the night those mocking dreams, that phone jolting out of sleep and the knowing the knowing of her pain and my impotent inability to heal and transform. Three in the morning, province of the mad and failed lovers. Hankering.

Reading this diary I see now that I saw it coming, always my genius, my epitaph. He saw it coming when it was gone. He always did.

As I walk through these indifferent estates I realise I have never been so alone in this world. Never with such utter totality and it has all been my decision to let all that fullness slip through, the carelessness of a child stripping petals from a rose.

So this is it. I break tonight . . . fully and completely, a flooded release that does not stop. There is nothing here now but the furniture watching the crying fool, dissolute child sobbing for the toy he has thrown away.

The shouts, hysterical now, bounce crazily from wall to wall, no one hearing in the dead estate – sleeping peacefully. There is a pain here that will never go away. Tomorrow will begin again and again facing into a world of second best, living in a world where only the past tense exists. I sleep fitfully. Tomorrow will come soon.

BEGINNINGS 28/7/93

I wake up again. One o'clock. The dream again, mocking, laughing at the silence filling the house. Smile cynically. The sound continues, intruding, mocking.

I sit up shocked, realising it is ringing, jump and run, cursing, praying not to miss that last ring. I lift it.

Her voice is breaking, the words cruel and reluctant. "Seán, I want us to stop being lovers and just be friends". My mind is blank, shocked. It is so very, very different to hear this spoken rather than seeing it on the written page. For a letter has formality, this is intimate, the voice that told me she loved me now telling me she wants nothing, nothing but a fickle friendship, post-cards.

"Hi, are you going out to a disco, for a drink, the like?"

I grasp stupidly at straws seeking to rescue some of the precious things. Can we kiss, hold hands, hug? Can we do none of these things? The answer is final. It is direct, too direct. She has others now, needs to experiment, to find herself. Thanks love. Why the fuck are you telling me this? Why?

Were it said with less pain I would be more bitter, but I, for all my rhetoric, am caught with nothing, nothing to say except, "Nooo, Nooo, Nooo". This is wrong. I feel it in my heart, not for me, selfishly, but for us. But I have been stripped of all arguments. Is that not the awful thing? The silence when you can no longer defend something beautiful, something you believe is right.

She does not give me her phone number. To fragile, too dangerous for that yet. She leaves. Out of money. The despair of all crossed lovers. She will call again. I can only wait.

EXPLANATIONS AND ANALYSIS   30/7/93

We live in a changing world. Cliché. What is not a cliché is the need for a new kind of social welfare system to deal with this changing society, if a third of this state is not to fall into a chasm of self-hatred and disempowerment.

We need first of all to be blunt. The present system was designed as part bribe, part punishment. The bribe element is the realisation that if you do not provide for the poor and the unemployed you will face social revolution. Dole purchases peace.

The punishment ethic lies in the decision to pitch the level of support there or thereabouts on the poverty line; attempting to make unemployment such a miserable existence that no-one could possibly desire it.

That is all very well in times of low employment, not so good in times of high. The present system, with its genesis in Victorian social engineering is outdated in an age which knows that full employment is a myth and that we will be faced with mass unemployment for years to come. The next question is, do we desire a society where the lives of up to one million of our people barely surpass that of animals? If so, we are on the right track.

Of course, the majority of us do not. Just as we want peace in Northern Ireland, the end of famine in Africa, a society where all the buses and trains run on time. The solving of these problems would be nice. We are not, however, sufficiently concerned or frightened to face up to the task of a radical redefinition of employment and, as a consequence, unemployment. Doubtless in this area as in all else we will want to see what Britain, America and Europe does and then follow. So much for independence.

There exists some debate on these issues. This, even in Ireland, is not surprising. The concept of paying three hundred thousand people not to work is sufficiently absurd to belong to the world of Swift and we are not mad enough . . . yet . . . to take our place amongst the Yahoos and Lilliputians.

Some of these ideas could potentially work. The idea of work-fare is one example. It recognises that people possess an intrinsic need, be this natural or through socialization to be creative, to possess some sense of worth or value in their lives; and that this is generally achieved through work which acts as the objective realisation of these needs. Hence the desirability of work-fare.

This, however, is lost when bastardised by our Irish Tories, the P.D.s using the oldest guise in the book, concern over the waste of our old friend the tax-payers' money. This scheme will be turned by them into some form of punishment/community service for the unemployed. This will be particularly the case if it is made compulsory, for the essence of employment (unlike the dole) is that it is voluntary. We choose to work. If work-fare becomes compulsory we will have thousands of people being thrown into totally unsuitable jobs for the sake of the tax-payers of Ireland and the whole worth of the thing lost.

Some sort of a start has been made by the S.E.S. schemes in redefining the nature of unemployment. What is particularly valuable about these schemes is that people can work part-time jobs outside of the scheme without their income being affected. This challenges the most gruelling effect of unemployment, the grinding poverty, the cheapness of that life.

This benefit should be extended to all the unemployed, particularly the long-termers. The present situation where, if one works, your benefit is reduced accordingly after a very small level of payment, is ludicrous. It is this which leads to the black economy and welfare fraud. In cases where the long-term unemployed obtain part-time work their supplementary benefits should not be affected and surplus income taxed as normal unless the part-time work becomes regular.

What incentive has an unemployed person to work for nothing which is the reality under the present system? What incentive has he to declare income? What incentive has he to leave benefit, to work for a month only to be thrown back again on the lottery of assistance? To the parties of enterprise and incentives I suggest they absorb these little truths in their attitudes towards Social Welfare.

What I am advocating is a radical sea-change in our attitude towards unemployment. We need to create a system which allows them also some quality of life. This, of course, will require imagination and courage and as these qualities cannot be drawn down under E.C. structural funds they are consequently in short supply in Irish politics.

This will also require a reversal of the belief that it is good for unemployment to be seen as a shameful thing or everybody would be at it. That is all very well given a scenario where work exists for all. Anywhere else it is a wasteful, stupid and dangerous cast of mind. It means that the unemployed, because of this shameful condition, must possess no quality to their lives. This is a boon only to be possessed by the middle classes, most of whom, surprise, surprise, vote unlike the demoralised non-possessors, few of whom vote and are consequently politically and economically worthless.

This politics of envy will yet reap its own whirlwind. It will be a bitter one of two nations existing in a silent enmity in the one state. It will be a harvest even more bitter than the one reaped by our Northern ancestors. Our new Planters will weep their folly too in their high security homes.

But what of learn-fare, I hear the concerned ones of our society ask. Surely that will help build a better world. I am very dubious about this. Learn-fare belongs to the school of thought that believes there is nothing which cannot be solved by education or government commissions or articles in *The Irish Times*. Way to go lads; if it is the centre pages of *The Irish Times* then it cannot be wrong. At this stage in my cynical world I incline to the opposite view.

There is another reason, outside of the people and institutions that support it, why I do not believe in learn-fare. We have the biggest system of learn-fare in the Western world under F.A.S. and as a result what do we have . . . the most over-qualified unemployed workforce in Europe. Learn-fare on its own achieves nothing except the creation at first of false hopes and then of a more realistic cynicism. It does nothing but train people for non-existent jobs that existed only in the days of full employment and Fionn McCumhail. The present plethora of schemes, based on the dream that there are thousands of jobs there waiting outside if people were qualified, foster nothing but other schemes. We are now ironically fostering a schemes dependency culture.

Actually, I am being too charitable in saying the people in charge of F.A.S. actually believe there are thousands of jobs out there waiting. This is a myth. It is also a government device, a ruse to pretend they have devised a response, that they really possess solutions to the unemployment crisis. It is something to put off the day of reckoning, the admission that we have no solutions and that this is your lot. And so the mythical dance continues, the government, F.A.S., the media all singing the same tuneless song.

At least, I hope this is the case. They don't seriously believe the patter they put out. If they do and if these are the people charged with resolving the jobs crisis, then God help us all. I would rather be lied to by knaves who are clever than consoled by fools who are well-meaning.

AUGUST

SHOCK 1/8/93

The pain pours slowly down the line, slowly and with such bitter, bitter clarity. I realise, shocked, that I, loving, giving Seán am responsible for this and I realise with the bitterness of her pain that I am shocked too, shocked that she has the capacity to hurt me so fully, so very thoroughly, as fully as I can hurt her.

I ask her to talk. How can she? She is too drunk, too hurt. She tells me to fuck off. Don't intellectualise. She is in the process of exorcising me from her life, and I can do absolutely nothing about it. This is horror, so so different from trying to win her, for now I am trying desperately not to lose her.

Oh! this pain. It is not right and yet a thrill goes through me to hear her voice even in pain. Contact with that which is in my heart so deeply still, and a joy also, a joy because part of her still loves me even in that very hate and pain, that this sleeping around, for she tells me that she has, is death for her. Oh love, I would make you live! I would heal and protect you, transform your life as I did once before. But now there is this awful finality, I no longer have the right!

I feel a cold ache at this sleeping around, not jealousy but pain that my cold self-regard has so devalued something once precious to us. I have been the architect, the secret little builder of all her nightmares.

She tells me she loves me, and I? I love her too, though I have disguised it so very well. But are we strong enough to reach over the distances, the great empty spaces we have built in the severance of our two lives. Do we actually want to?

She tells me she loves me but she cannot see me, she needs the space. I echo for it is right, it is necessary for her, for me too or I would flood, deluge her. I am so confused, so uncertain after it all. How can I feel bitterness at this separation. I love her too fully to give that gnashing hate free rein. I feel it lashing about below. Hidden. What good would it do? She and I have loved each other too much for this. The world, the landscape, everything is barren now. Even birdsong at the morning. Empty . . .

UNEMPLOYMENT AND CIVIL WAR 2/8/93

Am amused to read Mike Allen's warning that civil war is inevitable if nothing is done about social exclusion. I have more serious things on my mind right now. Mike is a leader of an organisation called the I.N.O.U. which apparently represents me. This is a break I could do without.

He is correct in his analysis at one level . . . and indeed one level only. Yes, unemployment will lead to civil strife throughout Europe if it remains at current levels. But this will not achieve civil war.

The P.D.s can rest easy. There will be no rioting, no street demonstrations unless their friends, the no-turning back group of Tories manage to re-introduce the Poor Laws.

What will occur is the escalation of the process of social breakdown, a ghettoisation of society on the American model between those who possess and those who do not. The unemployed will become the Hispanics of Europe, their discontent subsumed into scapegoatism. Racism, Neo Nazism, Le Pens National Front are all symptoms of this.

The dispossessed lack the ability or self-confidence to act politically. For many, their frustration and anger will be released in muggings, theft, crime, rape, heroin and hate, the politics of the powerless. The politics of those too demoralised to expect anything more out of life. Those who do, see their unemployed brethren as a threat, competitors banning their escape from limbo.

The process has already begun. Ireland and the U.K., Europe, the sense of community seems frailer, society full of warring little factions. Ireland is a harsher place today where only winners and wealth creators possess value. And our politicians wonder why the rest do not accept this!

Some historians believe the end of history is in sight, that the present level of socio-economic development represents a peak which will not be surpassed. Looking at the nature of society today, that I hope is another illusion. Ironically it may yet be the case that Marx rather than these self-satisfied historians of the liberal elite will be proved correct. It will not, however, be mass poverty which destroys capitalism. Our rulers are too cute to allow that happen. Instead it will be mass unemployment. Already it is eating at the roots.

PRELUDE   3/8/93

Oh my love, love, love, life is not living without you. So clichéd I know but is this all not stupid. A mature twenty-four year old crying at silly, stupid shitty love longs and all the time the pain, the physical grinding awful pain.

I have stopped crying at night now, love. I am too empty, have used all my tears, away into the indifferent bed. Sometimes I feel your presence also. Feel your sorrow and know you are thinking of me.

I hurt for your sorrow, hurt that I have betrayed us to the point that I, if you forgive my arrogance, I who healed you so much cannot heal you now.

I am your past now, have joined the rest of your nightmares. You will talk about me to another lover and he will wonder how I could have been so foolish, arrogant as to let you go. Just as I once thought about your previous lovers.

I no longer eat these days. I had zest for food only when I was with you. I was fat because I was happy.

At night I dream of you, my *speir-bhean* haunting sleep with your generous smile, your body below twisting into me, giving, for I am in your blood, your mind, memories, dreams. Past? Oh, no, no, no, not that. Our dreams are different now, though, aren't they, love? For in my dreams of you, you are a knife twisting, hurting, even when I dream of you kissing me. For then I wake. Thinking, your distance like the Christy Moore song I sang once to put you to sleep:

> *Ride on, see you*
> *I could never go with you*
> *No matter how I wanted to*

Did part of me know its truth even then?

CHOICES 4/8/93

This is madness. This is insanity. Two people who love, who still love so deeply apart and the tragedy that it is all so right.

In this life you make choices. We chose to love and we chose to separate. The radio is singing a cheap song, yet it is not cheap. I feel warmth and know she is thinking of me. Illogical, is it not?

Yet we make choices. I know we must separate and that separation is necessary and that separation will be good for us. I know that but I do not want it. Yet part of me does, for it would be too easy for us to come together now. We need the full, full pain of separation to survive. To come back together now would devalue all that has gone before.

Ultimately you make choices. We made the choice to live apart with all that that brought. She chose a career over me. What did I choose? Failure, narcissistic dreams. I chose to distance myself from her. I chose to ask her to accept second best for that is what I have become. That was my choice and I am reaping the bitter, bitter harvest that it brings.

I know I am repeating myself. It is as though I am trying to teach myself, to force myself to believe in something that I do not believe, that separation is needed. But I do not believe that selfish me wants this to end. Seán does not want the medicine, Mammy.

The thing about choices is that they are final. You pays your money and you takes your chances. I could get the safe job if I fought hard enough, learnt how to drive, use a computer instead of this incessant narcissism. Look at me. I'm a hero. I've rejected society. I'm different.

I'm alone in my bed tonight and that is terrifying. That could be forever.

HORRIBLE LIFE ON THE DOLE AND BORD TELECOM   6/8/93

It is truly a horrible life on the dole, sorry . . . S.E.S. scheme. It's worse, however, for many others. The case of single mothers is a case in hand. Their cycle of deprivation is horrific in comparison to my small problems. Barricaded in council flats, just enough to survive, no educational opportunities or creches. All that does is to replicate a cycle of deprivation which offers to some only one opportunity, the life of a single mother. If we were a humane society we would offer them more. But we are not a humane society and these people are too disempowered to count. Our politicians and the media are more interested in golden circles than dole circles, more interested in Telecom and Goodman than those who do not vote.

Why do they get pregnant again and again? What else is there to do? What other source of comfort or warmth exists. Life is lonely in this country today. Sex is part of the passing sweetness of youth. We grasp it whilst we can, not only out of lust but the need for warmth, connection, security. Are our political economists and moralists to deny that also to those who have nothing else because of how these people have ruled our society?

Is it not comforting to realise that Dr. Michael Woods, defender of the family extraordinaire, is in charge of defending the rights of these people. But who is going to protest about this? Telephone calls are more important.

HOPE   8/8/93

So it is not dead. That at least is joy. My life now is a phone, that ring alone defining hope, offering a future. It is pain, knowing she wants lips other than mine, that she is in ecstasy under someone else. But she is not in ecstasy. She is seeking comfort, the knowledge that someone loves her, finds her attractive, desirable. She has not known that for so long now. But if she were happy, she would not be calling me now.

I am rather scared. In my old arrogance I had always worried about my capacity to hurt her. I never thought about her capacity to hurt me. What is this connection, what are these calls, a beginning, or trying to contain the break, a false trail, cherishing old memories.

I am recovering now, able to flirt again, cross eyes begin the game again. But everything is dead compared to you, my love. I am dead too, in a world full of dead people, the world of the commuter, the acquisitive ones, and I too have joined them.

I tell her I love her. She tells me she loves me. But what is that? *Papier maché*. Illusions. No.

BITCH   9/8/93
Let my bitterness run free today. Cold bitch. Feeding and emptying. You have finished with me. Another step in your career progression. Now you have had your wild romantic fling, broken the hymen, checked it all out. Now go get your middle-class man and leave me alone.

All this inspired by another call. I try to tell her, want to tell her what went wrong in our relationship. Because I know and if we know then we can save it. She doesn't want to know.

"Stop intellectualising, Seán".

Arrogant bitch, what the fuck are you doing with me.

"I want space. I love you but I want space".

Self-centred bitch. What the hell are you doing ringing me, feeding the night-mare, festering the break if you want space? I can feel it growing, feel the anger, the frustration, everything.

"What do you want?"

"I don't know".

I feel the anger. Breaking up something like us because she doesn't know. How stupid is she?

It all rips out, all the spite of six months like a spot bursting. Ugly. Arrogant. Self-righteous. You've fucked up every other relationship and now you're do-ing the same to me. You're breaking me apart. You'll die a barren old maid wishing. You? Me? Oh I'm fine. Phone drops. Silence.

It is only afterwards that I realise I hadn't coped at all. Nothing. All of this, the excitement, anticipation, hope!? It had all of it been a 'fabulous lie'. For we had not talked, we had not listened. I knew how to solve everything. I loved her and I would rescue her/us. But I had forgotten to consult Cathy in all of this.

And now we are left with nothing. A barren phone-call. A small death not even making the local news. Shock surprise.

"Oh, I never thought they'd break up," and now we have. Parting in bitterness, tears and incomprehension. No longer even able to communicate with each other. Nothing. Finally.

REVELATION ... OW!   10/8/93

Looking back at us it is funny Ha Ha just how self-important we were. We thought we were so special that the world had to be made specially for us. The idea will be a long time coming for the next one. And if things didn't go right it wasn't because of our faults, it was because of the maliciousness of others, when in fact all they were indifferent to our special relationship. Well, that has become quite ordinary now.

Sometimes I think I am just going to go fucking insane. When is the truth, the truth? Why is tomorrow always the same as today? This country must be laughing at me. I must have been chosen out of the hat for fool of the year. This cannot be normal. Please, this cannot be how it really is, this mad living in this snickering Kafkaesque world, its beehives of indifference. This is a world of mirrors where questions are always deflected, parried, where no answer is ever straight but where those at the bottom certainly know their place.

I try to tell me I don't love her, curling the lip, everything. Yet I know, laughing at myself, that it's not true, only another defence. After this year I definitely and most sincerely sympathise with Alice in Wonderland. I can see myself evolving into Yosser Hughes. I can see myself going insane, shooting up McDonalds. That way I'll be able to cope in a society where only our mad hatters are prominent.

It is finally time for me to begin the slow, reluctant, final process of exorcising you too, my love. Goodbye Catherine.

S.E.S. SCHEME   11/8/93

This place is a punishment for excessive wit or sarcasm or intelligence. The people here look so defeated it spooks me. They're like those wild animals you see at a zoo, confined, their lives tired and lethargic. I feel a sinking feeling in my heart, an acute embarrassment going in there every morning to a job that is a lie, a thing that is a farce.

Not that anybody says anything. The pretence must be maintained. Yes the people are very nice. A lot of them are intelligent but something is missing in all of us, except perhaps one or two, something oblique, indefinable pride, self-belief, confidence, none of that is there.

I could say it is a start, or that something will come of it but that goes against my gut feeling that this place is somewhere to place people when there is no-where else they can be put.

There is another college graduate here. He looks the most beaten of us all. I don't want to know him, I'm looking at him out of the corner of my eye. Is that the mirror of my future, this hunched mewling thing who loves housework, baking, looking after the baby etc. etc? He probably carries the baby around in one of those bloody pouches to increase bonding. And the tragedy of it all is that when the child grows up it will probably despise this poor weak man. I will never . . . or at least hope that I will never allow myself be beaten down like that, allow myself go as gently as he into that long dark night.

For many of the women the scheme is not such a bad thing. For those who are either separated or married but want to return to the workforce the scheme is a liberation, a gaining of confidence and self-respect. That is why they are the happiest ones here. In this world they are the ones in control, the ones who attract all the attention. For men it is an admission of defeat, the final battering away of confidence and self-respect. For some it is almost a total de-sexing.

OFFICIAL AND UNOFFICIAL IRELAND   12/8/93

There are two cultures, two countries living side by side in Ireland. One is the official culture, the successful people. These are the ones milking the system, the politicians, county-councillors, Dunnes Stores managers, civil servants, primary school teachers, professionals, always seeking and acquiring, cuckoos within the social compact, demanding tax breaks, incentives, shares, houses, cars, special treatment. Our new colonisers. These are the ones in control, the lobby groups, complaining, always complaining, over-taxed, single mothers, dole spongers. Yet, God bless 'em, they're hanging in there.

These are the ones who own the country. They make the decisions about Mullaghmore, who control the media, R.T.E., the papers, their voices incessant, drowning everything else out; demanding, always demanding their agenda and their agenda alone. The whole mish-mash of unthought, incoherent, inchoate Social democracy as epitomised by the Labour party is fulfilled. It is their sons and daughters who go to college who become the next wave of trend-setters and opinion formers, our Arts Officers and cultural masters.

Then there is that other culture, the dissidents, the disinherited and dis-empowered, guests in the little island of ours. They are the people who do not scream loud enough, who are not part of the lobby groups that Ministers Ahern, Cowan or O'Higgins listen to. They are the ones who have rejected the strident self-importance of our new interest groups or have never been given the opportunity to join.

In Ireland 1993, Emmet is still waiting, and I am not talking about Mr. Stagg. The only difference between now and the past is that today people are too cynical, too disempowered to become revolutionaries. The new manifestations of civil discontent are silent, apathy and alienation; the silence of the people of Mullaghmore, the silence of the people not invited to *Questions and Answers*. Their weapons are toothless; apathy, alienation, incomprehension of the new rules.

CHAOS   13/8/93

I receive a call. She is in chaos. Join the club, dear. It was so foolish really, all those calls I waited for so avidly. I only half listened to them, so when she was screaming her need for me, I did not listen to the other part demanding separation. Oh, I noted it, took it down, signed the contract, but I believed none of it. And then when she rang me and said I could not have what I wanted I reacted like a spoilt bastard. Flinging away the joy of what I possessed because I wanted more, even though I did not deserve it. I, I, I, dotting these pages, the signature of our collapse.

She asks, oh fuck, what have I done, what have we done. All I know is that bitterness and hate I, we screamed down the phone is not us, is a part of us yes, and we are better for knowing that, for knowing the fall. We are not in love now, not because of the bitterness but because of the total and utter absence of connection in that last call.

I do not know what will happen to us. What I do know is that if we fall in love a second time it will be better. The first time we fell in love, each believing the other perfect, wanting the other to rescue them. That faith, that selfish faith, is gone now. If we love again it will be a giving love, a love that has survived the betrayals, the anguish and the pain. It will be okay. I am calm, cool, distant. I do not love her anymore. I do! . . .but differently.

SEA   16/8/93

I go to the sea tonight. Ironic really how clichéd we are in heartbreak. All the broken-hearted lovers walk along the shore. The sea calms me, its vast peace. I feel my heart in those waves lapping into the shore, knowing my love is as vast and as full as those sighing waves. I am those waves, love, lapping around your cold heart waiting to collapse it with the sea of my love, waiting to turn the grey cold of your dead eyes blue again. Glittering.

RECONCILIATION   17/8/93

I am crying now, love, and I am crying tears of joy for you have rung me and told me that you love me and that my love is living to me. Oh, we had shrivelled so much. I had become so ungenerous. I had become your most humane killer rather than lover.

I thought after that last call you had exorcised me from your heart. I had certainly lost my divine aura a little, had I not? I know so little these days, only the strength of my love and the strength of my pain.

It is funny. I am heart-broken yet I am living again. You meet so many dead people in this strange world of the dispossessed. Shifting around 9 to 5 with nothing to do and slowly and irrevocably you join them too until you also have slipped away over the shelf into the world of the non-living. Welcome to the world of the living dead, Seán.

How could I love Catherine, I who could no longer love or respect myself? How could I listen to her, I who could only listen to myself? I had become the cuckoo in your life, taking and always taking, and yet despite all we are not dead yet. I hug that, hug the final smouldering embers. Hope. I would not like to be exiled from you too long, my love.

I am living again. I am to see her next week, see the person I thought I would never see again, except when haunted by dreams, passing faces, a familiar car, its registration desperately scanned.

This coming together will be dangerous my love. There is no danger of kissing, touching over the phone. But if we meet, if we kiss, then we are gone. And I want to be gone.

I will see you at the weekend. Scared. As though it is all beginning again.

WAITING   18/8/93

My heart is in pieces this week. I can think of nothing else. I am to see her. See her again. See the person I love. I hate the beginning of each day, loving its end. What will happen? I have no expectations, only joy, joy at seeing that face, hair, eyes, hands, the joy of seeing, knowing, touching.

Yet we will not touch and that is agony. Unnatural. For we were made as lovers, not as friends. But we must remain separate now and that separation is good, is necessary, but not too long my love, oh, not too long.

Forgive my arrogance, love, but I am the person who makes your heart sing. The thought of losing you, for we were swans, is gall, gnawing at me inside, tearing, breaking. I will not lose you, love, will not.

The song teases, entering my head, "Come running back home to me, come running back again". That arrogance is gone now, love. I no longer expect you to come running back. But Christ! I want you to. Want . Want. Want. So badly and want you to want that.

Oh, pet, were we so petty, so frail as to be unable to survive? It is not nice to see the spell of that small room where we first made love, broken? Discovering that we were ordinary in this East Bloc world.

CONCLUSIONS   19/8/93

Conclusions are like beginnings really. Perhaps that is because they have their genesis in them. We are all like the great tragic heroes of Shakespeare and Greece, if you will pardon the small pomposity. Our fate/failures are decided by flaws which, in our pride, we do not know we possess. What are mine? The text like all confessions reveals those. The worst perhaps is that to survive in an age of change one must be in synch with that society, must share its goals. I do not. That alienation is my most profound defect, the catalyst for all my defects.

It has been a curious year. I cannot say it has been an interesting one. Too much of it has been killed off, disposed of, useless. But it has been a frightening, a revelatory one also. You cannot hide from yourself or the reality of your society when you are unemployed. Everything is stripped bare. I would not like too many others like it.

The great tragedy of human existence is consciousness, of ourselves, our weaknesses, sin, death, betrayal, conscience, evil. If God punished us in that mythical garden, that was our sentence. For many of us in our society today our great tragedy is that our consciousness of ourselves, our self-worth is, as Marx noted, defined by work, by what we do. For too many of us now that is nothing.

They say people who have retired wither. I never understood that before. I do now. And in that withering everything contracts, self-worth, pride, ambition, love, relationships. And with that also comes a terrible alienation from one's self and your society.

We all want to assimilate, to blend in. That I cannot achieve anymore. I feel so separate from conventional society, those who are in the business of making it, professionals, teachers, sales reps. etc. etc. What are they squabbling and struggling for, these tight, tense faces in their heavy serge suits.

I question all that. The sale of a life. And for what? A mortgaged home, a mortgaged car, a mortgaged life. They frighten me, these bland self-imprisoned lives. Yet part of me wants that, wants it so badly, but not at that cost. All of my family, my ancestors, have been cottiers, first to the landlord, now the capitalist. I don't want that. I want the dream of everyone to be special.

I know that will happen.

RENEWAL   20/8/93

She is in the car when I arrive. Smiling. Her eyes shine. She is happy. I can see it. It is long, oh so long, too long since I have seen her at peace, content. My heart beats fast. Happy too.

I feel disconnected, floating, as though I am a ghost, a dream from another world. I move towards her, across the sun-baked tarmacadam stumbling. My mind is uncertain, defensive about what will happen next but inside I feel fiery pillars of love and pain fighting and mingling.

Her face and shoulders are freckled from the summer's sun, the white dress elegant, classical, contrasting with her vivid features. Her face crinkles, alive, vibrant.

What do you love about the person you love? The uniqueness and yet the knowledge. I can almost see the breath from her lips drawing, pulling, the scent I know so, so well, her eyes, the timbre of her voice exploring, seeking.

I am putting my bag into the boot of her car, beside the hot water bottle, the unworn Doc. Martins, *City Girls*. I want to be inside this woman again, not sensually, but inside her mind, her heart, her memories, her past, her future.

I look up and she hovers above. A terrible brightness in the white sky. I feel dizzy and she swoops and I feel only a brilliant lightness of being, skin caressing the warmth of the sun, the sun shining brilliantly into my eyes. Connection.